WI

D1090225

WAHIDA CLARK PRESENTS:

THUGS: SEVEN

The Highly Anticipated Novel by

WAHIDA CLARK

This is a work of fiction. Names, characters, places, and incidents either are the product of the author's imagination or are used fictitiously, and any resemblance to actual persons, living or dead, business establishments, events, or locales are entirely coincidental.

Wahida Clark Presents Publishing
60 Evergreen Place
Suite 904A
East Orange, New Jersey 07018
1(866) 910-6920
www.wclarkpublishing.com

Library of Congress Cataloging-In-Publication Data:
Wahida Clark Presents: Thugs Seven
ISBN 13-digit 9781947732455 (Paperback)
ISBN 13-digit 9781944992736 (eBook)
ISBN 13-digit 9781944992712 (Hardback)

LCCN: 2017904241
1. Sex - 2. Drugs - 3. Infidelity- 4. African American-
5. Mobsters - 6. Violence - 7.Relationships- 8. Crime-
9. Thugs- 10. Family

Cover design and layout by Nuance Art, LLC
Book design by www.artdiggs.com
Edited by Linda Wilson
Proofreader Rosalind Hamilton
Printed in USA

DEDICATION

To The Staff and Team of WCP. Staff: Nuance aka Lil Wahida, Hasana, Sherry Porter and Nobel. There are none like you. Thank you for your sacrifices.

To the Ladies of WCP included WCP YA (Young Adult): Tash Hawthorne, Sereniti Hall, Tiffany Anderson, Tahanee Roberts, Aisha Hall Sunshine Smith Williams , Jamila T. Davis, Nancy 'Mama' Jones, Reds Johnson, Sheila Goss, Charmaine White, Gloria Dotson-Lewis,

To the Men of WCP and those on W. Clark Distribution who have kept it real until the end: The Victor L. Martin, Mike Sanders Intelligent Allah, Allah Adams, Grandmaster Caz, Mike Jefferies, Dean Hamid, Shannon Holmes, Missy Jackson, Saaid Salaam, Hood Chronicles, Said Sahid, Mike Enemigo, Shawn 'Jihad' Trump, Willie Gross and Dr. Henry Muhammad. Thank you for riding with me.

To all of my Brothers and Sisters on Lockdown. Stay Up and Stay Focused. Don't waste time.

WAHIDA CLARK

ACKNOWLEDGEMENTS

All Praise is Forever Due to Allah, the Most High, The Honorable Elijah Muhammad.

My Editorial Team for Thugs 7 drafts 1-7. You guys rock and I had a blast. In no particular order because everyone did their part and remained in their lane. Lol Linda Wilson, Little Wahida, Hasana, Maxine Thompson, Kwame Teague, Treena Burnette, Reds Johnson, Nafeesah A. Goldsmith, Antonio Faison, Po' Boy Natalie Sade and Katira Motley.

To My Prodigals Team. Big Shout out to Prodigal Sons & Daughters for their diligence in the shining a spotlight on Mental Health, Incarceration, Substance Abuse and the raising of our youth. I've never seen such a dedicated Team.

To all of my readers: Thank you for your continued support and love.

Wahida Clark

Chapter One

TRAE

"*Lock Down! Code four on the yard! Code four on the yard!" the loudspeaker blared, filling the prison corridor with static and tension as a twelve-man team of riot control officers stormed toward the prison yard.*

"Down! Down! Everybody on the ground now! Down on the fuckin' ground now!" bellowed the riot control sergeant as he entered the yard.

His team had every inmate on their bellies, hands locked behind their backs. He approached the weight pile where three nurses were gathered around a black inmate sprawled out on the ground in a pool of his own blood.

"If it were up to me, I'd let the bastard bleed to death," the sergeant grumbled to the officer sprinting beside him. The captain was standing next to the head nurse when the sergeant arrived.

"Captain Murphy, what do we have here?" the sergeant questioned.

Murphy shook his head. "The usual bullshit. But we probably would have lost him if we didn't get here when we did. The nurses are stabilizing him for transport to the outside."

"That bad?"

"Could've been worse."

"Matter of opinion," the sergeant chuckled, but when the captain didn't crack a smile, he covered the chuckle with a cough and asked, "Who's the vic this time? Somebody on our radar?"

"That's the not so exciting part. It was Mr. Big Time himself," the captain replied.

The sergeant's eyes widened. He already knew who the captain was talking about. They were just discussing the pull that this inmate held. "Macklin?" The sergeant confirmed.

The captain nodded.

"Knew it was only a matter of time. If we don't move fast, we're not asking, we are begging for a got-damn bloodbath!"

I gasped for air as I jumped up from the hard, cement like pad they called a mattress in the shit hole cell I was confined to. I was sweating bullets as I tried to shake off the fucked-up dream I'd just had. *Fuck!* Ever since I found out about my early release, I had been having weird ass dreams about getting hit. I was starting to think the shit was a sign, some type of warning that something bad was going to happen. I knew Mr. Li using his powerful connections played a major role in my early release, but damn! I didn't want to acknowledge that we had made a deal with the devil himself.

RICK

"Ohhhhh Rick, shit! Fuck, right there, baby. Stay right there, daddy, damn!" Kyra sexily cooed as she ran her fingers through my hair.

"Mmmmm." I moaned as I sucked gently on her nipple. She had me going crazy calling me daddy. I was enjoying the taste of one of the loves of my life. That shit may sound fucked up to some, but it was the truth.

"Roll your hips for me, mami."

Not turning my head loose, she spread her legs wider and was throwing the pussy at my hard dick. "Oooooh . . . I like . . . I like . . . it feels so . . . ohmygod. Big daddy." She groaned.

I stared straight into her eyes knowing that I was putting it down. "I know you love this big dick!" I bragged as I long stroked her pussy. I had Kyra on fire; she was spread eagle on top of her vanity table.

"Come on. Fuck this pussy reeeeal good, daddy." She begged.

Knowing that she was on the verge of a full body orgasm, I pulled out, stood straight up and looked down at her. I wanted to go back to sticking my dick deep in her pussy after seeing how she had my shit glistening from her juices. *Damn, I love this woman.* But, I had more important matters to get to the bottom of.

"I need you to have that conversation with Nina."

Kyra opened her eyes and fixed her gaze on me. "Rick, please." Her breathing was heavy, and she was looking confused. "What the fuck?"

The frustration in her voice told me that I had her undivided attention and that was exactly what I wanted. Kyra's nails were piercing my ass cheeks, crawling at my flesh as she was trying to get me to put my dick back inside of her. But it wasn't that type of party. I was on some serious shit. I needed her to do something for me. I was tired of playing around and being a pussy about the whole situation. I was a real nigga that was about real ass things. Besides, my patience was long gone.

"I'ma get y'all two on the phone later on. Y'all need to start somewhere."

"Rick, please." She was squirming, still trying to get me to give her the dick.

I decided to tease her a little and let her know that I was the one in full control. If she wanted the dick, then she had to do what I needed her to do. I slid the head in, stopped mid stroke and pulled out.

"Give me all of it now, zaddy." She was trying her damnest to get fucked.

I couldn't front and act like the shit wasn't turning me on even more, but I had to keep my game face on and stay focused.

"Actually, I think you and Nina should Facetime each other, do a google hangout or something."

That got her attention.

"What did you just say?" She was no longer wearing her fuck face, but her *nigga, you done lost your muthafuckin' mind* face.

"You and Nina need to talk today. I'm setting it up."

KYRA

Here it was, the first day of fuckin' summer and all I wanted to do was enjoy my day and get some good loving from *my man*. But of course, Rick was on some ridiculous bullshit. I let his ass slide the first time he mentioned her name. I had hoped that me ignoring him would make him leave it alone and continue giving me the dick; but now, he had me fucked up! All the way fucked up in every way, shape, form and fashion. This nigga has lost his damn mind. I mean, completely lost his fuckin' mind. I was not trying to do this with him right now. Shit, I wasn't trying to do this with him at all! The only thing I was thinking about was getting me some of this dick. That's it. That's all. I had been avoiding this so-called "conversation" with him about me sharing him with another woman. *Who the fuck does he think he is*? And what the fuck do I look like playing house with him and some other broad? This is not the Playboy Mansion and he damn sure ain't Hugh muthafuckin' Hefner. *He got me fucked up!*

"I need you to have that *conversation* with Nina, today." He repeated. His voice interrupting my thoughts, but I didn't respond. All I could do was stare at his fully erect penis which was standing tall. I was ready to salute the dick, *a-ten-tion*! As he was mouthing off about this Nina bullshit, my eyes were following the dick. *Damn, I had to admit, I was dickmatiz.*

"Rick, why do we have to do this now, baby? Come on, please." I pulled him close to me, kissing his lips. With sweat drippin' down his chiseled chest, I wrapped my right hand around the dick and began to stroke. He moved my hand and stood back.

I rolled my eyes in frustration. He was really getting on my fuckin' nerves!

"Kyra, I'm dead ass serious. I need you to understand where I'm coming from. Why should I have to choose? I love and take care of you both and the situation is not up for negotiation; I'ma get y'all two on the phone later on. Like I said, y'all need to start somewhere."

I pushed him away from me. "Seriously, Rick? You can't keep that bitch off your mind, even while we're fucking? Get the fuck out!" I didn't want to end up on *The First 48* for murdering his bitch ass. And that was exactly what he was at this moment, a bitch ass nigga! He had the nerve to just stand there, staring at me as if that was going to make me change my mind about sharing him.

Tasha always preached that being mad at your man when you were pregnant, was a *no-no*. She swore this was the time that you could get all the love and attention you ever needed and wanted. She said a good man pampers, caters to and spoils the queen carrying his seed. But I couldn't claim him as *my man*, even though he told me I could. And why? Because he was still with *her*. They have a family and she just had his baby.

Aisha, my eight-year-old daughter, loves Rick. Since her biological father, Marvin, is dead and Trae was locked up, she latched on to Rick. Hell, she spoke to him on the phone more than I did. That was what I loved about him. He was a real man when it came time to step up to the plate. But he doesn't love me enough to leave her.

With everything my daughter has been through. It's been rough on her, to say the least. At one point she thought that I was dead, only to find out I had been in a coma and didn't remember her or anyone else. And honestly, I still wasn't sure how to deal with her anymore. After being in a coma, I started doing the counseling thing, but I was over that. On one hand, I hated putting folks in my business. But on the other, I thought it would do us both some good to go and talk to a therapist, because I still didn't feel whole and I didn't think my baby girl did either. Tasha offered to take her when they packed up and went to New York. I wish I would have let her go.

I put my robe on, pissed, sexually frustrated and hurt. "I can't believe you are asking me to do this. Where is the nigga I fell in love with? What type of nigga are you?"

"That type you fell in love with. The one who will go through anything to be with you, protect you, take care of you. You know who I am Kyra. And all I'm asking you to do is talk to Nina.

He turned and headed out of the bedroom. Rick was really acting as if I was the problem and I didn't like this prison talk. I went after him. Still wanting to fuck him, and yet I wanted to kick him in the back and send him tumbling down the fuckin' stairs. "Are you prepared to leave her?"

"How many times do we have to have this conversation? I'm not leaving her just like I am not leaving you. You need to get used to the idea of me, her and you. And my babies."

"You a funny ass nigga. A bitch ass nigga at that! But this ain't Iowa, and we won't be one big ol' happy family. I don't need you, Rick. My baby and I are going to be all right. So, you want that bitch? Well, I'll give you that."

RICK

Kyra was getting on my fucking nerves just as well as I was probably getting on hers, but that was the least of my worries. Instead of going back and forth with her, I packed my shit and hopped a flight to Arizona to go and try to talk some sense into my other woman, Nina. Even though we were not together for a long time, we still had a deep history. Read *Golden Hustla* by Wahida Clark to learn more.

When I pulled up to the house, Nina's three children, Jatana, Daysha and Jermichael, were outside shooting water guns. When they looked up and saw me pull into the driveway, they threw the toys down and ran to the truck.

"Hey, Rick!" Daysha greeted.

"Rick, you just got off the plane? My mom said you went on a trip and you wasn't never coming back." Jermichael told me.

"Your mom said that?"

"Uh-huh." Jatana, the youngest of the siblings, chimed in.

"Well, she was wrong. I'm back now. And Jatana, why are you growing so fast? Who gave you a magical growth potion?"

She giggled. "I'm almost bigger than Jermichael. What you bring us back?"

I popped the trunk before getting out of the truck. "Don't touch the big red box. That's your mother's."

They squealed with delight as they ran to the back to see what was in the trunk.

Nina was sitting at the kitchen table squeezing a lemon into a teacup and looking like she needed a breather. I stood at the kitchen entrance staring at her. She reminded me so much of Kyra. Her complexion, her weight and height as well as her feisty spirit. She finally looked up at me, rolled her eyes, stood up and went to the sink. I turned and headed for the nursey.

"Rick!" She followed behind me. "Don't wake him up. I just put him to sleep."

"I know you're going to let me see my son. And why did you tell the kids I was never coming back?"

"Rick, why are you here? And don't wake him up. He just went to sleep."

"Can we have our talk without screaming and hollering at each other? I have something we need to discuss." I told her, still heading down the hall to the baby's nursery.

Nina looked at me with her arms crossed, rolling her eyes. I could tell she missed me. But I could also tell that her and Kyra's minds were in the same place. They weren't about to allow me to be at peace with them both by my side like I intended for it to be.

"What's up, Rick? Say what you came here to say. But do not wake up *my* baby."

"Your baby?" I stepped into the bedroom where my son, Rick Jr., was sleeping peacefully. I rubbed his back, in awe of my creation. This was my first child and I hadn't seen him in almost a month.

"Rick, please don't wake him up," Nina pleaded. "Let's go back to the kitchen." She grabbed my arm and led me out of the baby's nursery.

I took that as an open invitation to swoop her up into my arms.

"No, Rick. Put me down. Say what you came to say and then leave."

"You know I love you, Nina, and I love Kyra. We thought Kyra was dead, so I went on with my life."

"Put me down! I don't want to hear none of this bullshit."

"You told me to say what I got to say."

"But you're trying to convince me to accept why you're trying to openly fuck with the two of us. Get the fuck outta here. And put me down, Rick."

"Be quiet and listen." I snapped. "We thought she was dead. You have my child and she's about to have my child. I love you and I love her. So, this is what we are going to do. I'm going to set up my security business in PA and I'm going to be back and forth between there and here. One month with you and one month with Kyra or two weeks, however we decide. Only until we can agree on a better living situation. Bottom line, we eventually will all be together as one big happy family."

"The hell we will! Get the fuck out of my house!" Nina yelled as she tried her best to wiggle her way out of my arms.

"I thought you didn't want to wake the baby." I held her tighter. "I'ma tell you this once: chill the fuck out and hear me out. If y'all can't get y'all shit together, I'm walking on both of y'all. Nina, you know my situation and history with Kyra. Now, I'm trying to be a father to my children and a husband to the both of y'all. So, what the fuck do you want to do? You going to rock with me or do I gotta pay child support every month?"

"I curse the day I met you, and that dead bitch of yours." Nina said in a calm voice. "Get the hell out of my house!"

I decided to act as if she didn't just say that; I put her down and then turned and walked away. I wasn't going anywhere, not just yet. I was looking forward to spending some time with the kids and my new baby son before I made my way back to the East Coast.

Chapter Two

Saturday morning

KAYLIN

I decided to enjoy the fruits of my labor before I prepared myself for the baby shower Angel had been planning; she was going all out for her girls. I stood admiring the view from my 23rd floor window inside of my plush, corner office at Game Over Records. I had locked the door and rolled a blunt just to get a little peace and quiet for a few minutes. This was how I cleared my head and enjoyed some time being *still*. Our team was celebrating a profitable 2nd quarter, and I was celebrating and showing gratefulness for having dodged the Mr. Li bullet. The previous quarter suffered because I was busy putting out the Li Organization fires. Matters that could have easily resulted in my death as well as Trae's. We weren't a hundred percent out of danger, but at least the Li situation was contained, and I could breathe easy for a few.

I liked to be *still*. I liked the quality of thoughts I had, whenever I took the time to be *still*. So now that the bad smoke had cleared, we had to switch shit up a little bit. Tasha and the boys were back in New York with me and Angel. Faheem and Jaz were in Jersey, and Kyra and Rick were trying to get settled in Pennsylvania. The Tri-State area was our playground all over again. And now that everything was as close to normal as it could be, my focus was on getting Trae released before Tasha had the baby. Even though Mr. Charles Li, whose organization was internationally known and ran with an iron fist, was the source behind Trae's charges getting dropped, he had yet to be released. It was a little frustrating to a nigga, but I knew I had to remain patient and allow things to fall in place on their own.

The only thorn in my side, presently, was my dumb ass cousin Kendrick. I was having trouble accepting the signs, but in my *stillness*, I knew that Kendrick had to be dealt with before the Kyron episode came back to bite us all in the ass . . . especially my ass.

KENDRICK

I stood at Kyron's gravesite hugging a bottle of Ace of Spades. I finally cracked it open, then poured half over Kyron's grave. "Cheers, my nigga!" I swallowed a couple of gulps.

"Got-damn, beloved, I still can't believe you're gone." I took a long chug of the Ace. "And the fucked-up part is that bitch ass nigga Trae is still breathing. How the fuck that happen?" I took another swig. "Nigga, don't worry, 'cause you know I'm 'bout it 'bout it. I'ma have that nigga handled sooner or later."

But even revenge couldn't dry the tears streaming down my face. Revenge couldn't even begin to bring my favorite cousin and road partner in crime back.

"But what's got me fucked up is your brother, Kaylin. Your own brother! Man, how can that nigga keep fucking with Trae knowing what he did? I mean, I know y'all didn't always see eye to eye . . . but got-damn, y'all brothers: y'all are supposed to be bonded by blood."

I took another hard swig of the Ace of Spades as I shook my head in disappointment.

"I'ma get at that nigga and have a long talk with him. I ain't give up on him yet. After I put his head on straight, we can talk about that formula. Yoooooooo cuz. Trae fuckin' with that crazy, rich Asian bitch . . . that play right there, set him up lovely. I don't know what type of deal your brother cut with them, but they definitely rocking on some boss shit. Yeah. And we all get a piece of the action because we played our part. They called; we came. So the formula is all of ours. And trust me when I say it, the shit is gonna rock niggas socks! Wish you was here. We would be taking over and running things like we used to. But trust when I tell you, shit about to pop. You already know what's good. For real though. The only problem I see is convincing them niggas to let me get on right now. They tryna sit on that shit. I'm like nah we got the formula so let's work it now. Why the fuck we gotta wait? Let's get this paper while we got the chance, shit. Them niggas talking that 'wait until the time is right' bullshit. Like you always say, when it comes to the game, them niggas is pussy. They still talking about keeping shit squeaky clean and—"

Ding!

My cellphone went off and I looked down at it and smiled. My plan to get Trae's bitch ass back was about to spring into action sooner than I thought and I was happier than a muthafucka.

"Well cuz, pretty soon I'ma have that nigga Trae sent straight to you!"

JAZ

I stood on the porch as the moving truck backed into the circular driveway, preparing to unload our life into East Rutherford, NJ. We were about forty-five minutes to an hour outside of New York City. I cringed. It was a lot to take in. I would have never thought I would be back in Jersey, at least not to stay. I did not want to leave Georgia, but things had gotten hot and we had to go.

Lil' Faheem was murdered less than a year ago, but it still felt like it just happened yesterday. Faheem acted as if he was releasing himself from the tragedy of his son being gone. But he really wasn't. It broke my heart to see Faheem go through such a trying time, and the fact that Oni, Lil' Faheem's mother, had caused the death of their son due to greed made things worse.

Although I didn't give birth to Lil' Faheem, I mourned for him because he was the child of the man I loved. I knew it hurt him. And when he was hurting, I was hurting. I would catch him every now and then glaring off into space. And other times, he would pick up his Qur'an and read for hours non-stop. Those were the times that I think he would reflect on his son the most. Faheem's parents had been Muslim, and they had raised him as one. Even though he ventured to the dark side, he never stopped praying and praising his God.

When Kaeerah asked him how long she was supposed to feel sad that her brother wasn't coming back, he simply told her, "Until you choose to be happy. No one comes in this world or leaves without Allah's permission, so stop feeling sad."

He told Kaeerah that Allah would bless her with another baby brother, and he looked over at me and winked. That's when I got up and walked out of the room. I wasn't sure if I was ready for another child yet. Hell, I wasn't ready for another child at all.

ANGEL

I was super excited because Tasha and Jaz were back on the East Coast. I took two weeks off from the record label that Kaylin and I owned. My girls needed me, and I needed them just as much. I wanted to spend time with them; plus, the children needed to be together. Jahara and Aisha are seven. Kaeerah is eight. Tasha's twins, Kareem and Shaheem, are almost seven and Caliph is five. Kaylin's oldest, Malik, is eleven. We called them the Wrecking Crew. I remembered when we were all single with no kids, now we were coming up on a small village. With both Tasha and Kyra being seven months pregnant, I wanted to bless them with a ton of goodies for the new babies. They both were in funky moods, protesting my baby shower every step of the way. But it was too bad. We needed something other than our normal drama to come together for; something fun. Hell, I was going all out. And so far, my family gathering/baby shower was coming together flawlessly.

I shouldn't have invited Rick, and I promised Kyra that I wouldn't, but I did. She told me the only way she would come was if I didn't invite him. But of course, my hardheaded ass didn't listen. I just hoped it wouldn't blow up in my face.

KAYLIN

Today was a good day. I had some much-needed quiet time to get my thoughts together, and not only that, the baby shower and everything else was going as planned. I couldn't wait to reveal my surprise. My wife, Angel, was happy, because she now had a legitimate excuse to spend my money. She flew everyone in using a double baby shower as the excuse. I didn't object to it. She needed to spend time with her girls.

I finally got Red's attention and signaled for her to meet me in the kitchen. As soon as she walked through, I grabbed her up.

"Bae, what's up?" She looked at me skeptically. I pulled her close and kissed her on the neck and began easing her toward the stairs.

"You know I got a thang for redbones, don't you? And watching you work the room in this dress, well um, I think you can pretty much feel what I'm up to." One of the things I loved about Red was she knew how to dress. The white, sleeveless dress hugged every inch of her body. She paired it with the gold

Louboutin's she tricked me into buying for her. She was looking bad and bougie. I had her at the back stairwell before she objected.

"Kaylin, no."

"Why do women always gotta say no?" I placed her hand on my dick.

"Not. Now. Kaylin." She removed her hand, but I pulled her close to me. She tried to squirm away, but her wiggling on my dick was only getting me harder.

"We are not going upstairs. So, bae, not right now. There are too many people walking around." She giggled, feeling my erection pressing up against her.

"Who said anything about going upstairs? I just need you to bend over, right here, right now." I was able to maneuver one of my hands between her smooth, silky thighs.

"Kaylin. Baby, later."

"What? I only want a kiss."

"Why are you lying." She pressed her breasts against me as she whispered in my ear and then began teasing my earlobe.

"Stop lying, Kaylin."

"Just a kiss." I lifted her and began walking up the back stairs in the kitchen. She held her arms out, palms pressing against both sides of the narrow walls. All that did was put her in the position I needed her in. I was teasing her clit, and I wasn't letting go. Angel was getting wetter and wetter.

"Kaylin. Somebody is going to come." She made a feeble attempt to muffle her moans.

"You are." I unzipped my pants and released my bone.

"Somebody is going to come, baby." She leaned in and covered my lips with hers.

"Shhhhhhhhh. I got this." I didn't waste any time sliding up in her while fighting to not bust a nut. The pussy was knee buckling. Another reason I married her.

"Kaylin, we got... companeeee. Babeeee," she muttered as she began to ride my dick. I only needed to stay up in the pussy for a few minutes.

"Ay, yo, Red. You feel good, baby." She was riding up and down, already trembling. She was trying to hurry and get her nut off before someone came. Pun intended! And in a few more seconds, we both released almost at the same time.

"See. I told you I only needed a minute."

"That was two. Two good minutes. Really good minutes, bae. I love you." She kissed me like she meant it and was still jerking from that orgasm.

"See, and you almost missed that." I slid her dress back over her ass, just in time. Voices were chattering right behind us as I put my shit away and my cell rang. "I'll get with you later. Time to make that run." I slapped that ass playfully, just to see it jiggle.

"She blew me a kiss and said she had to go freshen up right quick. I glanced at the caller ID. It was *Mari.* I let it go to voicemail.

Chapter Three

TASHA

I felt fuckin' sad. Like, damn a bitch was really going through it. Trae was still locked up way across the damn country, and I hadn't seen or heard from him in almost a month. I was back here in New York with the kids living in our closet-sized apartment. The walls were closing in on me. *I hate New York.* Or maybe I was overreacting from being depressed. I couldn't even see my feet, and If my calculation is right, I still had six more weeks before my due date. In addition to that, the boys were driving me bonkers. They wanted and needed their father. I let out a deep sigh, *this shit is beginning to be a little too much.*

And now Angel had this brilliant idea to throw a baby shower, which I was not in the mood for. Hell, baby shower or not, I still felt angry at the world. But I was especially angry at Kaylin. He kept promising me that he was going to get Trae out, but I didn't see anything happening. I cussed him out several times for stringing me along, and today I planned on cussing him out again; that is if the nigga would even bother to call me back. That's how he got the nerve to be doing it.

We pulled up in front of Angel's home. *What the hell?* She had valet attendants and staff carrying baby shower balloons with trinkets attached passing them out. There was a catering truck, and waiters carrying trays of food and drinks. I instantly got annoyed. She told me it was going to be a small, private get together. *I am not convinced.*

My baby, Caliph and the twins, Kareem and Shaheem, took off running toward the backyard. I didn't even have the energy to chase after them. Which was all the more reason that Trae needed to get his ass home to his family.

My phone rang. I looked at it and it was the brother who I was mad at and who I came over here to see. "Kay, we need to talk."

"Aww shit. I'm Kay. Not Kaylin. And I can tell by the way you just said my name you are upset. Baby sis, you mad at ya big bruh again?"

"We need to talk, big bruh. Where are you?"

"Where are you? It's your baby shower. Don't you think you should be there?"

I was sick and tired of Kaylin playing my warden. "I'm here. I just pulled up. Where are you, Kay?"

"Good, this will be good for you. It's a celebration. You should be trying to enjoy yourself. It's a party for you, your girls and the baby. But I had to make a run. Sit tight, and I'll be right back."

"Kay, I swear to God. You better stop playing with me and get my husband out of jail. How much longer?" I was really an emotional wreck. My eyes welled up. "I would have never moved back here if I knew it was going to take this long. If I could have stayed in Cali, I would be closer to him, Kay, visiting him. You said he would be home by—"

"Bye, Tasha."

I looked at the phone and it said, call ended.

"No this nigga didn't just hang up on me!" I stormed up the front steps and into the house.

"Surpriiiiiise!" everyone yelled out. I found myself backing up as they gathered around me.

Kyra was the first to grab me and give me a big, long, tight hug. A little of the tension I had pent up was released. Our bellies collided, and I stepped back to get a good look at her. She was glowing and looked much smaller than me, although we were both almost seven months. Jaz, Faheem, Bo and Shanna gave me hugs. I couldn't believe Angel went all out for just the few of us. After I greeted everyone, I asked Angel where was Kay?

"He's not here. He'll be back."

"I was just talking to him. I thought he was here."

Angel pulled me to the side. "You just missed him. He had to make a run. What's the matter? Is everything okay? You don't look too good. Are the boys okay? You know Aisha and Jahara have been bugging me about when they would get here."

"They ran around back." I headed for the stairs.

"Where are you going, Tasha?"

"I'm not feeling well. I'm going to lie down, Angel. Is that okay with you?"

"Tasha, don't even try it. I know you. Stay your ass down here. You need to be around the family. They traveled far to see you."

"Fuck family, Angel! I'm sorry but that's how I am feeling right about now. I told you I don't feel well. The only family I want to see is my husband. And right about now, I need him more than anything." Tears streamed from the corners of my eyes.

"Tasha, you know what? No! I am not going to ruin my peace and this family atmosphere that I worked so hard to create arguing with you! Yes! Go lie down for a few and get yourself together. But rest assured, Trae is a soldier. He's good. You will see him soon. But I can see by your stinking attitude, you ain't trying to hear any words of encouragement. Go and lock your angry ass in the basement for all I care. I don't give a shit." She waved me off and walked away.

That was exactly what I was going to do. Lock my ass in a room somewhere. I wasn't feeling festive. All those pink balloons and streamers did nothing to uplift my mood. I climbed the stairs, made it to what used to be my old room, slammed the door, fell across the bed and allowed myself a good cry. It was just too hard to pull myself out of this slump.

FAHEEM

"All praise is due to Allah," I whispered to myself.

I must constantly thank Him for getting myself and my family out of Atlanta safe and sound. I owe Him everything. I knew it was time to go after Jaz had Oni and Steele, the man who kidnapped my son because Oni and her brothers stole his drugs, killed. Well, she thought she had, but I was behind the scenes giving Snell the orders on how to carry out the murders. Now I was planning to kill everything moving that had anything to do with me losing my son and that included Steel's people and Oni's brothers. Leaving was the smartest move I could've made, because while initially I was telling Jaz to chill on the murders, once I tasted blood I wanted more. I was on my way to jail or hell if I had stayed another day seeking to avenge my son's death. I thank Allah for giving me the strength to let go and leave. It was the hardest thing I ever had to do.

So, here we are back in Jersey. It felt strange. Almost as if I shouldn't be here. A feeling that I couldn't shake. A feeling that wasn't allowing me to get comfortable. Allah gives life and He takes it away. I had to remind myself of that guidance daily. My son was in my life for less than a year before he was taken from me. Burying your child comes with a type of anguish that you can't even begin to describe. I keep asking why did I even have to meet him? It was a fluke that I did. I mean, who meets their son for the first time by bumping into him at a strip mall? That alone was surreal. Oni never told me she was pregnant. She upped and moved to Atlanta, and when my son bumped into me, she had the nerve to try to take him and run. Just thinking about it made my blood boil.

Yes, I admit, I shut down after I lost my son. I wasn't asking for trouble in the A. I wasn't hustling. No guns. No drama. I was just laying back and laying low before life threw me a curve ball. However, with each passing day, I was feeling a little stronger, getting my mind and spirit back right. I know they say there are five stages to grief. I hadn't mastered step two: anger. But I was getting there. Going back and getting revenge was a constant thought in my head. I had convinced myself that it was the only way to get over my anger. Jaz kept saying if I went back, I would be walking into their trap. But revenge is an emotion strong enough to motivate taking the chance to find out.

Chapter Four

RICK

New York was still my city. I made my career here. I was even considering moving back this way. Start all over. But for now, I was more concerned with Nina and Kyra getting with the program. My program. There is only one of me and they both need me. So, why can't we just do this shit? The brainwashing and negativity this society subjects us to when having a one man, two women relationship is a muthafucka. When a grown woman knows that she is the other woman, she willingly plays her position. She waits and sneaks around to talk, fuck, hang out . . . the relationship must exist on the low, as she creeps, she handles the shit with exceptional skill. Oftentimes for years. So, what was the problem with a nigga placing all the cards on the table? Why couldn't I openly confess that I loved them both? Later for all of that sneaking and creeping around bullshit. This is a new day. They both claim they are in love with me and want to be with me, so why can't we all just get along and coexist in harmony? They both know my situation is unique. I love two women. One who I thought was dead, and the other one who I fell in love with after the fact. What the fuck am I supposed to do?

On another note, it was cool for her girl Angel to throw her a shower and to invite and fly me in. I stepped into the house, hoping that when Kyra saw me, she wouldn't start tripping. I spotted her talking animatedly with Jaz and Angel. When she turned to see who they were looking at, it was too late. I was already grabbing her hand.

"Angel!" She gritted her teeth. "You promised. You gave me your word."

"She promised you what, Kyra? That I wouldn't be here for *our* baby shower? That I wouldn't be here to celebrate our special occasion? You really need to stop the bullshit." I pulled her toward the door. "Let me talk to you, Kyra."

"Rick, I told you to let me deal with this my way. You are not helping the situation." She paused for a moment. "Actually, you are making it worse. Much worse by coming around trying to convince me to join your agenda."

"So, what are we supposed to do in the meantime?"

"Leave me alone so I can wrap my head around our situation."

"What is there to figure out. We love each other. You're having my baby."

"You know it's more than that. What about Nina?"

"Nina is fine, as you should be."

"No she isn't. I need you to respect my space, Rick."

"Fine, Kyra. I'm on the verge of giving you all the fucking space you'll ever need." I left her standing right there in the kitchen.

KAYLIN

How the fuck did I become the designated driver when it was time to pick up the niggas just getting out of the bing? As soon as that question left my mind, I got my answer. Be thankful you are doing the picking up, instead of somebody picking your ass up. True. True.

"Where this nigga at?" I glanced at my wrist and jumped out of Angel's girlie GLK. She asked me to pick it up from the detail shop. Jahara and her little buddies spilled Lord knows what all on the backseats and floor. I got out and leaned against the car waiting on my partner in crime, Trae muthafuckin' Macklin. My brotha from another mother, who I had been running with since grade school.

After about ten minutes, I was getting impatient. *Aiight, nigga. You said two o'clock. No text. No call. Whaddup?* About fifteen minutes later, the plane finally hit the tarmac. It had to be a boss feeling to leave prison and jump onto your own private jet.

After what felt like forever, the door opened, and the steps were rolled up to the side of the jet. Trae made his way down the stairs with two suitcases and a backpack. He set them on the luggage rack and raced back up. *Damn. How much luggage can he possibly have?* This time he came back down with shopping bags. *What the fuck?* How this nigga had time to go shopping, I didn't even want to know.

He looked over at me. "Yo! You gonna just stand there and look, or help a nigga out?"

"Do I look like the help? With the kind of bread you spent on gas leasing this bitch, the pilot need to have his ass out here," I yelled out and popped the trunk, trying to contain my excitement.

Trae was all smiles as he made his way over to the ride pushing the luggage rack. "Nigga, you know you glad to see me. Thanks for your help." He was, of course, being sarcastic. We embraced and followed that up by giving each other dap.

"Welcome back to New York, B!" I joked as my brother from another mother tossed the last bag into the trunk.

"Lazy ass," he mumbled. "Tasha still don't know, right?"

"Nah, nigga, she don't know shit."

"Is she pissed off?

"You know she is. She would fight me if she got the chance. But she still don't know shit."

"Good."

TRAE

Oh yeah! I could have done a backward flip and five cartwheels. This was one of the greatest feelings in the world. I couldn't wait to see my family. From the time Kay picked me up from the airport, he was running his mouth a mile a minute, trying to bring me up to speed on some shit I wasn't even concerned about. My thoughts were on my wife and kids. I was finally away from that shit hole and those nasty nightmares. Hopefully.

As we pulled up to the house, I damn near jumped out of the car but not before I noticed a valet in a white jacket and white gloves who tried to take the keys from Kay.

"This my house, playboy. You ain't gettin' my keys," he told him.

I chuckled. "Damn. A valet, nigga?"

"Yo, you know how bossy Angel can get. This her thang. She wanted to go all out for her girls. Wait until you see what she got going on inside."

He stepped into the house and immediately told everyone to keep it down. I was glad and thankful to be back around family. Nobody knew about me coming home besides him and Angel. And he didn't even share with her that I was coming home today. Angel was practically jumping up and down.

"Trae! How are you? So glad to see you in the flesh." She gave me a big warm hug. "I'm sooo glad you're home." She squealed as she grabbed my hand and led me upstairs. *Why was Tasha upstairs and not at her party?*

Angel motioned toward the room with the shut door. I turned the doorknob, but it was locked. I looked back at Angel, who was fumbling with her camera, and then at Kay, who motioned for me to be quiet.

He banged on the door. "Tasha, open up this damn door! The party is downstairs, not up here in the room with you."

"Later for you, Kay! And if I was you, I would get the hell away from my door. I am not talking to you right now, and I am not feeling you right now."

"*Your* door? This is *my* house."

"Kaylin, leave me alone."

"What did I do, Tasha?"

"You know damn well what you did. Where is my husband, Kaylin? What the fuck is really going on? What aren't you telling me?"

"Tasha, open this door. I told you I was working on it. These things take time." Kaylin smiled as he was talking to her. Angel was trying to hold back her laughter. And now just about the entire party was standing behind us. But from the bass in Tasha's voice, I knew she was pissed. "Open the door! These things take time. I told you that."

"Fuck that, Kay! Your time is up. I'm going back to our house in California this week, and you won't be able to stop me."

"Your ass ain't going nowhere until Trae says so. He asked me to keep an eye on his family, and I can't do that with you way across the country. So, your ass ain't going nowhere! Even if you have to be here another year, or however long it takes."

That was when the door flew open and my wife looked as if she was ready to draw blood from my man. I stepped from behind him; when she saw me, the look on her face was priceless.

Angel yelled out, "That's right! Surprise, bitch! I got your evil ass on video. You feel stupid right about now, don't you?

Go ahead and say it. You feel stupid, don't you? Oh, I can't wait to put this on blast."

Tasha stood there speechless and in shock. Finally, she found her voice.

"Babeeee." She covered her mouth as the tears welled up in her eyes.

"Now what? Say it, Tasha! Tell me I'm the man," Kaylin boasted while pounding on his chest. "Go ahead! Tell me! Say it! I told you I was gon' make the shit happen!"

"Nigga, leave my wife alone," I told him as I grabbed her and hugged her tight. "Daddy's home now." I backed my wife into the bedroom and kicked the door shut. Everyone burst into laughter and applause.

Chapter Five

TASHA

Oh, my God! This was finally happening. The room was spinning, but my heart and head were no longer heavy. I couldn't believe it. *My baby! He's finally home. Whoop! Whoop! Whoop! My baby is home!* A few minutes ago, I was one angry, miserable— did I say angry—bitch! I could no longer hold it in. I was right at the edge, and God sent me an angel. My angel. Oooh, I was so happy. I had to pray right then and there.

Dear God, thank you from the bottom of my heart. If I didn't think you were real before, I am a believer now. You came to my aid when I needed you the most. I bear witness to your power. I needed this nigga. My nigga. My husband. Oh, I needed him!

"Babeee!, I squealed with delight I can't believe you are finally here."

"Daddy's home now." I melted into his arms as he kicked the door shut, pulling me close and holding me tight. I was so relieved and thankful to be in his embrace. The weight of the world was lifted off my shoulders. I felt as if I had been locked up too. When he was away, my entire universe was turned upside down. But now, I knew that my life was about to get back right. I broke down and cried like a baby. He patiently waited for me to get it all out as he rubbed my back while whispering in my ear. "I'm here now."

The room was quiet except for my sniffles. When I finally got myself together, he stepped back and spun me around. "Can I get a good look at my wife please?" I was ashamed to let him see me this big. This was the most weight I had ever gained during any of my pregnancies. "Damn yo ass is fat!" He exclaimed.

The way he said it, wasn't coming off as if he wasn't pleased; it was more like shocked. Because a bitch was insecure as hell because of all the extra weight I gained. He obviously read the unsure expression on my face.

"I like it a lot."

I rushed back into his arms. Realizing that he could have called me a fat ho and I wouldn't have cared. Fuck what people say about not needing a man. I needed my king for everything. I never loved anyone the way I loved him. And I would always need and want him by my side. I wanted to grow old with this nigga. As long as he loved me and treated me like a queen, I'd be that ride or die and he'd be my king.

He wiped the tears from my cheeks and kissed me softly. "Bae, stop crying. You trying to make me sad?" I hugged him tighter, not even realizing that I was still crying. We just stood in the middle of the floor, enjoying the moment. The moment when no words needed to be spoken. This was our moment, and I didn't want it to end. They say you don't know how much you miss something until it's gone. I had gotten tired of missing my husband.

"You gonna tell Daddy all about it, or are you going to just keep crying? What's on your mind?" His hands slid down and were now gripping my fat ass.

"Don't do that, Trae. You are making me feel fatter than what I already am."

"I told you I like it. You gonna let me grip this fat ass or what? I love how soft it feels."

"Well, I don't. I'm fat. I'm miserable. I hate New York. The kids are driving me crazy. They miss you. Kaylin kept lying to me and being sneaky. You stopped writing and hadn't called me in forever. I didn't know what was going on or what happened to you. I'm pregnant as hell, as you can see. And it was looking as if I was going to be going through this pregnancy and birth without you. I'm raising three rough ass boys and have another baby on the way. I am beyond stressed out. Baby, I was at my boiling point."

"Damn. Is there anything else?" he teased, as he leaned back waiting for me to add more shit. I felt forty pounds lighter after getting all of that off my chest.

"Whatever, Trae. You know it's not everything. But hell, my baby is home now, and I feel my Swagswayzee coming back already."

"Oh, so your man is bringing your swag and your sway back?"

"My swag and my sway," I teased, propping my hands on my wide hips. "Swagswayzee." I liked the sound of that. I was actually smiling.

"Well, good. Now wipe the snot off your face. You got my shirt all messy."

"Whatever." I kissed him on the lips, snot and all. I wobbled to the bathroom to get myself together. I swear, I loved that man so much.

When I came out of the bathroom, Trae got right to the point, as usual. "We both are going to need your swag and your sway to get us back right, the way we were and the way we are supposed to be." The elephant in the room needed to be acknowledged, and Trae wasted no time doing so.

Shit, eight or nine months ago we were living separately, beefing like a muthafucka, and I was on my way to filing for divorce. And it was all behind that egg noodle ass bitch, Charli Li. The number one reason I couldn't stand the smell of Asian food to this day.

I had been up against my share of crazy bitches, but this ho had money, determination, and she wasn't trying to leave my husband alone. So, I retaliated by tripping the bitch, causing her to tumble down a flight of stairs, ashamed to say, while pregnant and by fucking the next nigga, Kyron Santos. I hated saying his name just as much as I hated saying hers. But Kyron wasn't just any nigga. The nigga was close to the family. Hell, he was family. It was fun getting that revenge but then it turned fatal.

I only cheated for retaliation and nothing more! I enjoyed Kyron's time and attention, but I was on a mission. A mission that consisted of showing hell has no fury like a woman scorned! Trae was going to feel my fuckin' wrath. But he, on the other hand, cheated for different reasons that broke my heart and fucked up my mental something serious. I had dealt with a lot of shit from Trae, but him fucking with Charli and getting her pregnant was the ultimate betrayal. He made me feel so low, lower than I had ever felt in all the years I had been with him and I was pissed about that.

TRAE

"You know we got shit to address. We need to get it out because if we don't, if some new bullshit gets thrown our way, our marriage is going to have a hell of a time trying to withstand it."

Tasha pushed me away. "Trae don't start. As long as you don't try to blame everything on me. I never want you to forget that it was you who started the shit. And no, I don't feel the best about what we *both* did. And I'm sure that you feel some kind of way, but I was just following the leader. You led and I followed."

"Tasha, you fucked a nigga and got into a relationship! Am I still fucked up about it? Yes. But it is what it is. I'm not even on that no more."

"Trae. Oh, my God. Baby. Do you hear what you're saying? You're conveniently leaving out how you fucked a bitch and got her pregnant. Which would likely have been a *relationship,* if I hadn't ended it by trying to kill the bitch and that fucking bastard that she was carrying. And not to mention you fucked the other bitch, or have you tell it, got drugged by another bitch who fucked *you.* Yeah. You didn't think I knew about that? Then you gave me some shit that I had to take pills for. That shit could've been HIV, syphilis or some shit like that, so again, don't get it twisted." She poked me in the chest. "It's funny that you can't let this shit go, but when you were doing it to me it was fine? I agree, a man can't take it when a woman does to him what he did to her. You fucked me over, and I did the same in return so let's just call a spade a spade. You need to be glad I'm still here."

The fuck? Tasha was talking to me on some straight G shit. I didn't know if I should be pissed right now or turned on.

"What's that supposed to mean?"

"You know what the fuck I mean! And if you don't, then take it how you want to, Trae."

"No. I don't know what you mean. Tell me."

"Trae, you haven't been home a full twenty minutes, and we are already fighting. What? What are we going to do? You're right, let's get all the shit out now."

"I know, but I wasn't going to bring that up Tasha. Let's squash any and all bullshit. I'm not talking about that. Every deed has a consequence. You put them dogs on ole girl. I doubt if they gonna let that go. So shit is real. We are not living in a fantasy land. We have to know and prepare ourselves for a clap back or we have to make the first move. That's a conversation we need to have sooner than later.

And the other shit is you had a paternity test. You had to get one for a reason. What Tasha? You was suspecting that the baby was his?"

It looked like I took all of the breath out of Tasha. I knew I should have waited to bring the bullshit up because I knew it was going to get heated. Now I had to diffuse the situation or mess up my homecoming and all of the trouble we went through to pull this day off.

"Trae, I wasn't sure. I wanted to be sure. And I'm so glad, this little person is us. This is us baby. Our baby girl. Me and you."

"Then we are going to do what we always do. Get through it. Because, for real, that shit ain't about nothing. I just needed to get it off my chest. I'm right here with you. Nothing can break our bond. Nothing! I'm willing to put in the work to get us back. Is it worth it to you? It's damn sure worth it to me."

"Yes, we are worth it. You know that. But I don't want to fight with you anymore. I'm mentally beat, baby. Can I enjoy my husband for a couple of days? No fights. No arguments. Please? If you want me or need me to still be that ride or die, I will do that. Just let me know if that's what we are doing. I was angry at you. You were angry at me. We are even. So, it stops here. Now tell me, Trae. Right here. Right now. What are we going to do?"

"Let's take it one day at a time. And for now, let's just enjoy the moment. I love you and I miss you."

I began rubbing the love of my life's stomach. The baby gave a hard ass kick. "Damn! What are we having? A karate kid?" I joked.

"I don't even care, as long as our daughter is healthy. Baby, I want to really, really, enjoy us again."

"So do I, baby. I can't believe I'm finally here with you. I can't front, sometimes, shit would be looking bleak. And I would wonder if I ever was going to see you again." Tasha and my kids were my world.

"But you're home now, baby. And I'm still in love with you."

Tasha moved close to me and kissed me on the lips. The kiss turned my dick from angry to happy. Now the challenge was to control myself until we got home. I had big plans for Tasha tonight. It was going down in the bedroom.

TASHA

Trae and I were still standing in the middle of the floor, hugging and talking, when we heard light but rapid taps on the door.

"Uh oh, Daddy. I think you have some little, anxious visitors. Somebody spilled the beans that their dad was in the house."

"Hey, Ma! Mommy!" We heard our sons' voices. The knocks were coming harder and faster.

Trae kissed me on the lips once again. "I love you," I told him, not wanting to turn the love of my life loose.

"Love you more. Let me see my little troopers." His eyes lit up.

Even though he always told me, "Tasha, you are my everything." I begged to differ. Those boys were his everything. "Okay, but you gotta let me capture this moment." I got my phone ready, and then motioned for Trae to stand to the side. I pressed record and opened the door halfway. "Guys, Mommy was trying to get some rest. What's up?"

Caliph, our youngest tried to squeeze past me. "Ma, Aisha said my dad was here."

"Is my dad here?" Kareem, one of the twins, asked.

"My daddy is here!" Shaheem, responded.

"My dad is not here. Just Mommy," Caliph chimed in, obviously disappointed.

I stepped back, and Trae appeared. They all yelled, "Daddy!" in unison and bum-rushed him at the same time.

Priceless.

"Dad, Aisha said you was in jail. Are we going back to California? Is the lady mommy sicced the dogs on going to be there?" Shaeem asked.

Shit! Nosey and grown ass Aisha had a big mouth. How the hell do they know about some dogs? I decided to let Trae answer that. *Let me see how he eases his slick ass outta this one.*

Chapter Six

KYRA

What a baby shower! I thought. Angel, as usual, had to go over the top. Ice sculpture, valet, DJ, catered with a wait staff. Me personally, I would have kept it old school. I would have fried some chicken, made some pans of tossed salad, cut up some fruit, made a hat out of ribbons or some easy shit like that.

She obviously had too much time on her hands so she used this as her way of having a reunion with the four of us. Angel worked her ass off, but I knew she missed all the ratchet shit we used to do. But the best part was that everyone had their man. So, this moment was bittersweet to me. I kept asking myself, why couldn't Rick be with me? And only me?

I was so happy to see Trae, because Tasha, with her stank attitude, was turning us all out. But now, every time I looked over at them, she was holding onto him for dear life. She was suffering while he was away. I didn't think she could have made it another day without him. I told her to count her blessings. I knew chicks whose men had been locked up for five, ten, fifteen or more years.

On the other hand, I didn't know why the hell Angel would play me out like this. I specifically asked her not to invite Rick.

Now, I would be wrong if I smacked the shit out of him, and out of her for that matter. I was not going to forgive her for this one and I meant that.

We were standing on the back porch, trying to talk quietly. "Kyra, the man wanted to come and be a part of your baby shower. You are carrying his baby, for crying out loud."

"You promised me, Angel. I asked. No! I begged, you not to invite him. Bottom line is, he's not leaving her, Angel. I can't deal with him and this bullshit." I couldn't hold back the tears. "Kyra look, I know it's a fucked-up situation but if we're honest, you knew all that when you fucked him on Tasha's porch and when you got pregnant. The good thing is, he doesn't want to leave you either. We thought you were gone, and we tried to move on. Now," she said and paused. "He-he's trying to incorporate you in the family. Try to deal with this a little better than what you are doing."

"Oh, please, Angel. Tell me this, how would you deal with this? What would you do?"

"I think I would deal with it a little better than the way you are."

"That's easy for you to say, when you are not seven months pregnant by a man who also has another family. Or should I say loves a woman who just gave him a son. He told her he's not leaving me either so I should forget about him leaving her? How would you handle that, Angel?"

"Kyra, listen., I'm not telling you to be in a three-way relationship with him, but I want you to have a safe pregnancy. You love him and he loves you. I think it's a beautiful thing to be pregnant and in love and with your love. That's all I have to say." She turned and walked away.

I was left standing on the back porch watching the kids running around carefree and having the time of their lives. Rick eased up behind me and placed both hands gently on my belly. "I miss you." He kissed me on the cheek, and then on my neck.

I closed my eyes. "I'm not going anywhere, Kyra. And every chance I get, I'm going to show you that."

"Take your hands off my stomach. If you came here to reiterate to me that you plan on being with the both of us, then you shouldn't have come. You really have me fucked up if you think I am going to go for your shit. I may have lost my memory, but I didn't lose my damn mind. So, again, let me make sure I have this right. You want me, you, and her to be one big happy family?"

"Ma, can I go spend the night with the twins and Auntie Tasha?" Aisha ran up on the back porch interrupting my rant. Kareem was right behind her. They both were dripping wet from the pool.

"No, Aisha! My mom already told you not tonight because my dad is home." Kareem ratted her out.

"Shut up, Kareem! I'm not asking you. I'm asking my mom."

"Aisha, watch your mouth. And Kareem, y'all go back and play. Me and Rick are talking." Aisha stomped off. Kareem was right behind her talking smack.

"Kyra, stop twisting this around to be something negative. You haven't even began to consider the situation."

"And I won't consider it. Listen to yourself, Rick. Your line of thinking is making me dizzy. I gotta lie down." I was feeling lightheaded, so I leaned up against the wall in the kitchen and closed my eyes. I felt Rick next to me.

"Kyra, are you all right?" He grabbed my hand.

"I'm fine. I need to lie down. I'm sick of going back and forth with you about your thinking. Every time I think of raising this baby without you it makes my heart sink down to my feet. I love you and I know that I want to be with you. Not you *and* her. So again, you got me fucked up. It ain't happening, so I suggest you get the fuck out of my life." I made my way to the stairs, and left him standing there, like he did me earlier.

MARI

I admired myself in the sun visor as I sat in front of Kay's house. My face was flawless and blemish free and my sensual curves were defined like a figure eight, but there was one thing I was missing. The one and only thing I craved, Kyron's seed. I was overwhelmed with the loss of my fiancé. His murder tore me up something serious and, in my mind, Tasha Macklin was carrying *my* baby, the baby I should be having.

I thought about the night before and how I promised Kyron that I wasn't going to stop until I avenged his death. The thought of me making promises to him as I gazed at the picture of him on my nightstand and fucked myself had my panties getting moist.

"Don't worry, Kyron. I'm going to get our baby back." I repeated the words I spoke to the love of my life last night.

Now that he was dead all his faults had died, too, leaving me with only the good memories; the loving memories that had to be buried with him because of Tasha's bitch ass and her selfishness. *How did I end up here*? I thought to myself. *Ugh!*

I thought about turning around and leaving but I couldn't. I grabbed my cellphone from the middle console and went to Angel's Instagram page. I looked at the pictures of Angel, Jaz, Kyra and Tasha posted up like they didn't have a care in the world, and although I already saw the pictures on her page last night; I found myself getting heated all over again. *Fuck it!* I thought to myself.

Tasha had me fucked up! She thought that she was just going to fuck my man, fuck up our engagement, and live happily ever after? "Oh, believe me, bitch... You thought I was going to lay down this easy? You best believe, I'm coming for you!"

I no longer regretted the pop-up visit that I was doing. I grabbed the envelope out of the passenger's seat and stared at it. I was beyond pissed, and lately, I had really been missing and mourning my fiancé, Kyron. He was murdered seven months ago, and I still had yet to come to grips with his death. *Damn, why him?* On top of that, no one had been charged.

I sent his brother Kay a text to come outside. The package I was holding onto was burning my hands. I had to see Kay. Plus, I needed to ask him, why was I the only one mourning? After the funeral, the only person who consistently kept in touch with me was his cousin Kendrick. He seemed more distraught than Kay was. Were the two of us the only ones mourning his death and seeking closure? Shit was suspect to me.

There were cars parked in the circular driveway and in front of their big house. I saw the pink baby shower balloons and realized that now probably wasn't a good time, but I had to pee. I stuffed the envelop in my purse, double parked and hopped out the car.

Kay was coming down the stairs. *Damn.* He resembled Kyron so much, especially when he smiled. It made my pussy thump, actually. *What the fuck is wrong with me? He's practically your brother!*

"Hey, baby sis. What's good? How are you?" He gave me a hug.

"I need to use your restroom. Do you mind?"

"Not at all. We're just having a little get together."

"I don't want to intrude."

"It's all good." He held the front door open for me and waved me into the house. I stepped into what looked more like a Christmas celebration than a baby shower. There were so many gifts spread all around. The mommy of this shower would not have to buy her baby anything for a very long time. "Red, look who stopped by?"

She turned around, surprised. "Mari?" Angel rushed over and gave me a hug. "What brings you all the way on this side of town? Is everything okay?" I could see her surprise turn into concern as she took a step back and looked me over.

"I'm okay. I needed to speak to Kay, and I figured since I was in the area, I might as well stop by. When I saw all of the cars, I started to turn around, but my bladder had other ideas."

"Oh, no worries. I'm throwing my girls a little baby shower. Follow me. And you know I'm always glad to see you."

Angel guided me to the bathroom, not introducing me to anyone. I caught a few glances as I followed close behind but my heart got caught in my throat when I saw Trae and Tasha. Together. I closed the door and rushed to do what I came inside to do. But I still saw her. I saw them. Or were my eyes playing tricks on me! Tasha and Trae were sitting on the sofa all cuddled up and lovey dovey. He was whispering in her ear. She was smiling and glowing. *Does he know whose baby she is carrying?*

I washed and dried my hands and pulled the envelope out of my Brahmin. Still stunned, I stepped out of the bathroom. I needed to make sure my eyes were not playing tricks on me. There she was. Glowing. Happy. All cozy up under her man. The more I watched their exchange: how she looked at him, how he looked at her, the way he whispered in her ear, how her lips curled into a permanent smile. I knew one thing; she had it all. So, why in the hell did she need to fuck my man? Why in the hell did she need to fuck up my happy home? Her happy ass was the cause of all the damn drama from the day Kyron stepped foot out of that prison. This trick ass bitch didn't deserve happiness. Her happiness was about to turn into sadness once I got finished with her. Fuck this, I now had a change of plans. Instead of giving it to Kay, I was giving the envelope burning a hole in my hands directly to Trae.

Chapter Seven

ANGEL

Lord have mercy! I called myself planning the perfect baby shower. The only drama I anticipated was with Rick and Kyra. And that was my own doing, and I could pretty much control it but come on! *Why is Mari here?* She came out of the bathroom, marched out to Trae then handed him an envelope and rushed back inside the bathroom. I *knew* she was up to some sneaky shit! *Dammit Mari!* A bitch like her made it hard for anyone to like or support her in her time of need. I banged on the door and made her open it but not before watching the exchange between Kay, Tasha and Trae. Now, me and her were huddled in the bathroom. She was crying, and I had no clue as to why, but still, I passed her Kleenex after Kleenex. The box was now damn near empty.

"Angel, you don't have to lie. Whose baby is she carrying? I understand that she's your best friend and everything. But you don't have to lie."

"Of course, she's my girl. She's like my sister, but lie about what?" I questioned. She gave me a knowing look. "Wait, you think it's Kyron's?"

"It has to be," she cried.

"Do the math. Kyron passed seven or more months ago. Yes, it's close, but not close enough. Plus, she had a DNA test done. So, chill out. It's not his baby!" I handed her the last Kleenex. *Where the fuck is her head?* She gave me the look that said she didn't believe me.

"Im not to sure about that. She released a deep sigh. "The more time that passes, the more depressed I get. I can't seem to shake him, Angel. And plus, it just feels like I'm the only one who wants to know what happened to him. Does anyone else even care? Believe me when I say I'm trying to let him go. I'm really trying. It's probably why I ended up here, because I can't let go!"

"Mari, let's keep it real. This is me you're talking to. You had a reason to come here. Unless you make a habit of coming to people's houses to use the bathroom with envelopes. What was in it? Why did you give it to Trae? You didn't know he was going to be here. What's in the envelope?"

She rolled her eyes at me. "*The sessions*, Angel."

"What do you mean *the sessions*?"

"Recorded sessions of Kyron. He didn't know that I arranged for him to have a sit down with a psychiatrist. I wanted to get to the bottom of what was driving him to be with her. What the hell wasn't I doing at home? What was I not doing in the bedroom, Angel?"

"Okay, but Kyron has been dead for a while now. To you, much longer than it feels, I'm sure. So, I don't understand why Trae needs to hear what *you* wanted to know about what was going on with Tasha and Kyron. That man just came home today, and you're here on some bullshit."

"Of course, you would say that. Tasha is your girl. And, yes, I am on some bullshit. My best bullshit. I don't care if he came home tomorrow. I would still make sure that he knows his wife was in love with my man. I shouldn't be the only one hurting."

What doctor would release private recorded sessions of their patients? Obviously, someone with nothing to lose. Mari had to be delusional. In love? Bullshit! Kyron was pussy drunk, and he fell right into Tasha's web. She got revenge, while getting dicked down. That's it, that's all. So, I didn't know why Mari was still on this *they were in love* bullshit.

In my opinion, my girl was in the right to get revenge on Trae. The shit he was into would drive any woman crazy. But Kyron didn't love or want Mari. She was in a relationship by herself. Now Mari was telling me that she gave Trae some tapes that would more than likely unravel their martial ties once and for all. I foresaw more harm than good in that envelope. I needed to get it from him. The last thing we needed was to start a new beef. I raced out of the bathroom leaving her messy ass in there by her damn self.

"Trae, let me talk to you for a minute." I was looking for the envelope, but I didn't see it. I grabbed his wrist in an attempt to pull him up but he wouldn't budge. I stood over him and Tasha. "I need to talk to you for a minute. And bring the envelope that Mari's messy ass just gave you." He simply looked at me, but he still wouldn't get up off the couch. Tasha was nestled under him, her arm snaked around his, unwilling to let him go. But I didn't give up. "Trae, where is that envelope? Let me get that from you right quick."

"And why would I do that?" he asked.

I stood tall, hands on my hips, looking down at him and his wife. "You know this is some bullshit, and y'all don't need this, trust me."

"Don't worry about it, Angel. I appreciate you looking out, but it's all good. We good."

I looked at Tasha, and then back at Trae. He was very relaxed and serene; too damn calm for me. Being home and being back with his family, he was in his element. And Tasha seemed as if she was following his lead. She was sitting there chillin' as well.

"All right then. Suit yourself. I am going to mind my own business." Since Tasha was so relaxed, why was I so worked up? They damn sure couldn't say that I didn't try. As if on cue, Mari came rushing by, heading for the front door. I turned and followed her.

"Are you going to be okay?" I asked, not allowing her to leave before I had my say.

"I'll be fine, Angel."

"Okay, cool. But Mari, I want you to keep in touch. You know you are like family, and because of that, I know you won't mind me saying that you shouldn't have given that envelope to anyone. Not Kaylin. Not Trae. Not Tasha. It is the past. Kyron is gone, and you need to move on. What's done is done. He's not coming back."

"It's not done, Angel. That's where *you're* wrong." With that said, she left out of the house, and then she looked back at me and said, "You're right, Kyron is gone and he's not coming back. But I'm not done. I will never be done." She didn't look back as she headed down the street and jumped into her truck.

Dammit! I had to admit that I had allowed her to fuck up my awesome mood. I paced back and forth trying to get myself together. I couldn't allow anyone to ruin my wonderful party. *Wait.* This is not my party! But it sure felt like it. Overall, I felt as if I was controlling everyone's good mood, but now that my mood was fucked up, everyone else's shouldn't have to be fucked up.

"Yo, what's up, Auntie? What up! What up! What up!"

Instantly a smile formed across my lips. Forget about Mari, for now. Kevin was here. Tasha's baby brother; my nephew. He was coming up the walkway with a young lady, who was rocking a cold pair of Sophia Webster's. She didn't release but a few pairs. I mean limited edition for real. This had to be a boss chick. She was holding the hand of a little boy who looked to be around two years old. I made it down the steps and met him at the driveway and gave Kev a big hug. "Glad you made it!" I squealed. "I didn't tell your sister because I wanted to surprise her. You know she's going to be so glad to see you."

"She just ought to be! Her ass been in New York all this time and didn't even call me or tell me that she was here."

"Don't be mad at her. She doesn't want to be here, and she has this big chip on her shoulder, a big ass belly, and a whole bunch of drama going on, as usual."

He started laughing. I then directed my attention to the young lady that he was with.

"My bad, Auntie. Auntie, this is Seven. Seven, meet my Auntie." Right on cue, the little boy started throwing up.

"Oh, Carlito!" she said.

The three of us stood there watching the baby hurl.

"Damn, little nigga! You almost caught my Giuseppes." Kevin looked down to check his shoes. "Go clean him up."

Carlito was standing there, head back, eyes closed, screaming at the top of his lungs.

His mother swooped him up. "Can I use your restroom?"

"Is he alright?" I was wondering why she would bring him out if he was sick.

"He's fine; thanks."

"I'll show you the restroom. I'm Angel by the way. And you are, again?"

"My friends call me Seven and it's a pleasure to finally meet you."

Kevin pointed to where he saw Faheem. "Yo! Is that Faheem? Yo, Sev. I'll be in there."

He slapped her on her ass and went to go kick it with Faheem.

KAYLIN

Before Mari could pull off good, I rushed to the truck to stop her while Angel excitedly greeted Kevin who had just pulled up. I wanted to holla at Mari for a minute to see why she tried to pull some fucked up shit at the baby shower of all places. I wasn't fuckin' around when I told her I needed to holla at her, and she tried to dip off.

"Yo, Mari. Wassup? Why you doin' this?" I asked her when I got to her driver side window.

"Doing what, Kay?" she asked with red, puffy eyes.

I could tell that she'd been crying, but damn, for what? She needed to let that Kyron shit go! Shit that was my big brother and I deaded the nigga and even I wasn't on it like that.

"You know what I'm talkin' about, Mari. Why did you give Trae that package?" I looked her dead in the eyes. "You really want them to hurt how you hurtin' right now? How can you live wit' yourself while you're tryna pull this wack shit?"

At this point, I was pissed. Angel went out of her way to make sure this day was special and here comes Mari attempting to fuck shit up. I knew that she was hurting, but I didn't expect for her to come around my home trying to fuck shit up for Trae and Tasha. That was some grimy ass shit and it had me looking at her sideways.

"Yes! I want them to hurt like I'm hurting! It's only right!" She screamed.

I shook my head in disappointment. I definitely thought about Kyron constantly, wondering if I had done the right thing at times, but Kyron was like a cancer in my life. A cancer that happened to be my own flesh and blood.

"This shit ain't right, Mari, and you know it." I told her.

She looked at me with pain and revenge in her eyes. "Promise me that you'll make them suffer. Whoever killed my Kyron, promise me that you'll bring them nothing but pain."

All I could do was nod and agree. I felt guilty at times; especially when I looked at my mother.

"They will." I replied, regretting that I had stopped her and hoping that would be the end of the conversation. Before I could attempt to walk away, Mari stopped me.

"I've hired a private investigator," she announced, adding, "It's not that I don't trust your methods, but I need to be hands on."

I couldn't hide my surprised expression. *This bitch is bananas!*

"A private investigator? Do you really think that's a good idea, Mari? Kyron had a lot of secret shit going on with a lot of people."

"I don't care about a lot of people, Kaylin. I only care about what happened to Kyron."

"Mari, I told you I'll take care of it. He was my brother. I was closer to him than you. So, trust me and leave it alone, okay? I got it. Leave it alone."

I didn't give her dumb ass the chance to get another word in edgewise. I hopped, skipped and swagged my black ass back to the house and left her ass right where she was.

TASHA

We finally came downstairs to chill and enjoy the atmosphere and of course, go through my gifts. I couldn't believe some of the gifts us mommies got for our baby girls. I'm talking about Gucci diaper bags, Burberry outfits, and the 2k stroller, which I had looked at, but refused to buy. After three kids, I was over all that name brand shit. Sike! *I can't believe I just said that.* I was so happy looking at this stuff because I wasn't prepared to have a baby, nor had I been shopping. And Trae, quiet as it was kept, was a shopaholic just like me and was enjoying going through the gifts just as much as I was.

Trae leaned over and whispered into my ear. "Yo, beautiful. I hope you're ready."

"Ready for what?"

"Tanite." He said in his Bernie Mac voice.

"Tonight?"

"You heard me. We fucking *all* night. And I mean *all* night," he emphasized.

I giggled as I kissed him gently on the lips; I felt myself getting moist. "I hope *you* are ready for tanite." I said in my Bernie Mac voice.

"Oh, yeah? It's going down like that?"

"You know it is." I was literally soaking my panties at that very moment.

"Bring it on then. But I'm telling you now, I don't want to hear you crying out, 'Oh, please, Trae, please. I can't come anymore, pleeeease stop.'"

"Whatever." I couldn't help but close my eyes and visualize it. My husband aimed to please me in every way that he could. And I wanted him I could beg and plead all I wanted, but when he got in that zone, he had tunnel vision. All I could do was hang on and ride the rollercoaster. I was enjoying the visual. But when I opened my eyes, I was in a bad dream. "Who . . . what—is that— Mari? I know damn well Angel did not invite her to my baby shower."

"Apparently, she did," Trae said. "And she's coming right this way."

"I swear, Trae, I am not up for any—"

"Chill out." He squeezed my hand.

"Hello, Trae. I wasn't expecting to see you here."

"Mari, I wasn't expecting to see you neither; what's up?"

"I stopped by to see Kay and to ask if I could count on him to make sure that you received this. But since you are here, I can put it in your hands myself."

She was holding a large brown envelope. I wished I could have jumped up and smacked the shit out of this bitch.

"What's inside?" Trae looked at the envelope as if she was carrying a ticking time bomb.

"Some recorded sessions that I think you need to hear. Also, I have something visual that I think you need to see. Take them, please. I have copies."

Kaylin stepped over and he and I stuck our hands out to grab the envelope. But Trae was quicker than both of us, grabbing it and placing it behind his back. "No. I'm good, dawg. She said it's just some tapes that I needed to listen to and something I needed to see. So, we're going to check them out."

The look on Kaylin's face let me know that he was going to get into Mari's ass.

I looked at the envelope, and I could say that now my festive mood was beginning to sink. Fast.

"Yo, didn't I just say it? Shit was going to be coming at us, testing our bond. I barely got the words out of my mouth." Trae reached back and held up the envelope. "Out of nowhere, Tasha. But don't worry. I promised you we gonna handle shit as it comes. Whatever comes at us, it won't shake us. Ride or Die. Our shit is unbreakable."

"We are unbreakable," I mumbled, trying to convince myself that the words coming out of my mouth were true.

"I can't hear you."

"Unbreakable," I said louder, while wondering what in the world could be on those tapes.

At the same time, I wondered if Trae was for real about us being unbreakable. Coming from Mari, I just knew those tapes held something deep and dark. Was it going to be some shit that was gonna fuck up our marriage once and for all?

Chapter Eight

RICK

After I fluffed up Kyra's pillows, I went to get a bottle of water and a warm cloth. Seeing her small body curled up into a knot on the bed had me worried.

"Kyra, maybe we should call an ambulance."

"Rick, I'm not in labor and I'm not dying. I'm just a little lightheaded." She unraveled and sat up. I opened the water and placed the bottle to her lips. She took a few swallows, bumping off half the bottle.

"I hope you're not dehydrated," I told her as she rested her head against the headboard.

"I'm fine." She closed her eyes, and I placed the damp cloth to her forehead.

"Kyra, I—"

"Please. Not–oh!" She grabbed her stomach.

"What? What is it, Kyra?" I got excited.

"It felt like she just did two backwards flips."

"How do you know it's a girl?"

"The doctor told me."

"When were you planning on telling me, the daddy, that I have a baby girl on the way?"

She didn't respond.

"Kyra, you know you on some straight bullshit, you know that right?"

She slid her blouse up, and I saw some lumps travel across her stomach. My baby girl was amped. "It's a little too much drama for you out here, isn't it? Destiny, is that what you're trying to tell us?" I asked my unborn baby girl. I leaned over and placed a few kisses across her belly.

"Destiny? I'm not naming her Destiny!" Kyra removed the cloth from her forehead and was now staring at me wide-eyed.

"So, now you want to engage in some conversation? A few minutes ago, you had nothing to say. Yes, I'm naming my daughter Kyra Destiny." I went back to gently kissing her belly. "Kyra, middle name Destiny," I repeated. And I liked the way that sounded. "Hey, baby, this is your father. Your daddy loves you." I kissed my baby again through Kyra's stomach. She kicked again.

"I'm serious, Rick, that is not going to be my baby girl's name."

"She's not your baby, Kyra. She's *our* baby."

"She's *my* baby, not *our* baby. I wanted you. I wanted it to be me and you." Tears welled up into her eyes. Her stubborn ass was trying to hold them back.

"It is me and you. Dammit, Kyra!" The tone and no nonsense in my voice must have startled the shit out of her. She began to tremble as the stream of tears continued to roll down her cheeks.

"Rick, I've made up my mind. I can't, but more importantly, I won't be a part of your fairy tale."

"Kyra, you haven't even tried, so stop talking this bullshit." I struggled to remain calm. I got up real close on her. "I am tired of repeating myself. You need to get in line with the way things have to be." I stood up and left. I meant what I said.

KEVIN

"Yo, Fah!" Faheem and Bo, Trae's cousin, were standing there facing the kids, watching them play in the pool. I was cool with Bo, but Faheem was that muthafucka. My nigga. Coming up, Jaz and my sister Roz (y'all call her Tasha), were the closest out of their crew. Of course, they would hang out a lot, and Faheem would always be around because of Jaz. He shared, very generously, I might add, much game about the streets. Matter of fact in Jersey, he gave me my first brick of dope.

"Kev, I thought that was you. What up, soldier?" Fah was a built nigga. He swallowed my small frame up. This nigga claimed he never lifted weights. He always told me to exercise the mind and the body would follow. I always wondered if he exercised for real.

"You know what it is. Just came by to check on my sister. Do the baby shower thang."

As we dapped each other up, I turned to Bo. "What up, man?"

"You got it. Good to see you." We dapped up as well. Then I ducked and a kick ball hit Bo smack dab in the chest.

"Yo, you got caught slippin', nigga!" Faheem teased. "You lucky that shit wasn't a bullet." We all laughed, and he went after whoever threw the ball in the backyard.

"Fah, how long are you in town for?"

"Nigga, you ain't get the memo? I'm on the East Coast for good. Just waiting on Jaz to finalize her school stuff, and wherever that is, that's where we will be settling down."

"Settling down? Oh, I forgot you on retired OG status!" I joked. But quiet as it was kept, Fah was one of them niggas who would probably die in the game.

Faheem smiled that humble smile. "I wouldn't call it that. I'm just chillin'. What's good with you? I see you doing the family thing."

"Nah, nah. Not yet. That's shorty's son. I'm just helping out. Trying to get in where I fit in. I work for food." I joked. I motioned for Seven, who was standing on the porch, to come to where we were.

"Seven, this is my unc, Faheem, that I told you about."

"Nice to finally meet you." She held out her hand and Faheem kissed it. "And this is my little man Carlito. Say hi Carlito."

"Carlito. What's good?" Faheem asked him. He clapped his hands together and then covered his face.

"Kevin, me and Carlito are going to go back inside with the ladies."

Faheem waited for Seven to get out of earshot. "Who ya girl? Where she from?"

A nigga was feelin' himself at this point. I mean, here I was, making major paper, didn't have to ask anybody for shit, and had a bad ass bitch on my arms. I was living the fuckin' life!

"So, you like that, huh, Unc? Her name is Seven. Shorty A-1. That's why I fuck with her. She owns her own used car lot Her bread all the way up. But for real yo, if you ever need anything, I got you. You looked out for me when it counted. I can't forget that. So holla at a nigga. I got you."

"Oh, you big now, Kev? It's like that? Don't forget what I told you. Every nigga in the game think they got nine lives. Shit, even me. But you done used up how many already?"

"C'mon, Unc. You preaching to the choir now? My parents were hustlers, my sisters hustle, Tasha married a hustler, my homies are hustlers. What else I'ma do? Get a nine to five? I'm not built like that. But, yo, I'm moving behind the scenes. These hands don't get too dirty."

"Just so you know, moving behind the scenes don't make you bulletproof or indictment proof."

"Kevin! Kevin! Come here, boy!" We turned around to see my sister, Tasha, as she walked, more like wobbled off the front porch.

"Unc, I'ma get back with you."

"Yeah, 'cause she look like she about to send you to the corna store or something."

"Whatever, yo!" I turned my attention on my sister. "Damn, sis, you stay pregnant! What number is this—six?"

"This will be four, negro!" she said, right before she smacked me upside my head. "But look who's talking! Why didn't you tell me you had a son? What is wrong with you? And where are my gifts?"

"Slow your roll, sis. He ain't mine." My sister glared at me, as if she didn't believe me. "Why would I lie? If he was mine, I would tell you. He doesn't even look like me."

"Yes, he does, Kevin."

"You know the old saying, if you feed them long enough, they will look like you."

"Yeah right!" She gave me a big hug. "It's something you're not telling me, but I miss you, baby boy!"

"Just like you didn't tell me you was no longer in Cali. What up with that?" I went to smack her upside her head, and she ducked, but not before punching me in the chest. "I miss you too."

"Don't try and change the subject."

"Who is the young lady? Is she wifey material for my lil' bro, a friend, side chick? What?"

"Damn, you still nosey, sis."

KAYLIN

Bo, Trae, and I were in the basement getting our smoke on and shooting a little pool. I couldn't help but think that anytime Red was doing anything with the girls, there was bound to be some drama. That thought reminded me that I hadn't seen Kyra or Rick in a while. Which meant that I needed to make my rounds.

"I'll be back in a few." I went upstairs to check the guest rooms. I tapped on the first door. "Kyra? Rick? Y'all good?"

The door flew open and immediately slammed shut. "Well dayum!"

It flew open again, and Rick said, "We good!"

"Dawg, you sure about that?"

"Trust and believe, before we come out of this room, we are going to be one big ass happy family." And he slammed it back.

"I hope so!"

I checked the other rooms, everything was good. Jahara's bedroom looked as if a tornado went through it. Because she was the only child in this house, whenever she got company she played the hostess with the mostess, just like her mom and dad.

I went downstairs to check on my wife. When she looked up and saw me, she said, "Kaylin, speak to your daughter."

"Jay, behave please, ma'am."

"Dad, I am."

"She is not. She's being rude. Any other day she wants to play with Derek and Ashley, now she wants to act all brand new. I'm not allowing them to come over anymore. That's not how you treat your neighbors, Jahara. Treat people the way you want to be treated."

"Jay, we spoke about this before, didn't we?"

"I know, Dad. But you said I didn't have to play with them when I didn't want to. And today I don't want to because I have enough kids to watch."

Angel rolled her eyes. "I need to be in the loop on some of these conversations with our daughter, Kaylin. Go back outside, Jahara. And treat people how you want to be treated," Angel snapped.

"Yes, ma'am."

I grabbed Angel's hand, and she tried to snatch away from me.

"What?" I gave her my most innocent look.

"Don't what me, Kaylin. You already know what."

"Come here, baby. Dance with me."

"You can't be going behind my back, Kaylin. You're not around when she's begging their parents to let them come play with her. And now I'm hearing that you said she don't have to reciprocate?"

I tried not to laugh. "Red, it's no big deal. Her family is over; she doesn't need them today."

"Kaylin!"

"Come here, baby." I embraced her. "Can your husband have this dance?" Ro James was playing quietly in the background; he was crooning about asking for permission. That song was dope to me and reminded me of Red and the first time I got the draws. "I just want to spend a little time with you," I sang into her ear as she tried her best to squirm away. She eventually decided to relax into my arms. I massaged her back and pressed up against her. Ro James had me waiting on permission and wanting that green light.

"Awwww, how sweet," Jaz teased as she walked by us, licking an ice cream cone.

"So what's up? You givin' me that green light or what?"

"Depends."

"On what?"

"If you behave yourself for the rest of the day and don't piss me off. Later tonight, I may allow you to do whatever it is you want to do to me."

"Whatever?"

"Whatever."

We swayed back and forth. Both of us caught up in the moment.

"It's a blessing and a curse that I know you so well, Kaylin. Your dick is hard, but you're tensing up. What's up? What's on your mind?"

"Who is and what's with the chick who Kevin came with?"

Angel already knew who I was talking about. I knew everyone personally that was in my house, around my family. Even though I hadn't seen Kevin in a while, he was Tasha's family. Even Angel vouched for him. I knew about Kevin and what a fuck up he could be. And for him to be there with a chick that carried herself with an heir of distinction, caught my attention.

"Those shoes she got on...Sophia Webster only made six pairs." Angel said as if I gave a fuck about how many shoes were made. However, this ain't no ordinary chick.

Her saying that only confirmed that she picked up on the vibes as well.

"Tasha is already on her."

"I know that, but what's her name?"

"She introduced herself as Seven," Angel replied.

"Seven, huh? What's the baby's name?"

"That's Carlito. Isn't he adorable?"

I kissed her on the forehead. "Adorable? We can go make a baby Carlito right now if you want to."

"Don't even try it, Kaylin."

I held her tighter as I watched Seven. She was sitting across from Trae and Tasha. She appeared to be doing all the talking while Tasha was giving her undivided attention.

"What is she doing?" Angel asked me.

"Still talking, but it looks like Tasha is getting ready to get up. I need y'all to keep her talking."

"I told you we got it."

Tasha rushed towards us. She was sure to glide by Angel. "I don't know what the hell Kevin been telling this chick. But I got to go to the bathroom. Meet me in the kitchen."

We went to the kitchen to get debriefed by Tasha while Seven sat there talking to Trae.

"Ol' girl is interesting. But Kev done told all of our business. He got this girl thinking we the Escobar family or some shit like that. I tried to tell her we ain't doing that shit no more."

"Where she from?"

"Ithaca and Scarsdale."

"Girl has her own exotic used car lot. Her mother died of a broken heart, and with no warning. So she says she moves through life just like that, with no warning. Whatever the hell that means. And that was the basis of our conversation."

"That's it? You don't have anything else? CPA? How else is she getting money?"

"How the fuck you think? She using my dumb ass brother. My brother is the front man; she put him on. Why she would risk what she built, I'm unclear on that, but I will have that find that out."

I hoped Tasha did find out. Her vibe had me open. Ithaca? And Scarsdale? What type of nigga is she? The last time I checked only muthafuckas with money were from Scarsdale. What was she doing with Kevin, a street nigga? That wasn't adding up.

I watched as Tasha went back to entertain our mystery guest. When she sat down, Trae got up and gave me eye contact. I knew that meant, *let's talk nigga*. I was eager to hear what he had to say, and I saw the excitement on his face. I told Angel to be sure they kept her talking.

I closed the dining room double doors but before I could turn around, Faheem and Bo was knocking and barging his way through.

"What y'all niggas up to? Why y'all in here?" He closed the doors.

Trae had both hands rubbing his bald head pacing back and forth. "This is my first day home and already shit is getting turnt up in my life."

"Nigga what up?" Faheem wanted to know.

"Yeah what?" Bo said.

"You never would believe who's out there in your living room?" Trae said to me.

"Who nigga?" I questioned through furrowed brows.

"Her mother is Lola King."

"Who the fuck is Lola King?" Bo and I asked at the same time.

Trae was looking at us as if we were stupid, as if we were supposed to know who he was talking about.

"Moe Mo Money King." He stood back looking at us and waiting for a response.

Moe Mo Money King was a fucking hood legend. Hood legend had it that Bumpy Johnson gave him the game and he took it all the way to the next level. They got money together. This nigga was the man! Royalty in the streets.

"Get the fuck outta here," Bo said.

"How do you know? If her mother is Lola King, then she is the granddaughter." I told him.

"She has a necklace with a locket around her neck. The locket. She showed it to me. It's a picture of Lola. She looks just like her. I'm telling you, that's how I know. It's his granddaughter."

"If that's the granddaughter of Moe Mo Money King, then that's . . . Shit! Fuck me!"

"Yeah nigga. Now you see why I said my first day out and thing can't get more turnt up."

"So what if it is his granddaughter?" Bo wanted to know.

"What does that mean to us?" Faheem asked.

"The shit is a set up; they had to send her to us. For what? Shit, I don't know." I said.

Trae went back to the doors and cracked them again. This time I stood behind him and we stared at Seven. She sat calmly, seemingly without a care in the world as she spoke to our wives. "Yo, that shit is spooky. We got us a problem," Trae said. Now, both Bo and Faheem were trying to get a peek.

"I'm not convinced," I told them after a deep sigh. "I need more confirmation; what they want with us, yo? We out the game."

"That's her, and that locket is the confirmation." Trae slid the doors shut. His jaw clenched. "They spying on us and we need to figure out why 'cause she's been in *your* house and around *our* wives and children."

Chapter Nine

FAHEEM

"**C**an someone explain to me what the fuck is going on? I thought we were having a celebration. Y'all negroes done turned the party dark. I mean, this is supposed to be a party not a funeral." I was dead serious. The tension had gone from zero to sixty in a matter of seconds, and I was trying to figure out what the fuck was going on, why it was going on and whose head I needed to bust all at the same damn time.

"Can y'all excuse me and Trae for a few minutes?" Kay had the nerve to ask us.

"What?" Bo asked.

"Exactly. How you going to insult us like that?" I couldn't believe that Kay asked us to leave the room.

"B, my sentiments exactly. At least grant a nigga the respect and let me know what the situation is and give me the chance to decide if I'm in or not." Bo snapped.

"My brothers, y'all know that I meant no disrespect. As a matter fact, my respect for you is why I'm asking y'all to leave the room. Everyone is at a point in their lives where they don't need any unnecessary drama or bullshit. We get enough of that with our wives. And we can deal with that. But why would I get y'all involved in something that could disrupt your existence? Where the outcome could be a toe tag or a jail cell?" Kaylin told us.

I wasn't trying to hear that shit. He and Trae knew that Bo and I were always down for whatever, especially when it came to the family. Trae was standing in the corner, head down, hands buried in his pocket. I needed to know what the hell was brewing.

"Trae, what's up?" That was Kaylin pretty much wanting to know from Trae if he wanted to involve us or not.

"Who did Kevin tell you that she was?" Trae had turned his attention on me. I didn't know he knew that I had a conversation with Kevin.

"He said Sev or Seven. She owns an exotic used car lot."

"Damn!"

"Look, y'all know that Moe Mo Money King is a hood legend, and he used to run with Bumpy Johnson. So, if I'm right, and I believe I am, and she is his granddaughter then y'all know she was raised amongst wolves. Her uncle died in jail. He was one of them New World Muslims. Them Elijah Muhammad fanatics, niggas unity tighter than any other Muslims. They loyal to the code, stone cold killers, tried and true and ain't none like them, nobody can touch them. Them niggas will kill you about Elijah. Faheem, your dad will tell you what's up."

"Y'all niggas need to know what's up. The New World 17; y'all the muthafuckas who need to google them."

"But ol' girl is on the Don's radar. He put a marker on her head before I went to Cali. An old beef." Trae told us.

"Shit how big of a marker? Who is she to him?" Bo asked.

"3.5 mil with some stipulations." Kay answered.

"If we are being set up, then by who?" I wanted to know. And for what?

"For what don't matter and Kevin. It's Kevin." Kaylin said.

"If its Kevin, what his relation to the Don? These muthafuckas playing games." I was convinced.

"Okay, so if it's a game, we need to know the rules before we can play. My first question is, do we call him and tell him she's here, or do we wait?" Kaylin wanted to know.

"Shit, I'm looking at the money," Bo said, "Find out if the contract is still good. If so, while y'all niggas trying to figure shit out, I want it."

Trae was staring at the girl through the glass door. "That is her. The million-dollar girl right here. Right now on my first day out. Kevin; he's setting us up. It's a test. I ain't fuckin' around with it. I'm not waiting around." Kaylin pulled out his phone and snapped a picture of her.

He sent the pictures off in a text. Then he said, "If he doesn't call us, then it's nothing. If he does, we will deal with it then."

"But in the meantime, I think we should pull Kevin's punk ass in here. I've always had my doubts about him. If he set us up, I'ma handle him personally." Trae was agitated, and it was obvious. After all, the man hadn't been home for more than twenty-four hours and now he was faced with this.

"If he's setting y'all up, who is he setting y'all up for? For himself?" These niggas weren't answering my questions fast enough for me. What the fuck were they into? I felt like I needed to be put on.

"Tasha said Kev has us looking like the Escobar family; shit, maybe they need help with their product," Kaylin said.

"Fuck they think, we some corner boys?" Trae seethed.

"They gotta know better than that," Kaylin said and thought for a minute. "…And what's with the covert spy shit?" he added. None of us seemed to be able to make sense of this shit.

"I bet it's Kevin. And I know how to find out. Let me go grab his little ass. I'll have some fun with him and get him to tell us what he knows. You carryin' right?" I asked Bo, and of course he was. "Just follow my lead." He pulled out his piece and handed it to me. "Y'all meet me in the basement."

I found Kevin in the backyard, happily playing with the twins and the little boy that he said was not his. "Yo, Kev!" He looked up, and I motioned for him to come to where I was. He swooped the baby up and came into the house.

"What up, Unc?"

"The fellows are in the basement about to get to blowing some trees."

"Aiight. Aiight. Let me get little man to his moms, and I'll be right there!"

TASHA

"Oh my. The dead has risen," I mumbled to Jaz as Rick and Kyra walked into the living room.

"Me and Rick are going for a ride." Kyra rolled her eyes, "I'ma take Aisha with me."

"Kyra, you know them kids are out there enjoying themselves. Let her stay here," Angel said.

"If you want to take somebody, take my boys," I joked.

"Yeah right. I hope you got that cleared with Daddy Macklin," Kyra remarked.

"I'm joking. I'm joking," I said. "But let her stay."

"We'll be right back." Kyra and Rick left out the front door, taking Aisha with them anyway.

Kyra and I looked at each other but couldn't say what we really wanted to say because we were sitting there in the presence of guests. But still, she had it coming.

SEVEN

"Seven, allow me to properly introduce myself. I'm Tasha, Kevin's sister. Pleased to meet you and little Carlito. He's soooo cute."

"Your brother carries a picture of you in his wallet and he calls you Roz. I feel like I already know you. He says that you are like his mother and his father."

His sister smiled. "Yes, we have a unique history and call me Tasha."

She was gorgeous. I could see where Kevin got his good looks from. Not that I looked at him in that way. Kev and I had an understanding. I am his silent business partner. Nothing more. He told me about his sister and her husband Trae. He told me about Kaylin, Faheem, Jaz, Angel and Kyra. I felt like I knew them all but now to finally meet them, I was feeling like a groupie amongst rock stars. *These people really exist.* I sometimes thought that Kev was making the shit up and these people were just figments of his imagination. But here I was. And Tasha's husband Trae! Faheem! And Kaylin! These ladies struck gold. Got me looking at Kevin in a whole new light. I felt totally relaxed, as if I was right at home. I felt such a relief to be able to talk to some adults. I had no close girlfriends, nothing even a little bit close to what these ladies shared, so it was refreshing just to be here.

FAHEEM

"Yo, that dro smells good. I see I'm in the right place," Kevin said as he raced down the stairs.

As soon as he hit the bottom landing, I grabbed him, put him in a chokehold, and pressed the barrel against his temple. "Who sent you here?"

I loved the element of surprise.

"What? Why–why the fuck are you choking me, Unc? What? What I do? Trae? Trae!"

"Trae can't help you. Who sent you here? Answer me, nigga!"

"No one. What do you mean? Angel called me! She said come see my sister."

I could smell the fear. I cocked back the barrel. "Don't make me get blood all over my shirt. My daughter gave me this for Father's Day."

"Trae!"

"I suggest you answer the man. Because look over there. He already got the carpet rolled and ready to take your body away," Trae told him.

"I swear! Nobody sent me. C'mon, Fah! What the fuck y'all talking about?"

"Then who is the girl?"

"Seven, man. Her name is Seven."

"What's her real name? Her government name? You playin' house with the chick, so don't tell me you don't know her personal shit. You ain't stupid."

"Lolita Calderon, man. C'mon, Unc! Why the fuck you have to hold a burner to my head, yo! You know me. I put in work for you! What is this about?" He had broken into a sweat.

"Let him go, Faheem," Kaylin told me.

I removed the barrel, and then pushed him hard, sending him crashing toward the rugs he thought were to wrap up his dead body. Bo snatched him up and forced him into a chair.

"What the fuck is wrong with y'all? Angel invited me. Y'all know that. What is this about?" His eyes were wide with shock.

I enjoyed this type of shit.

"Did she ask you to bring her here today?" Kay asked.

"Naw, man. I told you. I'm here because Angel told me to come."

"Who does she work for?"

"Who does who work for? What do you mean?"

I placed my arms around his neck and squeezed. "You know what the fuck we mean, nigga."

"Who does she work for? Why you bring a narc to my crib, Kev?" Kaylin asked.

He was gasping for air as I eased my chokehold. "Narc? She works for herself. I already told you, she has a used car lot. She buys and sells exotic cars. She do work for the unions and shit like that; she know all about shell corporation, off shore accounts, washing money."

"What else nigga?" I squeezed tighter for maximum effect.

"And she also fuck around with the work. She heavy in South Jersey. That's how I met her. We partners."

"She runs with who, nigga? You? If you want to live, I suggest you stop being so vague," Bo warned him.

"I'm telling you, nobody."

"She put me on; she bankrolled me. With her help, I got my weight all the way up. My name was ringing before, but now they singing my name in the streets. She put me on the best work in town, at the best prices. Ain't nobody fucking with me."

"Who's her people? Where's her parents?"

"Her mom is dead; all she says is that her moms dropped dead from a broken heart."

"Her father?"

"I don't know. She don't say shit about him and she's a bastard child. She said her pops kicked her out the house when she got pregnant and told her if she came back, he would kill her."

"And you believed that shit?"

"That's what she said. I don't know!"

"How did you meet her?" Trae asked.

"I was putting in work for the hometown, Trenton been good to me. I had got with this old head, Tracey. Fah, you know him. Tracey Syphax. He introduced us. We clicked and we started doing a little business that turned into big business."

"You didn't think anything was up? Faheem kill this nigga, wrap him up now. Get that nigga outta of here. I gotta take this call. Bo take scary Kev up the stairs to his little girlfriend and big sister." Kaylin teased Kevin.

We all gathered around the table.

"Don Carlos, all I need is confirmation?"

"This phone call itself is enough confirmation Mr. Santos."

"So, it is Seven? What do you want us to do with her?"

"You've done exactly what I needed you to do. I'll see you soon Mr. Santos"

This type of excitement was exactly what the doctor ordered. It looked like I may finally get my opportunity to meet the infamous Don Carlos.

"C'mon y'all, I told you she ain't no cop." He pleaded.

"Bitch ass nigga we only playin' with you, aww you pussy man!" Everyone doubled over in laughter.

"Why you fuckin' playin! Fuckin' fools!" He was fixing his clothes. Kay threw him a towel to dry off the sweat.

"We got your punk ass, nephew!"

"You still wet behind the ears. Come see us in about four years."

"Fuck y'all niggas." Kevin spat. He was madder than a muthafucka.

TASHA

I was enjoying my conversation with Seven when Kevin came racing into the living room and went outside, damn near knocking the door off its hinges. Me and Seven jumped up at the same time and went after him.

"Let me talk to my sister. Take the baby back into the house. I'll be there in a few," he said as he paced back and forth, his shaking hands fumbling to light a blunt.

"Is everything alright?" Seven asked.

"I'm good. Get your shit together though. Time to go."

She paused before turning and going into the house.

"What's going on, Kevin? What did you do?"

"What did I do? Them crazy motherfuckers just put a gun to my head!"

"For what? What did you do?"

I knew for damn sure Trae and them wouldn't do something like that unless some shenanigans were going on. Brother or not, I needed to know what he did for them to go that far.

"They was fuckin' playing around. Them niggas are crazy, Tasha, crazy. They don't know who they fuckin' with."

"What's that supposed to mean?"

"Take it how you want it."

Chapter Ten

The Board Walk
Coney Island, New York

RICK

Things were going as good as it was going to get with Kyra until she finally decided to be more open minded about the Nina situation. I couldn't front and act as if I didn't understand her because I did. I just wished she would understand me and realize that I was doing all that I could to make sure those I loved were taken care of and nurtured. This was my kingdom. The typical nigga would've been secretly dipping between the two and feeding them both lies just to feed his ego. But, that's not me and it would never be me. I was as real as they came, and I was not going to stop fighting for my family until I was at the head of my throne.

"What's up, baby? I want you to enjoy yourself." We had dipped away from the baby shower and went to walk around Coney Island on the board walk.

"I'm supposed to be fake with you and act like I'm happy?" Kyra pursed her lips. She was adamant. "You need to make a choice, Rick, because I am not feeling what you are hell bent on doing."

"Aren't you the same woman who told me, 'You know I am a fighter. You don't expect me to fight for you? Why not? I had you first.' Ain't that what you said?"

Aisha interrupted our soon to be battle and broke the ice a little when she pulled our hands together. She scooted around to my other side, holding me by the left hand. I was in the middle. "Look, we are a family. Look at our shadows."

People turned and looked at us in approval. "What a nice-looking family," an older black lady said.

"Thank you; I'm fighting to keep it together."

"That's what you are supposed to do young man. And you keep fighting." She pointed at me.

"Come on. Let's take a selfie," Aisha suggested. Kyra heaved a sigh, but then gave in. We took several selfies with my phone, and we did look like a family, a happy family at that. She even began to smile a bit.

"Text me that picture," she said. I knew she was going to put it on the Gram. I didn't care though. I wasn't lying or sneaking around.

As the evening wore on, we played games, rode a few rides, and shared an elephant ear. Later, I won—fair and square—a black and white furry horse and gave it to Aisha, who seemed to be having enough fun for me and Kyra put together.

"I'm tired," Kyra announced. We finally found an empty bench for her to rest on. She looked on as I taught Aisha some Tai Chi moves. I had a black belt, and she made me promise to teach her everything I knew.

"Hiya!" She chopped at my arm. "I won't have to worry about anybody bullying me!"

"That's my girl!" I high fived her.

At the merry-go-round, Kyra was trying to pay for the rides. "Don't even try it, Kyra. You taking shit a little too far now." I pulled out a knot of cash. "I got this."

"You never told me where you get all of your money?" Kyra's nostrils flared. "You always manage to evade the subject. What exactly is your hustle? I swear I don't even know you anymore."

"You would know me if you hadn't distanced yourself." I thought of the money Nina and I stole and how we'd been living off that money for a while. "If it would make you feel better, I'll tell you. I do some private contracting. You forgot that I am a cop. I have a few clients," I said offhandedly. That was partially truth. I had worked with Trae and Kay against the Chinese mob. I was a cop who broke the oath.i caught

Kyra looked skeptical. I couldn't tell her I'd gone underground, been declared dead by the government, and even had a funeral. I was supposed to have been relocated, but no one gave a shit about a nigga like me, so I figured as long as I stayed out of Cali, I was good. Just like Kyra had come back from the dead, so had I. We had more in common than she knew. We walked along the ocean after we let Aisha ride her little heart out.

"Who's hungry?" I asked Kyra and Aisha as I spread out the blanket I'd bought from a stand. I also had a big bag of snacks.

"Me! Me! Me!" Aisha shouted, jumping up and down.

"A picnic?" Kyra raised her eyebrow, but I could tell she was surprised.

I had picked up some grapes, mango salad, cheese, apple cider, and some wine glasses. I set up our little picnic, then began feeding Kyra grapes one by one. She was finally trying to relax.

Aisha started throwing the grapes at me, and I threw some back. "Food fight!" she yelled. "Food fight!" She laughed until she was bent over. Even Kyra joined in and laughed.

Afterward, we went to a different stand and bought cotton candy and soda. Aisha resumed holding my hand and made sure Kyra and I held hands, too.

Aisha got so excited watching people walk their dogs. "Mom, can I have a dog and put some cute clothes on her?"

"No, we have a baby on the way. No dogs right now. You can put cute clothes on your baby sister."

"Okay. But once my baby sister is bigger, Rick said he's going to get me a puppy."

"Did he?"

"Yes, but Mom, look!" Aisha was pointing at the setting sun which looked like a big ball of tangerine. "Wow! Who put that there? The sun is awesome!"

"Yes, that is a beautiful sunset, baby," Kyra said. "I haven't seen Aisha so happy since . . . since . . ." Her voice trailed off.

"Since Marvin." I completed her thought. I remembered Marvin, her late husband and Aisha's father. I had hooked up with Kyra while she was still married to that dope fiend nigga.

"Are you happy, Kyra?" I asked.

"For the moment, I am."

"Baby, it could be like this all the time."

She didn't say anything, yet she continued to hold my hand on the way back to the car. On the drive back to Angel's, Aisha fell asleep.

Finally, we made it back to the baby shower. With Kyra's arm around my waist, and me carrying a sleeping Aisha in my arms, we went back inside the house. Kay and Angel were still sitting in the living room. They nodded, looking happy that we were looking as if we had worked things out.

"You can take Malik's room. Aisha can sleep with Jahara," Angel said.

I walked back into the hallway after I laid Aisha down. Kyra was still standing outside the bedroom door. We looked into each other's eyes, and there was no need for words. I gently grabbed Kyra by the hand, took her into our room, and closed the door behind us.

KYRA

I am so mad at myself for sleeping with Rick. I wish the dick wasn't as good as it was. Not only that, but I loved him. And sometimes I wished I didn't love him as much as I did. I didn't know what to do. He was knocked out, snoring his ass off, while I was lying awake, wondering. Even though I was at peace my spirit was not satisfied. Where would our relationship go from here? How would we manage this ménage a trois? There was no way in hell we could work this out! I just didn't see it. I knew that I deserved so much better than to have to share this nigga with someone. How did I go from Marvin's shit to this whirlwind of shit I am swirling in the middle of?

I could just scream. And nobody understood how I felt. I waited for so long to find true love and to find a man who knew how to be a man. I felt so safe with him. It was the smallest things he did for me that made my heart sing. Like opening the doors and asking if I'm okay, or if I needed anything. But I hated that ho shit of him being in love with another woman. How could you love two women at the same time?

But I'd admit, it had been a wonderful day. I could get used to being a family with Rick involved. Getting pregnant spoiled. Seeing how happy Aisha was. This had been the first date for the three of us since I got pregnant.

"Fuck me, Rick! Fuck me, Rick," I remembered screaming. Just like the Ferris wheel we had seen at Coney Island, I felt as if I was slowly spinning. And I thought I could let him go, easily. I was really faced with a dilemma. Now it was time to be truthful with myself. No, I didn't want to let him go. No matter what. I loved him. I was madly in love with him. Rick entered my life and changed my entire world.

"I never stopped loving you, Kyra. Even Nina knows that," Rick told me. And yes it was real, and those words fed my soul.

Just as I was dozing off, Rick's cell phone rang, and he sat straight up. "Yeah," he answered. Immediately, his face screwed into lines of worry. "Okay. Okay. Calm down, baby. I'll be there as soon as I can get a flight."

A flight? He's leaving already?

"I don't want to leave you here. I want you to go with me."

"What's the matter? Go where?" I sat straight up, pulling the sheet over my naked body.

"The baby. He's in critical care."

"Oh no! What happened?" I had to be sure I heard him right.

"See if Aisha can stay here. Pack a bag. We gotta get to Arizona."

"But—"

"But, nothing . . . we family now. Right?"

I didn't recall saying that but there I found myself getting up and getting ready.

Chapter Eleven

CHARLI LI

Cedar Sinai Hospital Beverly Hills, California

"Miss Li. You healed quite nicely. But still take it easy," Dr. Bowers, my surgeon, gave me a warm, but stern look over his rimless glasses. The private hospital had been my home for the past six months, and the staff had become family. I was going to miss them.

"Thank you, Dr. Bowers. I'm so pleased with your work." I held the hand mirror and turned my face from side to side, admiring his handiwork. My eyes had been widened from their original slant. He had taken out some of my Asian crease through Epicanthoplasty. My pug nose now had an aquiline look. I no longer looked Chinese or part Jamaican. I looked—Caucasian! I burst into tears of joy. Imagine waking up with a new face!

"Well, thank God, modern science, and your father for these hands." He chuckled, ignoring my tears.

Dr. Bowers didn't even have to tell me. My father's money allowed me the best plastic surgeons money could buy. The right amount money would afford anyone to be transformed. The left side of my face had been scarred almost beyond recognition, and my right leg scarred in the pit bulls attack. Images of the dogs' teeth ripping my skin flooded me. My mandatory therapy sessions that Dr. Bowers required were more important than the surgery. Without those intense sessions I would not be alive.

* * *

"Now, Charli," my father said in a gentle tone as he pushed my wheelchair toward the curb where his driver waited in front of the hospital. "You can take as much time off as you need."

"No, Father. I'm ready to go back to work. Seven months is too long. You can understand that."

When we approached the curb, my father's driver jumped out the car and opened the back-passenger car door to the limousine.

Once inside the backseat, with the window closed for privacy, my father began the sermon I knew was coming. "Charli, I know you're a grown woman, but I forbid you to even think about that thug who was responsible for all this."

"But, Father—"

"We've had to pass on quite a few opportunities while you were in recovery. We lost time. We lost money and I almost lot you. He is responsible and I will take care of it."

I fought to maintain my composure. "I'm sure you will take care of it." I didn't dare say Trae's name, because I knew I would give my true feelings away.

"Good. You are my only child, and I hope you'll never experience what you just took me through. And for what? Nonsense." My father's voice broke as he became choked up, but he looked away and replaced his mask of steel. "That thug almost cost you your life." He took a deep breath, then continued. "You could pass for a Caucasian woman. Why don't you find yourself a good, Caucasian businessman and settle down? A Caucasian man will look past the scars on your legs and arms. My child, you must take this as a sign. It's time to settle down, Charli."

I paused. "I will, Father."

"Please come and stay with me until I am sure you are back to your old self again."

"I'm back to my old self now. And I feel fine. I want to get back home to get back to a sense of normalcy."

"Okay. But I'm leaving a guard at your house. You never know. Your mother has been worried sick—so much so she can't get out of bed. Be sure to visit her soon."

I hesitated. "All right, Father, I will."

"Be careful. And please . . . take it easy."

"I will, Father. I promise."

He nodded.

After my father dropped me off at my condo, I felt satisfied. I could drop the mask of the obedient daughter and embrace the boss bitch that I was. I had work to do. If only he knew how my heart was aching for Trae Macklin. He was blaming him for the sins of the wife. Recently, I found out through my private detective, Calvin Braggs, that she's pregnant—again. I cried my eyes out when I heard this bit of news. For one, I still mourned the baby Trae and I made, and that crazy bitch made me lose. The nerve that she is pregnant again!

I picked up the phone and called my private investigator. "Did you get it?"

"Yes."

"Good."

* * *

Once I got to my bedroom, I kept staring in the full-length mirror. I couldn't believe how full and cantaloupe-shaped my butt was. From the rearview, I looked like my nemesis— that crazy bitch, Tasha Macklin. When I showed the surgeon pictures of how I wanted to look, I had purposely chosen a woman whose shape was like the wife of my man.

My breasts are big, but not too big—nice C cups, just like hers. I used to be a B cup. My lips are full and the bottom one is pouty—like hers. But with my eyes widened, I could pass for a white woman. I even considered dying my hair blonde. I felt and looked stunning!

"Muah!" I air kissed myself in the mirror. Mr. Macklin was going to trip all over himself when he saw me.

But as for that bitch, Tasha, I wanted to sick some bull mastiffs on her ass and sit and watch as they ripped her to shreds.

Yes, I still loved Trae. I would always love him regardless of the ups and downs I'd had to endure to be with him. He was mine and I was his. And he would officially be all mine once I got Tasha out of the way. Permanently.

TASHA

The faint smell of breakfast woke me up. I opened my eyes to see the twins sitting on the edge of the bed watching television. Caliph was on the other side of Trae occupied with his tablet. *Trae.* Yes! *Trae.* My arms were wrapped around his waist. Feeling him, seeing him, breathing in his essence was my dream come true. And true to himself, he was basking in his morning ritual.

Smoking a blunt.

"Hey, sleeping beauty." He smiled down at me.

"Hey, handsome. What are you up to?"

"Waiting patiently for you to wake up."

I could tell that he was waiting because his dick was hard, standing straight up, forming a tent under the sheet.

"I told you I was gonna knock that ass out. Look at you. Oversleeping and shit. We done been to the store, cooked breakfast, went shopping, the whole nine."

"Stop lying." I smiled. I only believed the breakfast part because I could smell food. But yes, he did knock my ass out. We went several rounds last night. I stopped counting after orgasm number three. My kitty began to tingle at the thought. I needed every last thrust and grind. I was on fire the whole time at Angel's. I couldn't wait for him to take me home and make love . . . I mean dick me down. All night I had been having foreplay, touching Trae. His face. His biceps. Stealing a kiss. It was like I was seeing him for the first time. He was ripped like he was a personal trainer. It was as though I was in a dream. My man was home. Even with Mari, adamant about bringing all of her drama, I refused to allow anything to spoil the joy of having him back home. All I knew was I had forgiven my man, and he had forgiven me, and we were going to make it work.

Even though nature was calling, I held him tighter and wouldn't let go. "Why are you so quiet? What are you thinking about?"

"We're waiting for word to go see Don Carlos."

"Is that good or bad?"

He didn't answer. Something was going on. And it was happening too fast for me. Dammit! He just got home! I couldn't hold it any longer. My baby was dancing on my bladder. I jumped up, grabbed my robe, and turned my attention on my boys. "Good morning, guys. Y'all ain't calling my name or nothing. Y'all not thinking about Mommy since Daddy is home?"

"Hey, Mom! Daddy said we can go to the park today."

"I said we'll see," Trae reiterated.

"I still didn't get a good morning, guys."

"Mom. We know your morning is good," Kareem's smart ass said, as if he knew how good my morning was.

"Good morning, Ma!" Caliph and Shaheem said at the same time.

I headed to the bathroom, with thoughts about my brother. He was always in trouble. I emptied my bladder, washed my face and brushed my teeth. When I made it back to the bed, he had gotten rid of the boys and got back under the covers. I nestled up under my husband.

"Kevin said y'all pulled a gun on him, roughed him up and was wildin' out. That's my baby brother, Trae. What was that all about?"

"What? We were only fucking with him, Tasha." He reached down and pinched my nipple, which, as full as my breasts were now, stood at attention. I purred like a kitten.

And just like that, the case was closed.

"You ready for round five?"

"Oh, so you got jokes. *Are you ready?* That should be the question? I bet you can't give me a repeat performance," I challenged.

That made him smile. "How about I meet you halfway?"

I had to giggle at that. But I was down for whatever. Hell, I believe the last time we were together was when I got pregnant with my baby girl—that was the last time we made love. Pregnant sex had always been out of this world for me and Trae. Maybe that's why he kept me pregnant. I couldn't help but laugh.

"What's so funny?" he asked.

"Nothing. Just happy that's all." I rubbed his dick, knowing I was about to get another one of the best back-blown-out fucks of my life, even if I had to change positions again and again to do it. I was ready. And the way his dick was responding to my fingers, I could tell that he was too.

"Bae, slow down. I want you to relax first. Lay on your side. Where's the oil?"

"Probably under the bed, or on the floor somewhere." I giggled again and realized that I was doing a lot of that in the last twenty-four hours. He got up naked, dick swinging everywhere. I admired my baby as he went around the bedroom looking for the oil that we used last night. It was under the bed. "I told you."

"Damn. How did it get under the bed?" I lay on my side, and Trae began to work his warm hands up and down my back. He rubbed my thighs, legs, all the way down to the bottom of my feet. Then he turned me over and massaged my stomach. The baby even gave a kick. Gently, Trae kissed my stomach. I'd missed getting "pregnant spoiled" by my man. I had explained my pregnant spoiled philosophy to Kyra. Trae was a wonderful husband anyway, but he was awesome when I was pregnant. I didn't have to do shit. He waited on me hand and foot.

Once again, I was on fire. "Hurry up so we could fuck again." I wanted to say, but I lay back and let Trae work his massage magic on me. He was enjoying himself and I was loving every minute of it. And I kid you not, last night was explosive. It was all that I had fantasized about and more. Now again, feeling my man enter me after all these months, was almost mind-blowing. But as I relaxed, our old rhythm set in. The more my sugar walls gripped his dick, the wetter I became. With me on top, riding cowgirl, Trae started hitting my G-spot with each stroke, and I felt myself building to a climax. Within minutes, I was able to sit up, rock back and forth and before I knew it, I was comiiiiiing! "Trae, I love you!" I cried out.

But, Trae, the master of endurance and holding out, turned me over and I got on my knees. He hit my spot again from behind as he pulled my hair. I loved it when he did that. Seconds later, I was coming again. I was begging, "Bae, wait. Give me a minute." I wanted to catch my breath.

"Didn't I tell you I was gonna wear you out and have you begging for mercy? I love you, girl. Nothing will come between us." We lay there in silence catching our breath. I finally had enough.

"Then destroy that envelope Mari gave you . . . if you really love me."

THUGS: SEVEN

Chapter Twelve

TRAE

When we left Kay's house, my mind was on the call that we had made to Don Carlos. The Don never did speak loosely on the phones. All he said was he wanted to see Kay and me within the next forty-eight hours and to keep tabs on Seven without alerting her. He was too late; we didn't know what Kev was going to say to her.

My focus remained on Seven and our meeting with Don Carlos, and then my mind turned back to Tasha. I had waited for this moment a million times and fantasized about it for so long while I was locked up. I had to count my blessings.

She was my ride-or-die, my gangsta wife, I will admit. She went in on me when she thought that I stepped out on her. She became just as violent and vindictive as I was. First, she caused Charli Li to lose her baby, and then, later, she sicced two pit-bulls on her when she thought Charli was still trying to fuck with me. That shit was ridiculous and reminded me just how crazy Tasha was. She was a reflection of me.

At the time I was furious with Tasha. For one, it messed up my business dealings with Charli's mob boss father, Mr. Li, who had opened up the legitimate side of white-collar crime for me.

Legitimate side meaning, as long as you paid off all the key players, you had carte blanche. The sky was the limit!

I couldn't be too mad at the things she did to Charli. Hell, I tried to cut Kyron's throat over Tasha, so I too, went hard and didn't play that shit either. We were each other's soul mates and too crazy to be with anybody but each other. We definitely coined the term *for better or worse.*

So last night with that in mind, I decided to do something different and slow it down for her. I couldn't do enough for my wife, who had been by my side through it all.

"Babe, let me rub you down," I said, taking control. We were finally in the bedroom, butt naked.

"My neck, my back," she sang as she lay down on the bed, turning on her side, and putting a pillow under her stomach. I could feel her heartbeat as I massaged her. The baby even kicked.

"She knows her daddy," Tasha teased.

"That's a wonderful thing," I told her.

"Yes, it is."

So, this morning I wanted to do it all over again, but it didn't go quite like last night. By the time I penetrated my baby, with her on top, I knew heaven was found in the pyramid between Tasha's legs. She was still as tight as our first time. I had no idea how she did that shit, but she knew how to work that thang. We went at it for a while. Tasha came a few good times. I finally ejaculated, and it felt like i would never stop.

Spent, I collapsed cuddled up behind her. I don't know where it came from, but I began to wonder if this was Kyron's baby. I tried to push the thought out of my head.

"Is this how you felt when you were pregnant by Kyron?"

"Oh my God!" Tasha gritted, holding her stomach with one hand and banging the nightstand with the other. "Trae, that was another contraction. I think I'm in labor!"

WAHIDA CLARK

Chapter Thirteen

KAYLIN

I couldn't get the Don or Seven out of my head. The shit had been eating at me all night. I got out of my bed and went downstairs to sit on the back porch to think.

Was Kevin trying to set me up? Or was the chick trying to set me up? Or was it both of them? Did her family send her? Why did the Don have a price on her head? Too many unanswered questions. The Don was just that powerful for me to lose sleep over.

We had already put some feelers on the street. Street Intel was on the same level with the FBI. Whatever questions I had, I hoped would be answered and in detail.

Me and Trae were scheduled to see Don Carlos as soon as possible to find out what was really on his mind. The sooner the better. My gut was telling me something wasn't right. I just hadn't figured out what. But when I did, it was lights out for Kevin and that was a promise.

ANGEL

"Jahara and Aisha, y'all don't sound like y'all cleaning. All I hear is running back and forth and a bunch of giggling. Make the beds and clean up that room! This is my final warning!"

I made sure all the children had bathed, dressed, and were fed. I could still hear them snickering and running around upstairs. This would be the last pajama party that child would ever have! They were driving me bonkers. I didn't see how women could have a house full of kids. I just wasn't built for it. And on top of that, was when he received my text, he called and his only reply was not to lose her and that he needed to see us. I was still trying to figure out how I let Jahara trick me into letting our neighbor's two kids spend the night. Now, it wasn't even noon, and they were running buck wild, back and forth to Jahara's room. It only quieted down a little after my threats.

As I looked back over the previous day, I was glad the baby shower was over. I pulled off a near perfect event despite a few minor glitches: Rick, Kyra, Mari and the mysterious woman Seven. What the fuck was Mari on? I hoped she didn't fuck up Tasha and Trae's groove. I knew one thing, this chick was getting tired and overwhelmed with everyone's problems. I didn't know how much longer I could play the arbitrator.

My cell phone rang and it was Trae. *What the hell is going on now?* "Angel, Kay isn't picking up. Tell him I'm en route to the hospital with Tasha. She's in labor. Tell him I'm still on to fly out for that meeting, but I need somebody to meet me to pick up the boys."

"Labor? Already? Shit!" It was too soon. "No worries. I'll get over there. Which hospital are you taking her to? Her doctor is out of Mount Sinai, right?"

"That's exactly where we're headed." And with that he was gone.

"Kay!" I rushed into the bathroom. "You aren't going to believe this. We got more kids coming over. So, don't even think about going anywhere."

"What?" he yelled over the shower water.

"We got three more kids coming over. Tasha is in labor. So, cancel ya plans, playboy, and get out of the shower. I'm headed to Mount Sinai to pick up the boys."

I grabbed my keys. These girls were driving me nuts. I was glad to let Kaylin deal with them for an hour or two.

TRAE

I was flying at dangerous speeds and running through red lights as I rushed Tasha to the closest hospital in her Mercedes Sprinter. Her going into labor couldn't have come at a more inconvenient time.

Good thing it was Sunday morning and not a lot of traffic. Tasha was moaning like she was about to drop the baby any minute. "Hold on, ma. I got you. We gon' make it." I had to be doing at least 100 miles and it felt like I was going to flip over at every turn.

"OHHHH, Trae!" She grabbed my shoulder and sunk her nails in. "Heh. Heh. Heh." She released short breaths. "Baby, your mother was the one who told me this was supposed to be a breeze after the second or third child! She fuckin' lied, Trae! Don't ask me to have another baby. And you better not get me pregnant! Heh. Heh. Heh. I'm serious, Trae!"

"Let's talk about it."

"Traaaaaeee! And my water hasn't even broke. I'm not having any more kids. I'm hurting like hell. I mean that shit."

"Hang in there, bae."

The boys were in the backseat whispering amongst themselves, obviously enjoying the heightened drama and me driving as if we were on somebody's speedway. I pulled up in front of the emergency room entrance. "Y'all stay put and keep an eye on your mother," I ordered. "She's getting ready to have your baby sister."

I jumped out the truck and ran into the emergency room lobby. I stopped the first person I saw wearing a pair of scrubs.

"My wife is having contractions!"

She grabbed a wheelchair and followed me outside.

"Tasha, what the fuck?"

She was already out of the car with the boys beside her. The nurse helped her into the wheelchair and headed inside with me and my three little soldiers right on her heels.

"It's too early." Tasha was crying. "I'm only seven months. Trae, call Dr. Peta. Something's not right."

"Has your water broke?" the nurse asked as she took her vitals and the other one took her insurance card.

"Not yet. Heh. Heh. Heh." Tasha breathed.

A couple of nurses helped her onto the bed. One of the nurses turned to me. "Are you the father?"

"I am."

"You will have to wait in the waiting area with the children. We will keep you updated."

"Somebody will be picking them up shortly," I told her, and I dialed Angel.

She picked up on the first ring. "The GPS says I'm sixteen minutes away."

"Yo, hurry up. I'm not saying get into an accident, but hurry."

"I got you, my brotha."

I took this opportunity to go move the van that I double parked in front of the entrance. After I parked it, we stood in front waiting on Angel. The boys had a hundred and one questions about what was going on with their mother. Angel finally pulled up, and I told them to behave and I would see them later. I dashed back inside.

Once back in her room, the doctor, whose badge identified him as Dr. Monroe Fuller greeted me. "You must be the father?"

"I am." He shook my hand. "Well, you can calm down, Dad. This was a false alarm."

"False alarm? She was just having labor pains. Is she and the baby all right?"

"This seems to be a case of Braxton Hicks. The contractions have just about stopped. We're going to keep her for at least twenty-four hours, for observation. We've already notified her physician that she is here in our care." Doctor Fuller continued. "I want her on bedrest. No housekeeping. No cooking. No grocery shopping and especially no intercourse. No upsetting her. She has to remain calm."

"How much longer before the baby is due?" I asked. I was still a little suspicious in the back of my mind.

"She still has six and a half weeks to go, but if we can keep the bun in the over for at least five weeks, that will make us all happy."

Six and a half weeks to go. I thought about the timeline of events. The rape with Kyron happened immediately after we fucked. I counted back to when I went to jail in California almost seven months ago. The timeline was fucking with my head. I kept trying to dismiss it; I had to take Tasha's word for it. This was my baby. The DNA test said it was. I grabbed Tasha's hand. She was lying there with her eyes closed, IV in her arm.

"We've given her a mild sedative and something to stop the contractions, and she may be a little drowsy for a few hours."

"Thanks, doc." I shook his hand again and he left.

I leaned over and kissed her lips before placing my lips to her ear. "You think all that fucking we did caused this?"

My baby smiled but didn't open her eyes. "I told you to slow down."

"No you didn't." I laughed. "How you gonna place all of the blame on me? You the one who said you wanted to come until you fainted."

"Whatever. And I didn't say that."

"Yes, you did."

"I did not. But right now, I'm hungry. You never fed me my breakfast, only dick. Go find me something to eat, please."

"Shit, you should be full as fuck off this big muthafucka," I joked.

"Shut up, Trae! Please go get me something to eat."

"Not until you tell me you love me."

"I love you."

"That was mighty dry. Sounds like you just said it to get me to hurry up and find you some food."

"Trae, I'm hungry."

"All right. All right. I'll be back. But I'm still vexed that we can't have any more fun until after the baby comes."

"Me too. Now go get me something to eat. And I want to hear what my babies had to say."

"Yeah, now that's some funny shit. I'll be back."

As soon as I stepped out of her room, I reached for my cell to give Kay a call, but it went to voicemail. I called Angel and updated her about Tasha. I told her to tell Kay that I would still make the meeting tomorrow afternoon.

I got in the car and headed for the nearest spot to get Tasha something to eat. After I pulled into an IHOP, I called to ask her what she wanted. Turkey bacon, pancakes and eggs. I went inside and placed her order. Tasha also reminded me to bring her overnight bag out of the trunk. While waiting on her food, I went back to the car and popped the trunk. I grabbed the Louis Vuitton bag and it was on top of the envelope. I stared at it.

Fuck!

Did I really want to know what was inside? Now? Hell nah! I grabbed her bag, slammed the trunk, and placed her Louis Vuitton on the front seat. The envelope was calling me. *Nigga you know you playin' with fire*, was my first thought, but then I said *how much could it hurt?* I had twenty minutes to kill anyhow so fuck it. I went back to the trunk, grabbed the padded envelope, and got back in the van. I opened the package. To my surprise, there was also a flash drive and an iPhone inside. I touched the screen.

Chapter Fourteen

KENDRICK

"Checkmate, my niggah." I taunted B. Murder as he sat back from the chessboard and made circles with his blunt smoke.

He surveyed the board for the tenth time and smirked. "You got that off. I'm a little rusty."

B. Murder hated to lose but since me and the nigga was childhood friends, the relationship took some of the sting out of my taunts. "Rusty? Homey, you ain't beat me since the 8th grade. Come on. Let's rumble. Double or nothing. I'll let you get your face back." I wasn't finished with his ass just yet.

B. Murder stood up to his full 6'2, handed me five, crisp, one hundred dollar bills and replied, "Later, Brah. We need to meet these cats I told you about."

"They official?" I questioned as I pocketed the money.

"Do I fuck with anything less?"

This is true, I thought.

B. Murder and I made our way out and rode through the streets of Atlanta. My mind instantly went to that bitch ass nigga, Trae. "Yo, I appreciate you agreein' to handlin' that Trae situation for me." B. Murder shrugged as he drove.

"I remember Trae from back in the day. I ain't never have a problem with homey, but you family, so you already know how I'ma roll. My loyalty lies with you."

"Say no more."

I was pleased to know that sooner or later Trae was going to be dealt with, and maybe even Kaylin. All I was doing now was buying time until I got my hands on the formula I was trying to persuade Kay to give to me.

We pulled into the housing complex on Joseph E. Boone and parked. Everywhere we looked, dudes, females, even little kids were flagging red.

"Those niggas are Bloods?" I asked.

"What you see is what you get."

These niggas deeper than a muthafucka!

We got out and approached an apartment that appeared to be the headquarters. Everybody was flamed out and showing B. Murder love. The shit was like a hood hollywood movie. Once we made it inside, a skinny, dark-skinned dude with pimples, embraced B. Murder.

"What up, big homie?" Ace greeted.

"The rent my nigguh, you already know. But I want you to meet my man Kendrick." B. Murder introduced us, then turned to me and added, "This Ace, my lieutenant in the 'A'. Gresham Boy official."

I frowned a little, trying to think of where I had heard the name before but I let it go as I gave Ace a dap. "How you, fam?" I greeted.

"You down with big homie, so you already got the key to the city. Good to meet you," Ace returned.

The three of us sat down and sparked blunts.

"Now tell Ace why will be over distribution here," B. Murder said to me, ecstactic to be bringing to the table such a boss move that would allow his team to eat.

"Like I told B, what if there was some dope that was twice as addictive as heroine and twice as cheap?"

"Shit, something like that would make us twice as rich," Ace chuckled.

"Well yo, that's exactly what I'm telling you. I've got this good good that once produced, will turn the streets out, and make us billionaires. All I need from you is distribution down here."

"Access? You mean you got a connect?" Ace probed.

"Naw, homie, you heard him right we gonna be the connect," B. Murder clarified, adding, "This dope hasn't even been released yet. Our crew got the patent on this shit!" B.Murder gave me dap. "Now you see why I said you had to meet this nigga?" He said to Ace.

"Shiiiit! When do we get started?" Ace was ready to rock out.

That was the exact type of energy I was looking for.

"We'll talk on our second meet regarding percentages." I replied, in a boss like tone. I was feeling like the shit. "Right now, the logistics of the roll out are being finalized." I neglected to tell him that I didn't even have the formula. However, a nigga was confident I could get it from Kaylin. Even if I had to kill him in the process. But in the back of my mind, the question kept gnawing at the edges of my conscience. Who are the Gresham Boys? Why the fuck do they sound familiar?

TASHA

"Push, Tasha, push." Trae coached, wiping the sweat off my forehead. "You can do it."

We had always done the Lamaze thing, but this time it wasn't working for me and I was ready to quit. I did one final push, then heard the baby cry. "It's a boy!" the doctor announced.

"A boy! The ultrasound showed a girl; I was supposed to have a girl!" I cried out in shock.

I looked down at the baby; he looked like Kyron. My God! What is Trae going to……

Suddenly, a nurse came and took my baby away, wrapping him in a white sheet.

"Where are you going with my baby?"

I was weak; my legs were still in stirrups as the doctor stitched me up. The nurse had a sinister look and the way she turned her back, I knew she was stealing my baby. My baby! Nooooooo! Suddenly, I woke up drenched in sweat and screaming. A Dominican nurse came rushing into the room.

"Are you all right, Mrs. Macklin?"

I stared at her, then around the room. "Where is my baby?"

I felt my baby move, and I looked at my stomach. *Damn.* I let out a deep sigh of relief. It was just a dream. But it seemed so real and I couldn't help but wonder if my baby girl was in danger?

"Where is my husband? Is he back yet?"

"I last saw him in the waiting room. I'll have him paged."

It seemed like forever for Trae to come back to the room. Alone with my thoughts, I wondered if this was karma for pushing Charli Li down the stairs while she was pregnant and causing her to lose the baby. *Hell no!* This wasn't no damn karma. Trae went too far with that Asian bitch. He had me all fucked up if he thought I was gon' lay down, roll over, tuck my tail between my legs and take it.

Or was this karma for what Trae did when he dragged me down the stairs on the private jet and tried to throw me off, causing me to miscarry Kyron's baby? What the fuck was that dream about? Just yesterday he asked me some dumb shit about my feelings with Kyron being similar to my feelings with him. I heard him, but he acted as if I didn't. The false labor pains had me occupied.

Please God, don't let this be Kyron's baby. Please!

Chapter Fifteen

KYRON

Session One

"*Please. Have a seat, Mr. Santos.*" *The doctor gestured toward the burgundy couch.*

Kyron glanced around the small office space. He stood with his hands deep down in his pockets, frowned and then sat down. "Tell me why the fuck I'm here, yo."

"As you know, Mr. Santos, I have been assigned by the courts to conduct a mental assessment."

"What the fuck does that mean?" He caught himself. You and that bitch Mari are the ones that need a mental assessment. He chuckled at the thought. "Are you sure that it has nothing to do with that best friend of yours?" he questioned. Kyron was pretty much aware of Mari and how she was manipulating the psychiatrist like a puppet. He knew Mari was up to something, but he definitely didn't see this coming. Mari was over New York's probation department. He knew Mari had clout within the court system, but damn.

"If you decide to go against the court order, that's on you, Mr. Santos. I am not here to force you. I couldn't care less about you returning to prison." She swung around to her computer and began typing.

"What are you typing?"

Dr. Gillis did not respond, she continued to type.

"All right, all right. What do you want to know?"

She swiveled around, facing him. "The sooner you cooperate, the faster these sessions will be over. I need every detail leading up to the stabbing incident in that hospital. Also, the courts are requesting to see your next plan of action. But today, let's start with the relationship leading up to the stabbing."

Kyron leaned back onto the couch. He was going to have to play their little game for now. If not, it would be back to prison and things had just started cooking for him.

Dr. Gillis tapped her pen on the notepad and reached into her desk for the recorder. She waited for the red light. "Go ahead, Mr. Santos, whenever you're ready."

"You don't have to be so damn formal. You can call me Kyron, Dr. Gillis." He sat back and relaxed on the velvet couch.

Dr. Gillis took a deep breath, "Kyron, let's be clear. I cannot complete my assessment if you are not open with me. And if I don't submit a report, you will be in violation of your parole. So, tell me what I need to hear. The ball is in your court, Mr. Santos." Dr. Gillis folded her arms across her chest.

"Kyron. Call me Kyron."

"I'm listening, Kyron. Listening for inconsistencies. For embellishments . . . half-truths. For—"

"I get the picture, Dr. Gillis."

He stared into the judgmental eyes of Dr. Gillis, the New York State Department of Corrections psychologist. Mari beat everybody out when it came to being a controlling and thirsty bitch. Threatening to send him back to prison and putting his livelihood on the line, just so she could hear about how good he fucked another bitch? That was insane to Kyron.

And it pissed him off that the two of them with all this clout were working together against him. His pride said, "Fuck both of 'em, get up and walk out." But that would send the police to his front door.

"Fine, Mr. Santos. You give me no choice." Dr. Gillis stood and grabbed her purse, signaling that the session was over.

"Chill the fuck out, doc!" He half rose out of his seat but decided to sit back down to learn just how far Mari and Dr. Gillis were taking this charade. "You know you got a nigga caught between a rock and a hard place? I'm trying to wrap my head around this whole situation." He waved his hand around her sparsely decorated office as if he held a magic wand.

"What do you mean this whole situation?" She did that sista neck roll and immediately realized that he was bringing out the little ghetto girl in her.

"Y'all two hos think y'all the puppet master or some shit like that. Is that why my lawyer ain't here? I understand that for now y'all got a nigga boxed in, and I ain't got no choice in the matter. So, let's do this. Where do you want me to start?"

Dr. Gillis looked Kyron over for any hints of insincerity. She had known Mari for years, including the intimate and private details of her relationship with him. If her best friend wanted answers—or better yet needed answers, then dammit, she sure as hell better get them! She knew that.

Slowly Dr. Gillis sat back down onto her chair and placed her Coach bag in the desk drawer. "Start from the beginning, Mr. Santos. You were allegedly attacked in your hospital bed by your lover's husband, a Trae Macklin?" She picked up her legal notepad and pen.

"I don't know who attacked me, for the record. Let's get that shit straight right outta the gate." He pointed at her. "Also, for the record, I didn't have a lover. Shorty was just something to do. She wanted to get some get-back, and I damn sure didn't mind being used by her to get that get-back. She was on the get-back trip, and I was on the good pussy trip. It was a win-win for us both. And me, I couldn't help but win. As far as that little

move niggas tried to pull on me, bitch please. I got beef with a lot of muthafuckas out there. It could have been anybody. Even if I did know, that would be the one thing you wouldn't get on a recording. I'd never tell y'all muthafuckas."

"What does that mean 'shorty was just something to do?'" Her right brow furrowed.

"Wait a minute. Where are these questions coming from? You, or someone else?"

"Please answer the question, Mr. Santos."

"Me and shorty's relationship don't got shit to do with nothing. I said what I meant. Something to do. But yo, Dr. Gillis, I'm still trying to figure out what shorty was to me, or how much we fucked...what does that have to do with you treating me? This sounds and feels more like an interrogation."

"Mr. Santos, I haven't even begun treating you. How can I? I haven't even gotten a diagnosis. Now, does your 'just something to do' have a name?"

Bitch, you know her name. I'm sure Mari's ass told you everything, down to Tasha's panty size. *"Of course, she does. It's Tasha."*

"How did you meet Tasha, Mr. Santos? Is she someone you met while in prison? I see from your jacket that you had quite a few inappropriate relationships with several of the prison staff."

"Nah. She's not on that list. And for the record . . . is the recorder on?" Kyron glanced over at it.

Dr. Gillis nodded yes.

"I didn't manipulate anyone. Those women knew my situation. I was the one being manipulated. That is why the state is going to pay me for my mental anguish."

Although that statement shocked her, Dr. Gillis didn't flinch. She probably wondered why Mari hadn't mentioned that he had a lawsuit. "Save the bullshit for those state doctors, Mr. Santos.

Contrary to what you heard, or what you were told, I am not one of them. How did you meet Tasha?"

"The state writes your paycheck, correct?"

"Mr. Santos. This is the last time I am going to ask. How did you meet her?"

Kyron released a warm smile, but he knew for a fact that the chilling glare in his eyes prickled the doctor's arms. Three times she dropped her head while trying to maintain eye contact.

He leaned back into the velvety fabric, obviously to get comfortable. "The day my brother came to pick me up, she was with him."

"So, you were so excited to be in the presence of a woman you started mackin' the first one you saw?" Dr. Gillis smiled at her choice of words.

Before responding, he tilted his head right and thought about it. "Yes and no."

"Meaning?"

"Come on, doc." Kyron banged his hand on the not so sturdy coffee table in front of him. "You know I was getting plenty of pussy while I was locked up. So being around some new pussy wasn't nothing. It's just that as soon as I laid eyes on her . . . she was fine, but it wasn't just that. It was her aura. Her sensuality."
He licked his lips. "Nah, doc, I'm just fucking with you. It was all of that and some. But more than that, it was because she was forbidden. I knew I couldn't have her because she belonged to someone else. That made me want her more. But then the more I was in her presence, I saw how much of a boss bitch she was. She made me feel like I was that nigga. She made me feel like I could have her and plus our chemistry. We clicked! Do you understand what I'm saying? Is there a prognosis or diagnosis for what I'm explaining to you?"

"Yes. It's called lust."

"Doc got jokes. Seriously, I felt like I could have her. You understand?"

"I understand. What you're saying is that what you wanted with Tasha, was what she had with her husband."

"Hell no. That's not what I'm saying. I wasn't trying to be her husband." Kyron ran his finger back and forth under his chin. *"No, that wasn't it at all. It was an animalistic attraction. And for the record, I am not trying to be nobody's husband. Not even your girl, Mari's."*

"I'm curious. Take me back. Why was she with your brother when he came to pick you up?" Dr. Gillis needed to know, and Mari wanted to know.

"She had a big fight with her husband and left him out in Cali. She is tight with my brother's wife, so she came to stay with them to get her head straight and to get away. They obviously needed space."

"I see. Continue."

"Shorty ain't have nothing to do and wanted to take her mind off the drama, so I was like fuck it. I'm home, gotta get the crib right. So, I hired her to hang out with me and decorate and shit— do some shopping. And from there we just clicked. That's it, that's all."

"Have you been in contact with her since the hospital incident?"

"Of course."

"Well then it can't be, 'that's it, that's all'. You've obviously caught feelings for Tasha. So, on a scale of one to five, where would you say your feelings for her are?"

"What does that have to do with anything?"

"Please, Mr. Santos. Answer the question."

"I mean, I caught feelings for her, yeah. Hell, we were fucking. What do you expect?"

"I don't expect anything. Did she knock you off your feet? I mean, weren't you in a relationship before you decided to seduce her? You were in a relationship. She was married. Did you two ever discuss this?"

"Okay, doc, you just asked me about four or five questions. Which one do you want me to answer?"

"All of them, Mr. Santos. You said you were sexually involved. Were you surprised that you fell for this woman? How serious did you get?"

"It wasn't that serious. I wanted her to have my baby," he stated, matter-of-factly.

"So, are we talking a five?"

"You could say that."

"What was the conversation between the two of you, knowing that you each had active relationships?"

"I wouldn't discuss my shit with her. It was none of her business. But she let me know from the gate that I was just a fuck and that she was using me to get back at her husband for cheating on her."

"And you were fine with that?"

"Hell yeah! I mean, she is one boss bitch. She could use me to get back at her husband anytime!" Kyron moved to the edge of the sofa, getting excited at the thought of Tasha using him any way she wanted.

Dr. Gillis picked up on his excitement. She jotted down a few sentences before continuing. *"But why were you comfortable with her using you? Give me another reason other than the sex."*

The corners of his mouth turned upward in a smile. *"Because I knew over time, she would catch feelings for me. Being cheated on by her husband only made her ripe for the next nigga. So, I was like why not? When I was fucking shorty, she used to be going crazy! One thing about a nigga, my dick game strong and looongggg."* Seeing that his comments were making Dr. Gillis *uncomfortable, made him go in for the kill as he licked his lips. "And I suck the shit out of some pussy." Kyron tried to be as vulgar as possible. One diagnosis he could surely get was nympho and freak.*

"Keep in mind, shorty was hurt by her husband. And even though we fucked like crazy, she was still a hurt woman in love. I tried to do everything to turn her, but she's not that type of woman. On some real shit, that nigga Trae's fuck up was my come-up. He didn't deserve her."

Dr. Gillis shook her head no as she stood up and pulled off her cashmere sweater. "I think I'm missing something, Kyron. How do you know he didn't deserve her?"

"Oh, so I'm Kyron now? You're getting comfortable with me. Huh, doc? I was Mr. Santos a minute ago. What else do you want to hear, doc?" Kyron glanced at the platinum Breitling on his arm.

Dr. Gillis was silent as she scribbled more notes onto her legal pad. She was writing too muthafuckin' much as far as he was concerned. What the fuck is she writing? Probably shit like jealous, murder, infatuated, lust, and sex.

"So, what's up, doc? What else do you want to hear? Can we end this shit now? I did my part." He stood up. "You should have more than enough to do your report."

"You're right, Mr. Santos. We can end this session now. I think you now have a clearer idea as to what I want to hear. I expect you back into my office on this coming Tuesday. Is 1:00 fine?"

Chapter Sixteen

TRAE

This was just the first session. But could I blame her? Hell yeah! I mean, hell no. I don't fuckin' know! I hurt Tasha, I knew I did, but I damn sure didn't expect her to pull a me on me. This shit hurt like a muthafucka.

I couldn't get over what I just heard and saw. The disheartening part was watching Kyron talk about his relationship with my wife. Watching him express how good her pussy was to him. Him saying in a nutshell, that it was all my fault.

It was one thing to know your woman fucked a nigga, but another to actually see the video of it. I fumbled through the envelope; I still had about six or seven more sessions to go through, but I wasn't sure if I even wanted to watch them. This was a living nightmare. I got out the van and began to pace. I tossed that unbreakable bullshit out the window.

Even though I was determined to make things right with Tasha, it just didn't feel right hearing how they met, and especially listening to another nigga talking about fucking my wife. It damn sure didn't turn me on. In fact, I was sick to my stomach. Could I even stand to watch the rest of the sessions?

I fucked up by fucking Charli, but damn, this shit here was tearing a nigga up inside. I couldn't take it at all, and I wasn't about to act like it either. I mean, I did what I did for my own selfish reasons and nothing more. It was wrong, but I couldn't take it back. But Tasha really hurt me with this one, and I wasn't afraid to admit the shit.

It was crazy how the nigga was dead and gone and I was still being haunted by the shit him and Tasha did. The nigga was probably laughing at me from the grave. *Ain't this a bitch?* That muthafuckin' Kyron! I swear if he wasn't dead, I'd kill his ass again. And that goddamned Tasha! Before I knew it, I smashed my fist into the side window. My knuckles began to bleed, but I didn't give a fuck. I didn't even feel them. I needed to release that tension. Fuck the food, I jumped in the van and headed back to the hospital.

I was furious when I went back up to Tasha's floor, but I kept my fists balled up and contained my anger. One of the nurses stopped me.

"Mr. Macklin, what happened to your hand?" She pushed me over to a sink and immediately got to doing what nurses do. "Your wife had us page you. She woke up with a panic attack, but she seems to have calmed down."

I took a deep breath. Still not saying anything. Her instincts must have told her to shut the fuck up and mind her business. She bandaged me up, and I took several deep breaths.

"Are you going to be okay? Do you need some ibuprofen?"

"No, I'm good. Thank you. Let me go check on my wife."

By the time I made it back into the room, thankfully, Tasha was sleeping peacefully. They had brought her something to eat. But it looked like she barely touched it.

I eased out and went to go hang out in the waiting room. I had to clear my head. The shifts changed, and I went back into her room, and she was still sleeping. I got a few nods in while sitting in the recliner next to her bed. The nurses would come in and check her vitals, but that was it. She remained asleep.

TASHA

I had been lying in bed getting comfortable, after Trae brought me home from the hospital. He brought me breakfast in bed. And even though it was IHOP, it brought back memories of how things used to be. How we took turns spoiling each other, doing breakfast in bed on the weekends, and me giving him a mani-pedi. I remembered how we used to feed each other and eat off each other's plates. We were two peas in a pod. I missed that. I knew we could get back to that place. I was determined to get that comfortable love back again. But in order to do so, we have to dead that Charli/Kyron shit.

Why do men cheat in the first place? If a boss chick like Beyoncé gets her heart broken, then maybe I need to learn to roll with the punches? I wasn't the only one whose man cheated. But why do they do it? No chick who had that answer shared it with me. Trae and I had a beautiful marriage and fulfilling sex life before the Charli and Kyron bullshit. Why did Trae have to fuck up what we had? I would've never fucked Kyron if he hadn't done what he did. He drove me into another man's arms, and now he couldn't seem to get over it.

"We've got to fly out and take this meeting. As soon as Aunt Marva gets in, I'll be leaving." Trae's tone was cold. There was something odd in his voice that I didn't like. His hand was bandaged up and he wouldn't tell me what happened.

"Bae, talk to me. What's going on? You know the doctor said I have to take it easy and not get upset. What are these vibes I'm picking up from you?"

"I'm sorry, ma, but I fucked up. We said no more secrets, no more lies so I'ma just admit the shit. That envelope…it was in the trunk when I went to get your overnight bag. So, I figured while I was waiting for your food, I would check it out."

"Envelope?" I cut his ass off. "Trae! No, you didn't. Now you're fucked up. That's what you get, Trae."

I didn't know what to expect when Trae pulled out the cell phone and pushed play. He held it right in front of me, so I couldn't miss a thing. I watched the session between Kyron and a Dr. Gillis. It was creepy watching Kyron being questioned and sharing his feelings about me. Goosebumps popped up on my arms. How the hell did Mari get a hold of this? As I was forced to continue to watch, I found out that part of Kyron's court order was to see a psychiatrist, and the psychiatrist was Mar's friend. But who does that type of shit? What type of doctor videotapes confidential sessions and gives it to her girlfriend? I got something for them bitches. I'ma make sure they both lose their jobs.

Still, each word hammered a nail into my heart. How long was I going to have to pay for my actions? Tears kept streaming down my cheeks. To make matters worse, that wasn't all. Trae pushed another video in my face that showed me having sex with Kyron when I was drugged. That's when I lost it. That ho ass nigga had the nerve to tape himself raping me, and my husband thought it was cool to make me relive the shit? Why? Because his ego was bruised?

"Trae, that was a rape! You know I was drugged! Why are you showing me this bullshit!"

"I don't care. I wished I'd never seen this."

"Well, you didn't have to watch it. You should have destroyed the envelope like I said."

"Tasha, I couldn't resist; I fooled myself into thinking that I would get closure. This has fucked me all the way up."

"What about that diary Charli sent me with all the freaky sex y'all had! How you ate that bitch out! How do you think I felt? That was fucked up!" I was yelling.

"She was lying, Tasha, so calm down."

"Calm down? You the one pulling out videotapes and shit. You want me to go pull out that ho's diary?

"But that didn't mean shit, Tasha. It was business. You know that one was a fluke and the other one was business."

"What the fuck do you mean a fluke and business? What the fuck is a fluke? How was Charli business, Trae? You gave me trichomoniasis! You got Charli Ho pregnant! That meant you went up in both of them nasty bitches raw! You claim that you was drugged. But you know I was drugged. Therefore, what the fuck are we talking about?"

"You looked like you were enjoying that shit."

"Nigga, I was drugged! I wasn't Tasha, your wife, you fuckin' asshole!" I couldn't believe his line of reasoning. "You was sober! Did you enjoy fucking those hos? I'm sure you did. You came inside them nasty ass bitches. That means you enjoyed it, muthafucka!"

"Well, I know you don't expect me to accept this baby if it's Kyron's."

"You know what! Fuck you, Trae! So, what are you saying? You wouldn't love the baby, even though you say you love me? So much for being unbreakable, huh? So much for gettin' back tight!"

"I'm just saying, if this baby comes out with them light ass eyes, I know it ain't mine. We don't even need no DNA test. Just be truthful, Tasha. We said no more lies."

"You asshole! We have the DNA test results. What more do you need? You know what? Get the fuck away from me, Trae! I should have divorced your ass a long time ago."

"Yo, those videos have my head all fucked up. But it's a man thing, Tasha. You wouldn't understand."

"It's a woman thing, nigga, when your husband fucks other bitches, gets them pregnant and gives you trichomoniasis. And then has the nerve to expect you to be all right with that dumb shit. Like I said, get the fuck away from me! Go take your meeting and I hope your ass never comes back."

Kaylin

The Meeting with Don Carlos

Trae rode shot gun as I drove to the airport to meet with Don Carlos. He had a twisted look on his face from the time I picked him up.

"So, Tasha gave us the ol' false labor thing," I joked, trying to break the ice, although Angel had already told me this.

"False labor it was." Trae was curt and dry.

"Yo, you gotta get your head together for this meeting."

"I'll be ready by the time we land. You know that."

"Nah, nigga. By the time we land? I need you ready now. What's up? Is Tasha and the baby okay?"

"Yeah they good."

"So, what's the problem?"

"Maannnnn, I fucked around and watched those tapes."

"Watched what tapes?"

"That package that Mari gave me. That bitch gave me recordings of your brother and Tasha fucking. A recording of him at the psych doctor talking about how much fun him and Tasha had and how in love they were. The shit is on tape."

"Damn nigga, didn't I tell you to leave that alone? Why didn't you toss that shit? Now look at you. That shit is in the past. We got enough on our plate dealin' with the here and now. We got Seven and the Kings possibly on some bullshit, the shit with the Don and Seven. You just getting out. Tasha getting ready to have the baby. Nigga you better say fuck that old bullshit!"

"I thought I could handle anything. But that…."

"Man it ain't like you and Tasha just started a relationship. Y'all been married for years, nigga!"

"This shit is fucked up."

"Look. Get over it! Let! That! Bullshit! Go! Mari is sick about Kyron. Even though my brother didn't want her, she will never get it that Kyron was who he was. She's obviously not going to stop until you both feel the way she feels. She that type of bitch. If she could have her way, she'd ruin y'all. You gonna let her?"

"I'm done talking about it."

"You need to be. That shit is over. We got business we need to be on right now."

We rode in silence the rest of the way to the airport.

* * *

Don Carlos had property all over the world. This meeting was at his vintage Victorian mansion in Connecticut. It was one of the older homes, with a brick front. The house was decorated throughout in antique furniture, old, famous paintings by Frida Kahlo and Diego Rivera and expensive vases. Expensive tapestries covered and adorned the hardwood floors throughout, and a Persian rug runner trailed through the hallways under vaulted ceilings. It screamed old money.

Bossy.

The butler led us into an office study and library and then disappeared. The Don was seated behind a big oak desk. His chubby face looking as if he had gained a few pounds since we last saw him. He stood up to greet us, and then he sat back down. He got right down to the first order of business.

"You two have always been like sons to me. You know that. Our nationalities were never a factor. And Trae, you know how disappointed I was when you began working with the Li Organization. Charles Li is lower than a snake's belly. I trust that you have learned a valuable lesson from it. Like myself, I'm sure you are paying for your past actions and now your allegiance to him still hangs over both your heads."

Trae didn't respond, thankfully. His temperament could get ridiculous over the wrong things. His easy to ignite temper was his kryptonite. Don Carlos knew about the work our team put in for the Li Organization when Trae first went to jail. But if it meant that I had to dance with the devil to get Trae out, so be it. I had to do what need to be done. Yes, Charles Li was foul, but I had to risk it. I couldn't leave him hanging. During that brief time, I made a lot of money with the Li Organization. Don Carlos was right. Trae pulled me into the Li Organization. Trae's sins were now my sins. We were in until death.

It was Don Carlos' connections and work behind the scenes that got Trae out. I'm sure wasn't too easy especially since Trae collected a body while behind the wall. That nigga should be under the jail. The only way out with the Carlos Cartel was death. Especially since he collected a body while behind the wall.

For the second order of business, I pulled out my cell phone and showed Don Carlos the picture of Seven.

"Yes that's Lolita. And she's blood; she's my daughter," he revealed. I was stunned and I knew Trae felt the same but we each held a poker face. "Lolita was a mistake. A mistake that caused bad blood between friends and death. The stakes were very high during this time. The times were different.

"She didn't know at first. Her mother didn't explain her history until she was a teenager. I tried to do the right thing, make up for my past sins but it ended with her disappointing me. Now that I found her, I can make things right." He picked up my phone to examine the picture more closely. "Unbelievable. She just pops up out of nowhere. Magically reappears and of all the places. One of two reasons I sent for you." He put the phone down and looked back up at us.

"Her last marker was 3.5 million. 1.5 upon calling it in, and the rest when the job is complete. She requires an open marker. To complete the job, you must get your hands dirty. I don't necessarily want either of you to walk this out, but someone trustworthy and capable on your team. If you're in see Tino before you leave.

"I am ashamed to say that I have a grandson that I've never met. Do I feel at times guilty? Of course. And it gets better. As fate would have it, all the while she was right there under everyone's noses. Hidden in plain sight, Seven. Who was this Seven? Where was he from? Running drugs like a common criminal. Seven. All the while I'm looking for my daughter, Sina. The marker is for Sina. She is my seventh child. Not a guy named Seven. She has her old man's balls. Her mother must have told her that she was my seventh child, so she takes the name Seven."

"How did she end up at my house?" I asked.

"Now that, I can only attribute to fate, Mr. Santos. It was fate which brings me to the main purpose of this meeting." Don Carlos switched modes.

"I knew it was coming. I introduced the both of you to this business. I personally brought you into my world. I've always provided protection, which enabled the both of you to operate almost without restriction. And most recently, I made sure that Kay was able to orchestrate your release. I even got the blessings of Charles Li."

"You know. I'm grateful, Don Carlos," Trae interjected.

"Hear me out." He fanned his hand. "I don't call on you often. But the Li Organization is a thorn in all of our sides, and he can strike at any time.

Hmmmmmm. Something was brewing. Why would he strike? Them two are clashing heads? But why? Charles Li said one thing that stuck with me. "You can only get out of this life with blood." Now I see it was the same school of thought with

Don Carlos. We could never walk away from this life, wash our hands clean, and go 100% legit. Not without blood. "What are you proposing?" I asked.

"I need you two to go to Beijing. There is a Bitcoin and Cryptocurrency Private Roundtable that I need you to have a stake in. And there's some diversity needed. I assure you, you will be richly compensated— more than either one of you have earned with the Li Organization. In addition, we must solve our newly inherited territory issues. Both Beijing and the territory issues need to be moved on simultaneously. I trust that you will choose the right men for the job. I am aware that you both have baby and touring issues to be dealt with presently. But if you're in, sacrifices will have to be made because we must move immediately. You will receive further instructions once you get there. You will have protection for your family."

"Territory issues. Won't this bring war?"

"Always thinking ahead, Trae. But a war?"

"That depends on how we play our hand."

"Yes, there are territory issues in Beijing. But I also mean territory issues right here in my own backyard. Or should I say your backyard. But more on that later." Don Carlos shrugged. "There is still a marker on both of your heads, that I am trying to clean up. Kay, in that last meeting with Li, you were warned to get out of LA and never come back. But you did. You violated by going back and forth to get Trae out of prison."

"I had to do what I had to do. Trae wouldn't have left me hanging. Don't forget I have that information on the Li Organization that I used to walk out of that meeting alive."

"That's why your marker keeps going up. But you called in one of my markers, I've called in yours so that 3.5 is no longer on the table."

The Don looked serious. "He will never dismiss Trae's violation of his daughter. Do you really believe for a second that he is going to forgive and forget?"

I thought about it. Everything Don Carlos just said was true. That pit bull attack on his daughter . . . Charles Li wasn't going to let that slide.

The meeting lasted less than forty-five minutes. We were left with the illusion that we had a choice in the matter. And talking about coincidence? This Seven shit was unbelievable. Don Carlos' love child? And that love child who was running a territory, named her son after him. I couldn't make this shit up.

Chapter Seventeen

TRAE

We were back on the private jet. All I could think about was Don Carlos saying the Li Organization had a marker on my head. I knew those nightmares I was having while I was locked up were a fuckin' sign that some shit was about to go down.

"First order of business, our families," I said.

"Women and children are supposed to be off limits." Kay punched his fist into the palm of his hand. The Chinese Triad? Just the name alone lets me know that we can't be too fuckin' lax when dealing with these jokers. Nothing is off limits to them muthafuckas. We have to have a solid Plan B."

"Agreed. Again, first priority is to secure our families. Second priority put someone on Seven. The Don wants to move in on her territory as soon as possible. He wants to hit her where it hurts. Who should we put on that?" I asked him. I could see his mind churning to determine the best man for such a high-risk job.

"I'ma say Bo. He's out there anyway," Kay said.

"I say Faheem. He needs to replenish his war chest and it's his town. Use Bo as his backup. Plus, the nigga needs something dirty to do." I knew that was fucked up to say, but I could see it.

Faheem's spirit left with the death of his son. He was primed for what the Don needed done and anxious to get back in the game. He told me that himself.

"Then it's settled. What did you get from our meeting?" Kay asked.

"He said Li was a thorn in both of our sides. And he left that open. He got me thinking that this trip is about Charles Li. How and why? I don't know. And what the fuck he need us to attend some bitcoin conference for? It's not adding up."

"To me neither. But what choice do we have other than to go and let it play out?"

JAZ

"Girl, why didn't you call me? I heard you almost had the baby." I could tell Tasha was happy to hear from me. "So, now you're on bed rest?"

"Yes, but false labor, Jaz. My body is trippin' and Trae is seriously trippin'." She sighed.

"Tell me what's up? Trippin' about what?"

"He done went and watched a fuckin' video of Kyron...you know. The rape. Now the nigga can't even see or think straight. He is Dr. Jekyll and Mr. Hyde around this bitch."

"What the h—why?" I couldn't believe all the drama those two kept attracting and I was not ready for the bombshell that she dropped.

"I don't know. He was determined to check out what was in that envelope that Mari gave him and now he can't take it. The tension is so thick around here, I'm having trouble breathing."

"I'm coming over now!"

"Jaz, I'm good. Marva is here, and Angel has the boys."

"Where is he now?"

"He's gone. I'm not sure where and don't really care at this point when he's coming back."

"You know what? I'll be there after I run my errands. And where is Angel? Wait. Hold on." I called Angel and conferenced her in. "Angel, it's me and Tasha. Can you go over and be with Tasha? I can't get there until after I finish up at the college. I'm not sure what time that will be."

"Is in labor?"

"No. She needs our moral support right about now and I can't ...."

"Jaz, I have her boys, Jahara, and my neighbors' kids. Isn't Marva there? What happened? Tasha, are you by yourself? All I can say is bring her over here."

"Marva's here, ladies. I'm good. I'm not going anywhere. Chill out. Jaz, get here when you can. And stop talking as if I'm not on the phone."

"Tasha, what brought on the false labor? Too much dick? Slow ya ass down."

"Angel, shut the hell up! The doctor has me on bed rest until I deliver."

"So, it *was* too much dick. I told you to be careful. I guess Trae almost fucked that baby out of you." Me and Angel started laughing.

"I'm about to hang up on y'all." Tasha threatened.

"Wait. Not until you tell Angel what Trae did."

"Jaz, no. I'll tell her when I see her. You're lucky I told you. Just be sure to stop by when you finish."

"What? What did he do?" Angel probed.

"I'm hanging up. Jaz will fill you in. I don't feel like talking about it right now." Tasha said and hung up.

I looked up and my husband was taking off his clothes so there was no way in hell I was about to gossip with Angel. "I gotta go, Angel." I hung up. Faheem was standing in the middle of the bedroom butt naked, dick long and hard.

His determination to get me pregnant was getting on my nerves. He was trying to fill the void that Lil' Faheem left, but I knew I could have fifty kids, and it wouldn't heal his broken heart.

For the last few months, he had been trying his darnest. So, I knew he was going to flip when he found out I was on the pill. I was too scared to tell him that I wasn't ready to have another baby. I was dealing with too much stress. Trying to get situated with school. Relocating. Lil' Faheem. The baby showers. It was all a little overwhelming. I didn't need to have another baby. I would leave that to fertile myrtle Tasha; it was not my calling.

And not to mention the paranoia I was battling. I had been on ten. I made it a habit to go to the gun range at least three times a week. Atlanta was a real life experience. No Hollywood shit. I told Faheem that I was paranoid, and I wanted to always be ready.

"You only paranoid 'cause you don't know what you doin'. Baby, you not a gangsta," he had said.

I wasn't trying to be a gangster. But the paranoia was real, and it was getting worse.

FAHEEM

"Jaz, get your fine ass over here. You know what time it is."

Although Jaz was dressed to go to school, she stopped, took off her clothes, and dropped to her knees. I didn't know how I would have made it these last few months if it wasn't for my wife. She took care of me when I was in the hospital and when I got out. It was hard pill for me to swallow when I suggested that we move from Atlanta. We both knew we had to. There were too many niggas, with a little power, out for revenge against us. We were sitting ducks, waiting to get plucked.

I pulled her up off her knees, turned her around, and entered her from the back. The way I was fucking her, I was sending shockwaves to her G-spot. Her pussy was so wet, the smack of each stroke was growing louder and louder.

"Fa—oh fuck! I'm getting ready . . . you gonna make me come!" She gasped.

"Come on then. Come wit' big daddy. I'm ready." I told her as her juices creamed my long, hard shaft. She began to tremble. I didn't come with her, but I wasn't far behind. The extra creaminess of her pussy made me blast off deep inside of her. The force made me weak in the knees, and I staggered slightly. Fuck. I was hoping I made another son. This time it would be with the woman I loved and respected. I knew one child couldn't replace another, but it was the only way I could heal this hole in my heart.

After Jaz left for school, my cell phone rang. I glanced down to see who it was but the number was blocked. I answered it anyway.

A subdued voice whispered, "Nigga, don't think you got away with shit. We gon' find you, nigga. Find you and yo' family."

TRAE

After we left Don Carlos and flew back into town, I picked up my ride from the apartment and went to pick the boys up from Angel's.

"Trae, you need to be there now more than ever for her emotional stability. She really needs you right now. And fuck Mari! Fuck Kyron! Let that go!" Angel fussed at me.

I didn't say anything. I was still pissed, and yes, I knew my wife needed me. I just didn't want to be there for her right now.

"Daddy! Daddy!" Caliph yelled, running to jump on me. I used to be able to easily pick him up and turn him upside down. That was over now.

"Hey, Dad," Kareem said as he came and stood by me.

"Dad, are we going home now?" Shaheem asked.

The twins were calm and cool for six-year-olds. "I was thinking about stopping by the park," I told them.

"Yeah, let's do that!" Shaheem said and headed for the front door with his brothers on his heels.

"Did Mommy have our little sister yet?" Kareem turned around and asked.

"No, not yet. Let's go have some fun."

"Trae, you're not going straight home. You didn't hear what I just said?" Angel was still in fuss mode.

"I need to clear my head first. I'm sure Tasha does too. Thanks for keeping the boys." I kissed her on the cheek and left. She was still running off at the mouth, but I had tuned her out.

I took the boys to the park and let them run wild. We ate all the junk we could find, and I made them promise not to tell Tasha. My plan was to stay until it was dark; that way, I could be sure that the only thing they were up for was a bath and a bed.

"I'm ready to see Mommy now," Caliph screamed as he pumped his legs on the swing, trying to go higher. I knew the boys loved their mother, and until this Kyron thing, Tasha had always been an impeccable mom. I knew that she would have never did what she did had I not fucked around on her. Tasha told me up front: if she let me into her heart, she would not tolerate any cheating. I promised her that I would never break her heart. I had no idea of the drama that would come from breaking my promise. I should be able to take this like a man. I made my bed and I have to lie in it. But damn it stung. Now I knew how Tasha felt.

As the boys started to tire out, I thought about how I had seen all three of them born. I had watched them each take their first breath. Suddenly, I wanted to be there when Tasha had this baby—no matter what.

Chapter Eighteen

MARI

I couldn't wait any longer. I pushed the number programmed in my cell phone. "Hello, Trae?" I could hear the kids playing in the background. I had to admit it. I was jealous to know that Tasha had such a good husband and father for her kids.

"Who is this?"

"It's Mari. Kyron's widow."

I couldn't help but call Trae and ask if he had listened to the recordings and looked at the videos. I couldn't stand people like Tasha. She had a good man, but she was just greedy. Why did she have to fuck with my man and ruin what we had? I had waited years for Kyron while he was locked up, set up his business, and cleaned up his legal problems. We were planning on getting married. Now he was dead and gone with all my dreams and hopes for our future. I knew somehow, Kyron's murder was indirectly tied to Tasha. Although Trae had a good alibi, he was in California and locked up when Kyron was murdered, I still knew it was tied into Tasha.

As far as I was concerned, that baby Tasha was carrying should have been Kyron's and my baby, but he was too busy screwing Tasha when we went to Las Vegas. I knew that was

Kyron's baby Tasha was carrying. And since it was his baby, that baby might as well be mine. I was sure I could get Trae to give it to me, and if he didn't, I'd just take what belonged to me.

"Kyron's widow?" The line went silent, so I spoke.

"Yes. How are you?"

"What are you callin' me for? . . . What? You want me to agree to fuck you because that would make you feel better since Kyron and Tasha fucked, right? Let me save you some time. It ain't happening!"

No, he didn't just say that. It didn't sound like a bad idea though.

"That's where you're wrong. I was calling to see if you had a chance to check out the contents of my package. It's not hard to see they were in love."

"Look, Mari, I had you pegged differently. So, I don't want to be disrespectful, but that was some ho shit. And them tapes ain't shit. There's nothing on them that I care about." The line went silent again. I looked down to see that he had hung up in my face. I dialed him back because I wanted to discuss the baby or at least arrange a meeting, but it kept going to voicemail.

I couldn't help but smile. Obviously, he had seen everything. I could hear it in his voice. I was going to destroy their relationship like Tasha destroyed mine.

Then I would get that baby. It was an eye for an eye.

Next, I called Tasha's number, which I found in Kyron's cell phone. She sounded like I woke her up when she answered.

"Hey, Tasha."

"Who is this?"

"It's Mari."

"Mari, I hope you enjoyed watching the tape of your man being so obsessed with this pussy that he had to drug and rape me to get it. That nigga is fuckin' pathetic. I hope you see that."

"Tasha, I know you're behind Kyron's death, and you are going to pay for it."

"Bitch, eat a dick! And you better pray that you don't run into me because I'ma dog walk that ass!" Tasha hung up the phone.

TASHA

I couldn't believe the nerve of that bitch, Mari. Was she ever going to get over Kyron? The dick was good, but it wasn't that good for her to be trippin' over him the way she was doing.

As I told Kyron, he was just a revenge fuck. How was I to know a nigga would get pussy whipped, fall in love, and give me an engagement ring. Trae took that shit and flushed it down the toilet?

Just when Trae and I were trying to get back tight, this bitch, Mari planted this bombshell. I could be sitting here getting "pregnant spoiled" by my man, particularly since I was craving a big, juicy, sloppy cheeseburger—but now he was out, God knows where. From the look on his face when he left this morning, I wasn't even sure if he was ever coming back.

I had cried enough and decided to do something about my situation. This lying in bed was driving me crazy. I spent most of the time on my laptop cruising around on Facebook and Instagram. I even a fake account for myself. I checked Charli's Facebook account and it was no longer active. I checked Mari's Facebook account and it was still active. I guess she had friended me, or vice versa when Kyron was alive because I could see her activity. Damn. I must be bored, to be scoping out these bitches. Mari had changed her status to "widow." *Puh-lease.* They were never married. All her fake ass, dick-sucking followers were sending praying hands, quotes and giving her all types of comments of encouragement and support.

I knew Mari would be ecstatic to know her ploy worked. The tapes were a blow to Trae's male ego, but he was the one who said, that shit was going to be coming at us, but we were unbreakable. I believed him, and now I was determined to not allow air to come between us.

It was now dark and late, and I was beginning to get a little anxious. Even though I told him to never come back, I had called his cell all evening, and it went straight to voicemail. I'd also texted him several times. I went into the living room to wait on my husband and boys. Out of nowhere, Aunt Marva popped up.

"And what do you think you're doing?" Her hands were on her hips and her head was cocked to the side.

"Sitting on the couch. I am allowed to sit, right? You want me to get bed sores?"

"Girl, you only been on bed rest for a day. Two tops. How in the hell are you going to get bedsores?"

"I'm good, Auntie. Just waiting on Trae and the boys."

Reluctantly, she turned around and disappeared. I sat there for almost an hour getting more restless by the minute. Just when I grabbed my phone to call Kay, I heard the key turning the lock.

The front door opened, and my boys came in first, followed by their father. That was the most beautiful sight in the world. My little men and my Big Daddy were home.

TRAE

I was still mad, but I enjoyed seeing how the boys doted all over Tasha who was propped up on the living room sofa. "Ma! Dad took us to the park," they said as they rained kisses all over her face.

"Did y'all eat?" she asked. I could hear the suspicion in her voice. None of the boys responded. "Um hmmm. I know your dad let y'all eat junk food. You don't have to tell on him."

Seeing my boys with Tasha made me realize how much they loved their mother. Hell, I was madly in love with her, and our marriage was worth trying to save. I was really trippin'. After I seriously thought about it, I felt stupid. *How in the fuck can I let a dead man ruin everything I've built?* My wife and children are here with me, my baby girl is on the way, and I am free. Fuck is wrong with me? I should be fighting for my marriage.

Tasha kissed the boys all over their dirty faces. "I missed y'all. But y'all are all so dirty and smelly. Ewwww!"

The boys thought that was so funny. "We been with Daddy at the park, Ma," Caliph reminded her.

"We raced on fast bikes and shot some hoops!" Kareem bragged.

"You did?" Tasha sounded happy and amused.

"We had so much fun!" Shaheem added. "Ma, I'm glad my dad is back and he's glad to be back, right Dad?"

"Me too, baby," she said.

"Me too!" Kareem and Caliph chimed in.

Looking over their heads, Tasha smiled gratefully at me. "Time to take your baths, guys. It is way past your bedtime."

After I made sure the boys were down, I made my way to our bedroom where Tasha was. We both were quiet, as if we didn't know what to say to each other.

Tasha spoke up first. "Bae, that bitch Mari called here. She wants to start shit between us, and I'm not going to let her."

I didn't tell her Mari had called me, too. Yes, I knew Mari was out to break us up, and she was doing a good job of it, if you ask me. "What did you say?"

"I told her to eat a dick and that she better hope we don't cross paths and I hung up on her."

I had to smile. This was the chick I fell in love with. We looked at each other and smiled. The ice was broken—for the moment anyhow.

"Baby, I'm sorry. And I know I said some mean things," Tasha told me. She reached up, put both arms around my neck, and pulled me down onto the bed with her. She gave me a big kiss, and as much as I tried to act hard, I gave in. I knew she was sincere. Ever since that Charli/STD scenario, Tasha didn't always apologize, so I knew she was humbling herself for the sake of holding us together.

Within seconds I started getting an erection, and I moved away. "You know the doctor said I can't get none, so you need to chill." I placed her hand on my dick. Tasha began to massage it.

"He didn't say I couldn't give you head." Tasha gave me a wink and *that* look, and I knew it was on. "You want some of this?" she flirted, licking her lips seductively.

"I want all of it." I told her as I eased the straps off of her shoulders, down over her breasts, and began to feast on her erect nipples. Her breath caught in her throat. She grabbed the back of my head, loving what I was doing.

I knew my wife's body very well and used it to play a rhythm. I knew when to alternate between licks and sucks. Gently, I kissed and licked my way down to her belly button. She spread her legs wide in anticipation of what was coming next. I pulled back the hood of her clit and began to suck on it until she squirmed and moaned, as she tossed her head from side to side. My dick was rock hard and throbbing. As much as I loved it when she came on my tongue, I wanted to feel that shit on my dick.

"Put it in please. Just for a minute, babe. Please."

I snatched off my pants and got in between my wife's thick, juicy thighs and made penetration, but not all the way in like I wanted.

"Oh, Trae, I miss us and how we were so much," she groaned, tears of joy cascading down her cheeks.

"I missed us even more."

"Trae," she sang, loving the slow, steady, but not so deep, dicking I was giving her.

"Say my name again."

"Traaaaae!" She opened her legs wider, inviting me to go deeper, but I wouldn't.

"Yeah, daddy, just like that. Just like that." She pleaded.

I was giving her short, teasing thrusts that made her gasp for air until she began to come. I released with her.

"Oh my God! I love you, baby." She could barely catch her breath.

"I love you too. I hope we didn't fuck up."

We lay there in a cozy embrace as she drifted off to sleep. I couldn't help but to think about Mari's phone call. That bitch was a problem that needed to be erased.

Chapter Nineteen

KAYLIN

"Are you sure?" I was sitting at my desk at my office in Game Over Records. Angel pulled out the pregnancy stick and flashed it before me like a magic wand. It read positive.

"Yes, babe. You're going to be a daddy—again!"

I jumped out my chair, grabbed Angel, lifted her in the air and kissed her. I think I was more excited than when she was pregnant with Jahara. I'd never forget how Angel almost lost her life by clinging to me when I was kidnapped. She refused to let the hitmen take me without her, although I tried to stop her. We almost got buried alive. This baby was conceived out of a deeper love than when we first were married and I hoped it was a boy.

"Red, let's go out tonight and celebrate. We'll go to a nice restaurant and have a candle-lit dinner."

"No, baby. Let's celebrate at home. Let me create the mood. I don't want to go out." Angel was glowing.

I answered with a kiss as I scooped her up and laid her onto the sofa. I ran my hands along her thighs, pushing her skirt up to her hips, to get an up close and personal view of the pussy print that was all mines. I nibbled up her thighs until my nose touched the moistened silk of her panties as I inhaled her scent. My favorite scent.

"Mmmmmmmmm," Angel moaned, cocking her leg up over the couch. "I think dinner's already ready."

I didn't hesitate to feast. I slid her panties off, tossed them, and went to sucking her clit and fingering her at the same time. Her body trembled as she grabbed the back of my head and went to grinding her pussy into my face.

"You taste good, baby." I darted my tongue in and out of her, causing her to become wetter and wetter.

She gasped as she rocked her hips and kept moaning my name. I was loving this.

"Baby, I'm com–" she tried to say, but the explosion inside of her took her breath away. Then it was like she couldn't stop coming.

I got up and stripped. "Get up, Red, time to take a ride on this dick," I commanded as I stood there waiting on her to get herself together. I lay down on the couch and she straddled me, reverse cowgirl style, cocking both legs wide and bracing herself by putting her hands on her knees. I watched her fat, juicy ass jiggle as she went buck wild on my dick, taking every inch.

"I love this good dick," she moaned.

Smack! I couldn't resist. That ass cheek jiggled. She rode me harder. She loved it when I slapped that ass.

"Yeah, Daddy, you know I like that shit. I love that while you're fucking me!"

Smack! She released a whimper as I reached around and spread her pussy lips, grinding my dick deeper up in it.

"Ka-Kaylin!"

I pulled her to me, arching my back as my dick spit inside her. She was right. Dinner was already served.

* * *

After Angel left, my mind shifted back to Don Carlos. I had to keep up, and if I could, think ahead of him. He tried to make it appear so simple. Go to China, handle business for him and come right back. Yeah right. Every time he told us that, it always ended in gun play and or murder. Then there was Kevin and Seven. I couldn't shake the feeling that Kevin knew more than what he told us. Was that really how they hooked up? If so, who sent her to my house, if it wasn't Kevin? Or the Li organization. Or Don Carlos? On top of everything else, we had to get Faheem set up and prepared to put in work for Don Carlos.

But more important than that we were about to embark on some crazy shit. I felt in my gut that this was going to be a bumpy ride.

SEVEN

"This shit got that diamond dance going. Definitely flakey," Kevin said, cutting open the kilo and dipping in a tiny spoon to snort up one nostril. "Wow, that's fire there!" He released a long whistle.

"Good. Those Columbians never fail us." I frowned as I thought about my next sentence. "We need to be able to flip a little faster than what we're doing."

"Here we go again. Seven, don't be greedy and you won't get swallowed up. We have to pace ourselves."

We were sitting in the back office at my CPA firm. We were doing well, don't get me wrong. But since I had Kevin, the dope game was less hours and more money. My accounting practice was more hours and less money. I was anxious to travel, see the world and get more money. Kevin was in my ear about backing up from the dope game and keeping clean.

"I have a plan, Kevin. We just need to execute it. Let me show it to you."

"Sev, I need to bounce. And like I said, you too greedy."

"You only hatin' because I'm a girl."

"Moderation is the key. And you need to keep your nose clean. You have a baby. I'm out."

"You'll see my plan. You'll see."

Kevin waved me off. He did have to leave. Today, we had a U-Haul going to the flea market to drop product off to his runners. Usually, someone lower on the food chain did that, but our main man, Diesel, went to Texas to bury his father. So Kevin had to do it.

"Be careful, punk," I told him.

"I will." Kevin nodded. "Peace. I'm out."

* * *

"You have a prepaid call from an inmate," the operator's voice came across my cell phone. I had recognized the prison phone number, which was why I immediately answered and pressed 5.

The voice that used to be music to my ears cut right to the chase. "Sina, what's up? How are you? When are you going to come see me and bring my son?" It was Roddy, my son's father, who was doing a twenty-five-year bid for RICO charges. He had an appeal pending. I lost count of how much I spent fighting this fight with him. He was in USP Leavenworth. I refused to travel way to Kansas to a maximum-security prison with a baby. I did it once and vowed never again.

"Always quick to the point. I'm good. Your son is good."

"You know I don't have a lot of time on this phone. I want to see my son. My sister said she'd even bring him for a visit."

"I just sent you some new pictures." Roddy had gone to prison before Carlito was born.

"Pictures? Stop playing. I need to *see* my son."

"Roddy, I asked you to call because I wanted to hear your voice. Not fight with you. I can't leave my business, and I already told you we will see you when you get moved to a closer facility. I am not allowing your sister to bring him. He barely knows her; I might as well bring him myself. Me flying him to her in Chicago, then going back to get him…it doesn't even make sense. Again, I might as well bring him myself."

"You have one-minute remaining," the automated voice announced.

"Don't think I don't hear things 'cause I'm on lock. I know what you're up to. I just hope you know what you're doing and can handle yourself."

"You know better than I do that you can't believe everything you hear. And once more for the record, me and Kevin are business partners."

"I'm not talking about that nigga. I'm telling you that's why I need to see you."

"I'm hanging up now." I didn't want him talking my business over the prison network.

When Roddy got arrested, I was almost nine months pregnant. I met Kevin months later. He was at the flea market selling mixtapes and dope. I was pushing Carlito in his stroller, checking out the vendors, dressed like a tomboy.

"That's a cute lil' man you've got," Kevin called out from his booth. "Ma, come here; check out my tapes." He was being a salesman.

I know I was looking down in the face. That was where I was at that time. Depressed. Depressed about my state of affairs. Roddy. My mother who was my best friend. It was all wearing me down. Kevin picked up right away, and I appreciated that. I looked down at Carlito's fat cheeks and headful of curly, black hair. He was a beautiful baby. Kevin made me feel grateful. For the first time in a long time, I smiled. "Thank you," I said, and I went over to his table.

"Is he your first?" Kevin was just trying to make conversation.

"Yes." Suddenly Carlito began spitting up, and I hurried to get him out the stroller, so he wouldn't choke. He suffered from GERD; he would throw-up all of the time.

Before I could get the baby out the stroller, Kevin had rushed from behind his booth, took him from me, and was gently patting his back until he cleared his air passages. Kevin walked him back and forth until he dozed back off to sleep.

"You're a professional. How many do you have?"

He laughed. "Nada."

"Yeah, right."

"Seriously. I can't help it if I'm a natural when it comes to the babies. My sister has an army."

"If you're such a natural, why don't you have one?"

"Not the right time. I got moves to make."

Those were the magic words. *Moves to make.* I ended up staying at his booth until he closed up shop. That evening, Kevin took me to Cold Stone for some ice cream; we clicked and kept in touch. We ended up becoming homies. He was doing his thing, and I was trying to make moves. From that day forward, we teamed up and had been rolling as thick as thieves ever since.

That's my history with Kevin. We vowed to keep our relationship strictly business. And so far, it had been working. Hooking up with Kevin was the best thing that could have happened to me. He was loyal, trustworthy, and had a wealth of information. Yes! His family, his sister's husband, and friends used to be big in the game, but according to him they quit to go legit, but I didn't believe him until the baby shower. The energy, their swag; I wanted that. And I wanted more.

Chapter Twenty

KYRA

I had never felt more awkward in my life than I felt as I stood by Rick at the neonatal critical care unit window, gazing at his baby boy, Rick Jr., as he fought for his life. He was in an incubator and had tubes going in and out of his little body. I felt so bad for the baby. It broke my heart, and the tears welled up in my eyes. For a moment, I didn't think about Nina being my adversary. If she were here, I would actually give her a hug. I saw this precious little soul fighting for his life and my man hurting to see his firstborn so vulnerable and clinging to every breath.

"How's the baby?" Rick frantically asked the first doctor who came out of the room.

"And you are?"

"I'm his father, Rick Bryant." Rick pulled out his ID. "My name is on the birth certificate."

Before the doctor, whose badge identified him as Dr. Jeff Henson, could pull Rick aside, we heard a loud irate voice.

"Rick, no you didn't just sneak up here with this bitch!" I looked up and there was Nina, hands on her hips. The last time I saw her was when she was pregnant, and we came to blows. I balled up my fists, ready to beat this bitch's ass and have her laid up right next to her son.

She always had to be disrespectful whenever she saw me; when in all reality, I should be the one that was pissed off. Rick was my man first! And regardless of anything, if he didn't want to be with me when he found out I was alive, then he wouldn't have. So, her anger needed to be towards him not me.

RICK

"Nina, that is my son in there. Why aren't you answering your phone? I told you I'd be on the next flight out."

"I knew you were going to do this, Rick. Why did you have to bring her? You just keep making shit worse. This is a matter to be dealt with within our family. Not me, you and ya homewrecking skank!"

"Watch your mouth, Nina. She is carrying our baby's sister, so you might as well get used to it. I think we got bigger things to worry about. Like for instance, what's wrong with my son?"

"Rick, you really got me fucked up! If you don't get the fuck out of this hospital and take this hood rat with you, I swear I'm about to lose it. Leave me alone to worry about making sure that my son lives to see another day." Then she turned to Kyra, "I suggest you get your bitch ass the fuck away from here before I tear you a new one."

I looked on as the two women that I loved were locked in a stalemate. They glared at each other in a Mexican stand-off. I could tell by the look on Kyra's face that she didn't give a fuck if she was pregnant or not, she was just waiting for Nina to bring the slightest move.

What the fuck did I get myself into? They both were hell bent on not allowing our good thing to work.

ANGEL

Don't make a scene. Just walk with us, a voice barked. At first, I was thinking he wasn't talking to us. But when I turned and saw three dudes in janitor uniforms, I tried to remain calm. These niggas had rolled up on us with guns. We were about to get jacked.

"Yo, son, tell your wife to keep going. You have to come with us," the light-skinned one told Kaylin.

"Aiight. But just make sure you let my wife go."

I held Kaylin that much tighter.

"Baby, go ahead home. I'll be there later."

I panicked. "No!" I blurted out. "If they take you, they gotta take me, too." I balled up a fistful of his shirt. If they wanted me to turn him loose, they were going to have to cut off my arm.

Pow!

I woke up, twisting and sweating.

Kaylin was shaking me. "Baby, are you having that nightmare again?" I looked around the room. He hugged me tight. "Yo, we good, baby, you're safe. I got you. But, babe, same dream back to back to back. That's not healthy."

"I know, I know, but it was so real this time," I said, trying to stop trembling.

"You said that the last time and the time before that, Red." I hoped this wasn't an omen and I hoped Kaylin wouldn't send me back to therapy again. "We need to find out why this is happening."

KAYLIN

I took Angel to dinner at Daniel's, one of my fave five, a restaurant in New York. Jahara and Aisha were spending the night with Jaz and Faheem, so the night was all about us.

The lobster bisque was on point, but the intimate ambiance was really what you were paying three hundred dollars a plate for. It was worth every dime. The whole time I couldn't take my eyes off Angel. I was so excited to be having another baby, and she already had that pregnant glow. She kept her eyes on me. It was as though she and I were the only ones in the place. Red was using her foot to play with my dick under the table. We were giggling and shit, taking turns and feeding each other like we were straight honeymooners.

The foreplay had me overly anxious to get home and beat the pussy up.

When we got situated in the car, Red whispered into my ear, "I told you we should've stayed home." She unzipped me and began to give me some jaw action.

* * *

By the time we made it home, we couldn't make it to the bedroom. We stood up against the living room wall, her legs wrapped around my waist, and I pulled her thong to the side. I slid into her so effortlessly and was just getting my stroke on, causing her to whisper nasty shit in my ear, when suddenly, I started hearing a *"Rattattattat!"* and *"Pop, Pop, Pop."* Our windows rained shards of glass all over the living room floor.

I instinctively pulled Angel to the floor, covering her with my body. I didn't even have my burner on me.

The fire power seemed like it went on forever. Finally, I heard the car doors slam and rubber skidding against the road. Then there was silence.

KYRA

I was sick of this bitch! Who the hell did she think she was? She had me fucked up! Pregnant or not, I was about to show this ho who she need not to fuck with, period! I lunged for Nina, and this time I was the one pregnant, ready to battle. Rick stepped in between us, but I damn near tried to take his head off too.

"Stop it, Kyra! You're both better than this."

"I ain't gon' be no more bitches, skanks or whores!" I said, trying to swing on Nina. The blow landed on Rick's shoulder.

Nina was reaching over Rick, trying to hit me as well.

"Bitch, I'll call you that all day long since you gon' get pregnant by my man, when you knew I was pregnant." She enunciated each word with a swing, although none of her hits landed and vice-versa. Rick was like a wall standing between us.

"Bitch, he was my man first!" I declared. "We have history!"

I was praying I got my hands on her ass. I was going to rip her ass apart! *Ugh*.

Doctor Henson began calling on his phone. "Security! Security!"

All I felt was Rick's arms around me, keeping me from Nina; my enemy. The bitch he fell in love with. The bitch he was choosing over me! At least, that was how I looked at the situation.

"Let me go! Let me go!" I screamed. "You're choosing her over me!"

"I chose the both of you. But now I'm having second thoughts. Neither one of y'all is proving to be worth my damn energy and time."

RICK

I was trying to keep Kyra from hurting herself and the baby, but she turned on me like a rattlesnake. Her generally soft features transmogrified into something that looked like a demon. It caught me off guard.

"If you want that bitch, you can have her. Let me go!" Kyra ranted.

By then the security guards had shown up on the scene. "Ladies, I suggest that you quiet down immediately. This is a hospital. Or will we need to escort the both of you out?"

"I have this under control, thank you." I hoped I was putting the security officers at ease. They walked a few feet away and stood there watching and listening. "Kyra, I'm trying to calm you down. You're too far gone to be in a fist fight."

"Let her go," Nina hissed. "She fought me when I was pregnant. That's probably what's wrong with our son. If something happens to my baby, I swear . . . I swear, I'll never forgive you or her."

"Bitch, if you keep it up. The same thing is going to be wrong with you!" Kyra shot back.

I couldn't take this shit anymore.

"Ladies, will you please STOP!" I didn't mean to lose control, but I couldn't take anymore. The bass in my voice bounced off the walls.

Both Kyra and Nina looked as though I had struck them. For a moment, silence reigned. The two women stood as if they were frozen to the floor. Security was motionless as well.

Finally, Kyra snatched her arm away from my grasp, and stomped away, heading to the elevator. She turned to the security guards. "You don't have to put me out, I'm leaving." As for me, she threw words over her shoulder as she waddled away. "I'm outta here, Rick. Don't worry about me or my baby."

I rushed over to her and grabbed her arm. "The hell you are! You are staying your ass right here. You don't want to see this side of me, Kyra. But if you leave, I'm going to show it to you. Now, I need you here. Fuck all the bullshit. I need you. Be here for me and my son." I left her there to make her own decision daring her to leave.

* * *

I was worried about Kyra, but I knew she had a credit card and her license and could get a ticket anywhere she wanted to go. Plus, I had slipped about four-grand in her purse when she wasn't looking. I was more concerned about my defenseless baby. Why did women have to act so crazy? I mean damn, at least think about the kids. But I knew if she left, she would see what crazy was.

Of course, I stayed and found out about my son. It turned out Rick Jr. had a large boil on his stomach from a staph infection. The doctor had done the surgery, and now they had taken the tubes out of him. He was on the mend, so I was relieved about that.

Nina was silent after the doctor left. Wearing our white gowns so as not to pass any infection, we both camped out in the nursery. We stayed there all night, never speaking a word to each other. We both took turns talking to Rick Jr. Nina would rub his arms and legs and sing to him. When she sat down, I knew it was my turn. I went over to the incubator.

"You're a fighter like your dad," I whispered to my son, as he clung to my finger. "You are going to be all right."

Kyra sat in the waiting room all night. I knew she was hurt, but I was even more thankful that she stood by my side when I needed her most. She had passed my test.

SEVEN

"Kevin, how close are you to Faheem?" I had to tread lightly but at the same time I wanted to know.

"Close enough. Why?"

"Because I would like to bring him in on something."

"Sev, Faheem is out of your league. I'm telling you, you don't want to fuck with him. Stay far away from him. They were asking me who you were at the shower. Stay away."

"Who wanted to know?" He now had my full attention. I followed him to the front door.

"Stay away, Seven. Plus, he's married."

"I know that. I'm talking about business. Business and pleasure or business and relationships don't mix."

"You have a business partner. I'm your business partner."

"What if I don't want us to be business partners anymore?"

"What the fuck are you talking about?" He had opened the front door and now he had closed it back, his eyes cutting through me.

I didn't want to tell him, but the baby shower allowed me to see a different side of him. Seeing that all of the people he would talk about were real and they were exactly how he described...all bosses. The chicks and the men. Dayuuummmm. It gave him more credibility. Lately I had been having a hard time not fantasizing about them; and now I was looking at Kevin in a whole new light.

I stepped up to him and kissed him. There. I did it. And yes, he was caught by surprise.

"What are you doing, Sev? You know this ain't us."

"Why can't it be us?" I kissed him again. This time longer as I went in close. His hands were raised in the air, as if he was scared to touch me. "We can bring Faheem in and me and you can see where this goes."

"Sev, stop playing. We can't shit where we eat. And we damn sure can't mix business with pleasure." And with that he slapped me on the ass and left out.

KEVIN

What the fuck just happened? I had to get the fuck out of there as fast as I could. My dick was like hold up, nigga. Where you going? Why you running away?

I learned this lesson years ago. Never shit where you eat. Once we started fucking, the business would suffer. Don't get me wrong, Sev was mad hot but hell nah. All I could see were problems.

ANGEL

"Bae, you okay? Are you all right?" Kaylin sounded more upset about me and if I was harmed than the actual shooting.

"I think I am."

He disappeared and came back with two burners. My heart was beating a million miles a minute, but I took deep breaths. "Yeah, I'm fine." I touched all over my body and felt nothing. I buttoned my blouse back up and pulled my skirt down over my hips. Everything happened so fast. As soon as the gunfire had started, the shooting had stopped. Then we heard a couple of cars as they sped away. The smell of gun powder and smoke burned my nose.

Police sirens wailed in the background remaining in the distance as if they were chasing the shooters. That probably was all in my mind. Our house is in the suburbs, so I'm sure one of the neighbors called the police the minute they heard shots.

Kaylin came back over to where I was lying on the floor. He touched me all over. "You sure you're all right? Is the baby okay?"

"I'm fine . . . I guess. The baby is fine. But what the hell was that? What if our children were here?"

Kaylin didn't answer. He handed me one of the pistols.

"You know how to use this. I need to check around the house. Stay here. Red, shoot first, ask questions later," he barked. "You understand? Angel? Shoot first, don't ask questions." I guess I was responding too slow.

Before he went outside, Kay pulled out his cell. "Trae, get over here. They just shot up the crib. No, we're okay. I'm getting ready to check around the house. I think they're gone, but I don't know."

I wasn't sure what caused the shooters to stop firing, but they did. And I knew it was serious when Kay called Trae, instead of the police. I sat by the door, both hands on the pistol, ready to kill anyone who invaded our space.

Finally, Kaylin stepped back into the house.

"C'mon, I gotta get you to safety." He snatched me up by the arm. "Get the keys to your ride. I'll follow behind you. I need you to stay with Tasha for now."

"But—"

"Red. But nothing! Damn, just do what I say. Please. Let's go."

KAYLIN

I dropped Angel off and picked up Trae. When we made it back to my house, Bo and Faheem appeared out of nowhere.

"Everybody okay?" Faheem asked. I nodded.

"You checked the house yet?" Bo wanted to know.

"Quickly, yes. I had to get Angel out of the way first."

They both pulled out their pieces and went their separate ways, me and Trae leave. They checked the entire house. The downstairs, the upstairs, the backyard, and the basement.

"All clear," Trae said, coming up from the basement.

Bo came from the backyard. "It's good back here."

"Son, what the fuck happened?" Faheem asked as he bounced down the stairs, two steps at a time.

"We went out to dinner to celebrate the new baby, and before we could get settled in, bullets came flying through the house." I kicked at the shell casings on the floor.

"What if the girls would have been here? This is where I lay my head! Muthafuckas shot up my house where I rest my head, my wife, my children . . ." I found myself pacing. I felt violated. My world had just been turned upside down.

"Damn! How's my baby?" I asked Faheem anxiously. Then I remembered we were watching my niece, Aisha. "How's Aisha?"

"They're fine. They're with Jaz."

"Who do you think did it?" Bo asked the question that I was sure was at the forefront of everyone's mind. "Let's go run the security cameras and see who these muthafuckas are."

"If it looks like Kevin, I don't care if he is Tasha's brother, his ass is mine," Trae gritted.

"Let's see what we can see on the tape." Trae was familiar with my surveillance system because it was identical to his.

"I hope we see these niggas' faces," Faheem said just as there was a knock at the door.

I assumed it was the police. I needed to get my story together as to why I didn't call them. I made my way to the door only to find Jake, my clean up man. He was there to clean up the mess and cover the windows. Angel must have called him. I let him in; he asked were we all right, and I headed for the basement leaving him to do what it is that he does.

They were all huddled around the surveillance screen as Trae was playing with the quality. No matter how he enlarged the screen, all we saw were shadows. The men were wearing black masks, black hoodies, and black gloves; completely covered. You couldn't tell what race or color the shooters were. Now I was worried. These cats moved like professionals.

"Maybe we're looking at this wrong; y'all think it could be Don Carlos?" Faheem asked.

"No." Trae shook his head. "He needs us right now. Plus, it's not his style. We would've just woke up dead if it were him."

"How the fuck you gonna wake up dead?" Bo tried to make light of the situation.

"Nigga, you know what the fuck I mean," Trae snapped.

"Well, it could be Kevin's crew," Faheem said. "I think y'all underestimate that lil' nigga. I mean, think about it. What's the odds of him showing up with the Don's daughter? I did some checking and it wasn't until he got with shorty that he got his weight up. I'm telling y'all, shit not adding up. Y'all need to listen to me."

"Whoever did it got me all fucked up." I was in a rage. It brought me back to when I slit my brother's throat. These muthafuckas came to the wrong nigga's house. It was fucked up because now I had to constantly look over my shoulder. But once I found out who was responsible, it was going down. I hoped it was Kevin. At least I would be able to get at him easily. Right now, all this uncertainty had me jumpier than a muthafucka.

"First things first, we are getting the fuck up outta this house. Unless you want to be like Ock in the movie *Belly*, a sitting duck waiting on them muthafuckas and end up dead. So pack your shit. You can't stay here tonight," Trae told me.

"Santos! The police are here," Jake hollered down the basement stairs.

"Tell them I'll be right up."

"Where do you wanna go? There's more than enough room at my house," Faheem offered. "And your daughter is already there."

"She's safer there. But Trae is closer, and I need to make sure Red got her head on straight. At least until we figure something out. Tell my daughter that her dad will catch up with her later."

"She ain't thinking about y'all. She got Aisha and Kaeerah. It's one big ass non-stop pajama party."

Look at Faheem sounding like a soccer dad! That was who we all were becoming. But trying to remain legit seemed like a dark, fluffy, cloud high up above that we would never reach. Our hands stayed deep into some bullshit. The bullshit with Seven showing up. The bullshit with Don Carlos wanting us to go to China. And more bullshit with Mari opening her own investigation. Now this. We were going into that blind. And now more than ever, I really wanted to keep my nose clean, especially with the new baby on the way. But it didn't look like it was going to happen for me.

"In the meantime, Bo is going to put feelers out there in the streets. Believe me. We are going to find the muthafuckas who did this," Faheem assured me.

"I put that on my granddaddy," Trae vowed, running his hand over his baldhead.

"Angel just sent me a text that she spoke to Ronni, our publicist. If it gets out that a record exec's house got shot up, she is going to have to spin the shit out of this. She plans to get out in front of it before it hits the media. I'll catch y'all later. I'ma head over to the office after I talk to the police."

Everybody left, except Trae.

Chapter Twenty-One

ANGEL

I was on the pull-out sofa when I was awaken by my husband and Trae sitting in the kitchen talking real low and smoking weed. I faked sleep so that I could ear hustle, and I hoped that I would be able to figure out what the hell was going on.

"I want these muthafuckas found and taken care of," Kaylin said. "This shit was brought to my home, Trae. Where I lay my head. Somebody is sending a serious message, and I don't know who, but we need to find out."

"We will find out; and when we do, we gonna end the shit. You know that," Trae said.

"We will," Kay said in his calm, methodical tone. "We got too much at stake."

I glanced at the clock. It was almost 4:00 a.m. I didn't even hear them come in.

"We're going to have to get guards around the clock for our families while we go to China," Trae said.

China? I wanted to scream out. Kaylin didn't mention anything about China.

"Do you think it was the Chinese Mob?" Kaylin asked.

The Mob? Chinese Mob? Shit. My breathing was becoming erratic.

"I couldn't tell who the fuck it was. The muthafuckas were dressed in all black. And we been into so much shit over the years, it could have come from anywhere," Trae responded.

"We need to move our families to a safe place. How about that condo you had in the Hamptons? You still have that—right?"

The Hamptons? I don't want to go to no fucking Hamptons. I want to go home. What about our business? Jahara. Her school? My bed? My garden?

"I'll call the realtor later on."

Oh, hell to the nah!

FAHEEM

I called my cousin, G, and told them what happened to Kay's house. He told me and Bo to swing by and pick him up. The shit we were about to get into . . . It was finally time to ride to Jersey to my old stomping grounds of Trenton.

"You ain't said nothin' but a word," G said.

He jumped in the ride with a large duffle bag full of guns. If we were to get stopped and searched, we would have to go out blazing. Because with what we had, even with a license to carry, they would throw our black asses under the jail. At the baby shower, Kevin had hinted at where his trap houses were. Niggas talked too much and didn't even realize they were leaving a trail of information. Trenton's so small that a hot fifty to a dope fiend led us right to our target.

We sat on the street of one of his spots in a low-key ride. The house was on a dead-end block, looking abandoned. I hit the blunt. With each inhale, I thought about Lil' Faheem. Blood raged through my body, even though this didn't have anything to do with him. This was my way of healing. I needed to let off steam. I slid the mask down my face and felt myself transforming into someone else.

We shot up two spots and killed everyone who was working or getting high up in there. We took the product they had on hand and gave it to Bo to get off and we would all split the profit. They had about $50,000 cash between both spots. We divided that money up. The morning headlines would probably read, Tumerous Killed in Drug-Related War.

We just wanted to leave a message. Kevin was playing with the big boys now. It was not confirmed whether Kevin or the chick was behind the shooting of Kay's crib, but we all knew there was no such thing as coincidences. So, I confirmed my own suspicions and whatever he and Seven were up to, I planned on sending as many messages as needed.

That night, something inside of me changed. I felt alive for the first time since Lil' Faheem's death. Maybe I couldn't bring back my son, but I could avenge him by setting my crew back up and being ready and protected. I thought of the anonymous threat I had received on my phone. *"We will find you and yo' family."*

If Steele's men or Oni's people came after me, I would be ready. Hell, I had to raise more money at this point, because I needed money to fight them niggas off.

And the sweet thing was that I was back in my old territory. I knew it well. It should be a breeze taking over the little blocks that Seven and Kevin had. My mind was made up. I was about to strong arm them, and they could get down or lay down.

Later that evening, Kay and Trae were at my doorstep. We took a walk around the block, and they made me an offer I couldn't refuse. The infamous Carlos Cartel needed someone with my expertise.

Now I had an excuse to be back complements of Don Carlos. Without realizing it, I had just killed two birds with one stone.

Don Carlos brought me on to shut down Seven's operation, and tonight was the official kickoff.

TASHA

"Oh, my God!" I was moaning in pure fucking ecstasy.

Trae had slid behind me and went up inside the pussy against the doctor's orders just like I knew he would. But a bitch didn't complain because he had some good ass dick that I could never pass up. He was being very gentle, pumping slow and not going deep. Lord knows, I wanted him to fuck me harder so I could cream all over his dick. But he wouldn't. His breathing was growing harder and his pumps were coming faster. He was about to come, and I wasn't even close, damn. "Trae . . . baby . . . slow . . . wait . . . bae . . ."

"Uugghhh," he groaned.

The party was over.

"Shit." He kissed me gently up and down my arms. "Sorry, bae. I had to release this tension. I hope I didn't make matters worse. Did I hurt you? I was trying to be gentle."

"Yes, I'm hurt. I didn't even come."

He turned me on my back and spread my legs. "I'm leaving for China in a few days." He began kissing my pussy.

"What?" I dug my nails into the pillows.

"You, Angel, and all of the kids are going to wait for us out in the Hamptons at Sag Harbor until shit cools down."

"Oh God! What . . . oh my god that feels good. Right there. Baby. Yes! Ohmygod. Please. Traaaaae." Now it was my turn to come. "Oh, god. Thank you, baby. I needed that."

When Trae finally came out of the bathroom, I was sitting up. "Do you want to repeat that again? Did you say China? We are moving to the Hamptons? Did I hear you right?"

"Are you all right? Did we bring on any contractions?"

"Trae, how long will you be in China? What about the baby? Why the Hamptons?" I was either confused at what I just heard, or was I dick dizzy.

"It's for the safety of both of our families. That's why the Hamptons. It's not forever, Tasha. And I won't be in China for more than a couple of weeks."

"A couple of weeks?" I could feel my stomach hardening. "Will you be back before the baby is born?" Once again, I would be alone. I just got my man back and now he was telling me this?

"Tasha, it's business."

"It's always business."

"I'ma act like you didn't just say that. I know you are emotional right now."

"Are you sure you have to go? Can't you talk to them and get it postponed? C'mon, baby. I need you here at least until after the baby."

"I know you do. And you know I want to be here, Tasha. I really don't have a choice. It's a favor for a favor. Don Carlos is one of the reasons I am here with you now."

"I can't believe this, Trae."

"This is the life we chose, Tasha."

"We chose? You chose this, Trae. Not me!" I regretted those words as soon as they came out.

"You chose me, Tasha. You been about this life. From the wedding, to the murders, to the jail shit, we been living this life. And at no time did I ever hear you say, 'baby I'm out.' I need you to ride out with me and roll with the punches like we've always done."

"I know, bae, but damn. Why does shit have to be so hard and so dangerous? I'm tired of living like this. Why do you have to leave now? This is unnecessary stress. I could deliver at any time. The doctor said my stomach is dropping." I was grasping at straws, anything to make him feel sorry for me and stay.

TRAE

"Tasha, I need you to be strong. Don't send me away thinking that you are falling to pieces."

She was trying to be hard, holding back the tears but they came rolling fast down her cheeks.

I hated to see her cry. But once again she would have to suck it up. Although she cried easily, Tasha was as strong as nails. When I came from Cali to New York for Kay's wedding and was shot, she stayed with me in the ambulance against medical advice and sat at the hospital for the three months I was in the coma. Pregnant and all. The whole time I was unconscious, she talked to me, message me; and although I was out of it, somehow, I heard her, and I felt her.

And throughout all the drama, she still delivered our healthy son. She never gave up hope on a nigga. And now she finally got her baby girl and that's surrounded by drama. Now I had to dip on her and she was having a complicated pregnancy.

It seemed like every time we said we were out, one more obligation pulled us back in.

KAYLIN

"We're ready to go, but we need your help," I told Don Carlos.

"Anything I can do to accommodate, let me know."

"I need some bodies to watch over our families until we get back."

"It's done."

Later that evening four men were sent to Trae's apartment and four more were parked in a van out front of my house. We had to bring the Don's team up to speed on the recent shooting. We told them about the move to the Sag Harbor condo.

Obviously, Don Carlos was an expert at this shit. He immediately sent over a moving company, carpenters, electricians; the whole nine. Three days later, we were being escorted out to the Hamptons.

The China assignment came at the most inopportune time. It had me thinking the Carlos Cartel was behind the shooting, just so that we could call on them and be committed to the trip. The shooting locked us into the trip because it was now a favor for some favors. Coincidence? Never. However, according to Don Carlos, we wouldn't regret it. It was supposed to come with very heavy financial rewards, which wasn't my motivating factor.

Our record company, Game Over Records, was dead in the middle of an artist launch, and yet I was uprooted and on my way clean across the world. Angel demanded that I allow her to go to the office, but I had to sit her ass down. Not only because she was pregnant, but it wasn't safe. I had everything under control. She would have to wait until I came back. Thankfully, I had just hired new legal counsel, Frank Stephanopoulos, and a new operation manager, Seth Cohen, who came highly recommended. He was a staple in the hip hop industry. He had only been there two months, but I was confident in his ability to run the company in my absence. We had promoted him from A&R exec to Operations Manager. I had to trust and believe that everything would work out. If I had a choice in the matter, I would have no parts of China. No matter the payout.

But we didn't have a choice in the matter.

Once the wives got settled in and it looked like things were under control, Trae and I flew back to Connecticut to see the Don. We were given our passports, visas, first-class tickets, money, and our instructions as to who we were to meet in Beijing.

"I'm still waiting on the final word of who was behind the incident at your home. Don't worry about your home or your families, I will handle it. I just need you two to do what you do.

But do it even better in Beijing." He laughed. "I told them that I am sending my best for this assignment. No doubt in my mind about that, and I know you won't let me down," the Don told us as we were leaving. "I will make sure your families are protected, and I will see to it that you are protected while you're in China. I have my allies there," he assured us. "You may be skeptical now, but you will be able to set up your own operations. This assignment will be very lucrative for us all and I promise you will be legit and set for life."

I still wasn't convinced or excited about this trip. The timing was all off.

Chapter Twenty-Two

TASHA

My whole life had been turned upside down, yet again. We had to move to Sag Harbor in the Hamptons, which was a nice vacationing spot in and of itself, but why did it have to be under these circumstances? We were in hiding and had bodyguards outside our house around the clock. This was a new one for me. And our men were gone to got-damn China!

Angel was pissed off that she couldn't go to her office until Kay got back. They had to trust their new office manager to run things, and it was running her crazy to give up control. She was definitely a career woman. All day she was texting and talking to her office. She was like the Energizer Bunny. I'd never seen her in this light. I was amazed, and I saw why Kaylin treated her like a queen and loved her to death. But she still had too much damn energy for me.

To pass time while I was stuck in the bed, I stayed online with my tablet or my iPhone. I hadn't checked Mari's Facebook page in a while, so I went to see what she had going one. Today, she posted that she was adopting a little girl soon. Who would give this nut a baby? I felt a twinge—that old gut-wrenching feeling I got when things were not quite right. Something was yanking at my spirit. Maybe it was those tapes. Those damn therapy sessions. I swear, I wished Trae hadn't even opened the envelope. That envelope had a curse on it.

But now Trae wasn't here. And some weird shit was going on, and it seemed as if it had something to do with my baby. And that scared the hell out of me.

I last recalled the envelope being in the trunk of Trae's car. I threw on some sweats and went out to the garage. The house was quiet because everyone was sleeping. I figured that I might as well take advantage of the opportunity. There was also a flash drive with the written reports on them. This Dr. Gillis discussed not only Kyron's gestures, but her personal thoughts of his sessions. Her notes were very detailed. I could see and feel Kyron Santos. He was back from the dead.

KYRON

Session Two

"I'm glad to see you back and on time," Dr. Gillis *commented. She looked down at her watch and looked up approvingly.*

Kyron nodded as he sat comfortably on the burgundy couch, which was now a little more familiar to him. He knew the drill. His eyes took in more of the atmosphere this time. The room was sunny, and there was a huge plant in the corner and smaller ones scattered about the office. Dr. Gillis sat behind a large mahogany desk in a nice Queen Anne chair.

"In fact, I got here early. I don't want to be in contempt of the court order."

Dr. Gillis gave a look of disapproval. "Okay. You don't have to brown nose. I need you to participate whole heartedly in these sessions but keep it real. This is serious, Mr. Santos."

"Not a problem. I'm feeling great. What's on the agenda for today? I know you and others are all ears."

Dr. Gillis pulled out his file, skimmed some notes, then turned to her recorder and her laptop. She cleared her voice before speaking. "So, what did you feel about the pregnancy?"

The question was so blunt, it almost knocked the wind out of him.

"Oh, you know about that?" Kyron looked surprised. Right away, he knew she got this information from her girlfriend, Mari.

Dr. Gillis looked flustered, knowing that she had broken the confidentiality clause. She recovered quickly with a lie. "Yes. It's in the records. Let me reword this. How did you feel getting another man's wife pregnant?"

He paused and thought before speaking. Intuitively, he knew she was lying about her finding out about it in his file. But he didn't want to talk about how he really felt. To Kyron mourning the loss of his seed displayed weakness, and a nigga could never show his weakness.

"I felt good."

"Why would it make you feel good?"

"I started feeling as if this was my destiny. I'd never had a baby before. I'd been locked up most of my adult life, so I had it in my mind that I would never have any kids. So, to find out I was going to be a father, it was like—I can't explain it."

"How did you feel?"

"I was happy. Excited. I would now have somebody that I could claim. Even my mother said she would take or help with the baby if things didn't work out with me and shorty. I felt as if a baby would give me a chance to get my life right. Like my seed would redeem me. I thought it would be dope to have someone to depend on me."

"What do you mean?"

"See, I'd always been the black sheep of the family. My younger brother, Kay, was the bright star. He did good in school, then he was even good in the streets. He did something most street niggas couldn't do or don't want to do."

"What was that?"

"He was able to get out the game and go legit."

"Is that what you measured yourself by—your brother's success?"

"It wasn't just that. I envy him, yes. He is a stable family man. I stayed with him for a minute, after I got out the pen, and I peeped how he was a good father and a good husband. That's what I wanted for myself and for shorty."

"Didn't you think about the people you would hurt in the process—your partner? Her husband?"

"Let me tell you something, I was happy. I wanted that baby—despite the circumstances. I gave shorty a ring. Yeah, I put a ring on it. Shorty had it like that." He licked his lips, as if in remembrance of how good the sex was. "I wanted to marry her and make my baby legit. The baby would have sealed the deal...our deal."

Dr. Gillis couldn't keep the irritation out of her voice. "But didn't you think about the fact that this woman couldn't marry you since she was still married? That would be bigamy."

Kyron shifted in his seat. "She was filing for divorce."

"But why didn't she?"

His nostrils flared and his tone was angry. "Her husband forced her to come back home to LA. That's when he made her lose the baby."

"How did he make her lose it? Did she have an abortion?"

"He told me on the phone he was taking her to abort the baby. And since there never was a baby, I'm assuming that's exactly what he did."

"How did that make you feel?"

"That shit was suspect to me. So, of course I was pissed the fuck off!"

"If she really wanted to divorce him, why didn't she?"

"How do you know she didn't?"

"I don't know."

"He is a violent man. She wrote me this nasty letter that I'm sure he made her write saying it was over."

"She obviously wasn't afraid of him—if she cheated with you and went so far as to get pregnant."

He was flustered. *"Look. She was a boss, too. Her husband had cheated on her first. I already told you she did this to get back at him, but I know she was catching feelings for me."*

"What about the allegations of rape?"

"Rape? Hell no! That wasn't rape. That shit was always consensual. She threw it back at me. So, how could that be rape? She was enjoying that shit as much as I was."

"What about the drugging? That's what the police report says. You're lucky that you didn't violate your parole. Someone somewhere is looking out for you. Because technically, you should be back in custody."

Kyron knew that Mari's influence with the psychologist and her clout and position was the reason he wasn't back in lock up.

"Sheeeeeit, a lil' 'E' mixed with Viagra; that's recreational. Since when did that become drugging?"

"The report says there was another substance. But wasn't your fiancée with you in Vegas when this happened?"

"I don't know, was she?"

"Let's stay on track, Mr. Santos. Did you think about your fiancée's feelings?"

He chuckled. *"I don't know what the fuck you heard, but I don't have a fiancée. Where the fuck is you getting all this info from? Can we put that on the record? Because I feel that some of this shit ain't none of your business."*

"Fiancée. Girlfriend. Wifey. Whatever you call her. Are you two in a good place now that Tasha is back with her husband? Can you mend your relationship with your fiancée?"

"Mend? Who said it was broken?" Kyron chuckled again.

"Do you love her?"

"She's been good to me. But what's love got to do with this? She held me down when I was locked up.

But—"

"But, what? Do you love her or what? You either love her, or you don't."

"Let me say something."

"What is it?"

"It's something an old man told me."

"What did he tell you?"

"When you don't love someone, you just don't love them. That someone can't force you to. It's just not happening."

"Is that what you're saying about your fiancée?"

Kyron hesitated. "No. I'm talking about Tasha. I'm simply saying that I was good to her. I gave her me. I gave her a car. I gave her a ring. And she still went back to her husband. But I hope when I came in her that last time, I planted another seed. My seed. Now that shit right there . . . That would be street justice." He started laughing.

"But, what about your fiancée?"

"She can't have kids. Anyway, doc, I feel like you rode my nuts enough for today. May we finish this next time?"

* * *

I turned the tape off, and my stomach dropped to my knees. I was sick. Did Trae watch this one? What if the DNA test was wrong? It was close together; the time I was with Trae, and the rape. My head was fucked up. A sense of dread flooded through me, but I decided to take a nap and calm my nerves. But shit, what if this was Kyron's baby?

ANGEL

I guess you could say I'd gotten spoiled over the past three years since my baby started school. Jahara was eight years old and very independent. My life had been family, work, and time for myself. I had a spa day with a massage every Saturday. A day for a mani and pedi, and a private hairdresser who came to the office. I was in the office from 9:00 a.m. to 9:00 p.m., and I jumped on a plane at least once a week.

But since the shooting my life was totally different. I was no longer the lawyer at my husband's record company. I felt like I was just a housewife and I didn't like it. I couldn't see how Tasha did it.

I was trying to adjust to this new life of semi-hiding, morning sickness, and Kay being in China. For how long, I didn't know. We had tours and new album release parties that I had to turn over to our new manager, Seth Cohen, a young, smart, hungry, Jewish cat. I never realized what a control freak I was until I had to loosen the reins. I loved when we would break in new artists: the media frenzy, and how we took our artists to Greece, Spain, the UK, Africa. Game Over Records would crush it.

I was going through all these tumultuous emotions. Even with Aunt Marva's help, I was trying to take care of five children, three rough-and-tumble boys, and two precocious little girls. Some relief came when Kyra arrived, supposedly to get Aisha, but she wound up staying with us. Kyra was due in about four weeks, but she wasn't nearly as big as Tasha, who was still on bed rest. We had three able-bodied women to help with the twins, Kareem and Shaheem, Caliph, and the girls, Jahara and Aisha.

This morning I woke up and my first thought was, I'm going to stay in bed until noon and have some time to myself. This was going to be a me-day. I would do my own mani and pedi and enjoy myself. Suddenly, I heard Tasha yell my name.

"Angel! Marva! Anybody up? It's real this time. My water broke!"

MARI

"Has a Tasha Macklin delivered her baby yet? I am from the Department of Children and Family Services. We received a referral from her doctor saying the baby has chemical endangerment. They found doses of diazepam, which is the generic name for Valium, in her system and in the baby's system; it seems like mom was self-medicating. There are no doctor's orders on file. According to the lab report, this drug was in her system when she came in for a prenatal visit, and I need to detain the infant. The mother will be given a court date in the hopes of reuniting with her baby after a thorough investigation is complete."

I stopped the recording on my iPhone. I had been practicing my spiel daily. If my plan worked, they would be charging Tasha with "knowingly, recklessly, or intentionally" causing her baby to be exposed to a controlled substance in the womb—a felony punishable, in her case, by up to ten years in prison.

At least 50 times, I practiced my spiel. I had my New York Human Services badge, and all the appropriate paperwork. I changed my name to Megan Sloane, and I set up a dummy corporation that was a privately-owned Human Services Agency.

I planned to pick the baby up from the hospital, act as though I was taking the baby to a foster home, and then we would be on our way to a new life.

On the other hand, I didn't know what was going on. I'd gone by Kaylin and Angel's house and it was lifeless. Several of the shingles were replaced with boards. I'd called their office many times, but they were never in and had not returned my messages. What was happening? When was Tasha having the baby or had she had it?

I called Kaylin's number and it went straight to voicemail. I called Trae's number, straight to voicemail. I tried Tasha's number, but she had blocked me. They all had disappeared on me. I was back at square one.

Chapter Twenty-Three

JAZ

"*Steele. He's dead. The deed is done, Faheem. That was my call. You can thank me later . . .*"

"*Then why the fuck are you sitting here telling me that you handled it? What? Just because I'm banged the fuck up, you think I'm pussy, Jaz?*"

"*You can laugh all you want, because the deed is done, and I took care of it. You always wanted me to honor your thug, but you need to recognize and honor mines.*"

"*Jaz, I already told you, you ain't no thug. You got someone else to do it. You know why? 'Cause you ain't no killer.*"

"*Whatever. But like I already told you, the deed is done.*"

I could still feel the sense of liberation I had after I set my sight on a desired result and got it done. Me. It was me. I ordered the hit on Steele. I think it had a lot to do with taking over a man's job when my man was shot and out of commission. Although he was furious, and acted as if I'd taken over his manhood, I saw it as being his partner. I think that's why I'd been going to the gun range. I was empowered by that project so the next time, if necessary, I would do the deed myself.

* * *

"Good luck, Ms. Jaz."

"Ms. Jaz? How old do you think I am?" I asked my new friend, Anderson, a nerdy white guy, who wore large bifocals and had braces on his teeth. We were both applying for an internship at Robert Wood Johnson. "Don't answer that. But it's Doctor Jaz to you."

He thought that was funny.

I was finally enrolled back in school, in spite of what Faheem had said a few days ago.

"Jaz, maybe you should wait and start school next semester."

I was upset about what had happened at Angel and Kay's house, too, but I wanted to get on with my life. Isn't that why we left Atlanta? Besides, that was in New York. We were in Jersey.

I clicked my automatic door opener on my car keys as I walked to the parking lot. I checked over my shoulder as I always did these days. Something made me reach into my purse for my burner. I made it to my BMW, checked the backseat to make sure no one was in it, then jumped in and locked the doors. I put my glock on the passenger's seat, but kept one hand on it, just in case.

As I drove out the garage and onto the streets, from habit, I glanced in my rearview mirror. A black car with tinted windows was driving on my ass. When I turned right at the light, it turned. When I made a left, it made a left. The car tailgated me for a few miles. I was getting nervous, or was it paranoia? I really needed to get checked out. My left hand started sweating as I gripped the steering wheel. I sped up and swerved in and out of traffic, trying to lose the car. The car was keeping up with me though. I saw the upcoming freeway and I jumped on it, flooring the pedal. The car followed me on the freeway. It fell back a little, remaining about three cars behind me and would change lanes whenever I did. It wasn't paranoia. I was being followed.

My heart flip-flopped in my chest as the dark vehicle got one car behind me. I finally saw an exit, and I cut over three lanes, just barely being missed by two cars, and jumped off the freeway. Cars screeched to abrupt stops, just barely avoiding a big traffic accident. The car couldn't get over to follow me. I let out a sigh of relief.

I drove in a circle until I was sure no one was tailing me, then I headed home, looking in my rearview mirror the entire time. I was freaking out.

Rushing into the house I yelled, "Faheem! Faheem!" My breathing was jagged, and I was flushed.

"What's the matter, bae?" Faheem came out of the kitchen with a dish towel in his hand.

He was wearing an apron, looking alarmed.

I let out a deep breath. "Someone was following me." I rushed into my man's arms.

"What? Why didn't you call? Did they follow you here?"

"No, I lost them on the highway. I was driving like a madwoman, swerving in and out of traffic. Baby, I was scared shitless." I burst into tears. "I was really being followed."

"Jaz, this is it. You're going to have to come out of school until we get everything straightened out. I'm going to take you and Kaeerah over to Trae's with everyone else. They have round-the-clock protection."

This time I didn't object.

FAHEEM

"You sure this is the only way to handle this; can't we just move again?" Jaz asked, as I pulled up in front of the spot in Sag Harbor. "Why were they following me? Angel's house getting shot up had nothing to do with us."

"Jaz, baby I know. At least I think I know. We've got to get shit straight. It's too hot right now and I don't want anything to happen to you or our baby. I don't have any answers." We gave each other a deep kiss.

"Bye, Daddy," Kaeerah said, kissing me on the cheek.

"Bye, baby girl." I kissed my daughter back. "I'll see you soon."

As the Don's men got their bags and escorted them inside the house, I felt an overwhelming anxiety. Life, as we knew it, was already changing. Jaz had a point. Angel's house getting shot up shouldn't have had anything to do with us. So, who tried to run Jaz off the road and why? How did they know it was her?

Being in the game when you have a family is a negative. You expose innocent lives to the dangers that come with the hustle. You yourself become a sitting duck. You must always be ready to walk away. With a family it becomes damn near impossible. Your enemies and haters try to get to you through the people who are closest to you. They killed my son because of something his crazy mother and her brothers had done in the streets. They know even an evil person loves their seed. The easiest way to hurt a man or get revenge on a man is to touch his family.

The whole point of me retiring from the streets was to be a family man. While Jaz studied for her degree, I took our daughter back and forth to school. And I loved it. I had turned into Mr. Mom, hanging around at Girl Scouts meetings and shit. The irony is, keeping my family safe now, meant getting back in the game to get my bread up so that I could do just that.

* * *

I knew I would surprise Kevin by popping into their accounting firm in downtown Trenton. I needed to read his temperature in regard to their spots getting hit.

"Hey, Unc. What brings you here?"

"Just checking on you; what's been up?"

"Glad to see you. Shits been crazy down here."

"Oh yea? I wanted to talk to you about the baby shower."

His voice cracked. "Unc, I swear on everything I love that I wasn't trying to set anybody up when I came to see my sister."

I smiled. "Crazy shit has been happening since you showed up, including Kay's house getting shot up."

"Kay's house? Was anyone hurt?"

"Luckily, no one was home. You don't know anything about that?"

"I swear 'for God. Look, Unc, things have gotten crazy down this way as well. Somebody done shot up two of my spots and killed five of my men. I 'ont know what the fuck is going on, or who is behind it."

I looked that lil' nigga straight in the eyes, and my gut told me he might be telling the truth about not shooting up Kay's house, but he was lying about something else.

"Hello, Faheem," a female voice interrupted us. I looked up. It was Seven. She was rocking the hell out of a pair of Fashion Nova jeans, which were screaming like she was hurtin' them. Her belly top showed off her belly ring, and those six-inch red bottoms had her ass poking out.

"Hello, Miss Seven." I stood up. She held out her hand, and I kissed it just like I did at the shower.

"How can we help you? Do you need any accounting done?" She smiled at me.

"Nah. Not this time."

As a man I could tell when a female was feeling me, and I could tell when a woman was low-key flirting with me. Perfect! I would need to capitalize on this and hit her up at a later time. Shit was coming together effortlessly.

TRAE

As I looked out the window, all I saw were endless clouds and another plane far away. My thoughts went back to how

Charli's cousin, Kon Li, a wannabe black gangster, who thought he was Nino Brown from *New Jack City*, had drunkenly given me a piece of information.

"Dude," Kon said through slurred speech. "I'm not stupid, you know. I can teach you a lot. I know they want to replace me. But it's okay. You know why? Because I will be getting a promotion. The big boss is about to get even bigger. He's about to fuck up the whole banking system. And I'm going to help him. We about to get paid, dawg!" He clinked his glass against mine.

This bitcoin or cryptocurrency technology probably was the alternate banking system and had covered all types of black-market shit over in China from organ stealing, to white slavery, to drug trafficking. Even so, I still felt like we should have tried to delay this trip. The Don admitted there would be some risks, but he said we'd have protection from his men and his allies. The Carlos Cartel versus the Chinese Triad. It was like choosing between the rattlesnake and the anaconda. You're fucked either way. But my attitude at this point was let the chips fall where they may.

Suddenly I took a deep, calming breath, as the plane landed in Beijing after our eighteen-hour flight. I had come a long way rising from on-the-block mode to boss mode. I chose this life and I knew there was no turning back. Once again, we found ourselves in unchartered territory.

KAYLIN

"You see, bitcoin is the new gold rush, like the internet was twenty years ago. America is behind the times with it," Mr. Wong, our escort, said as he continued with his PowerPoint presentation. We were seated on the fiftieth floor in an office building in Beijing. I could see tall buildings all over the city from the glass windows which surrounded the building. China was crammed with people. Rich people. Filthy rich young people. "Since the big market crash in 2008, cryptocurrency has become the wave of the future. We are paying close attention to the growth. A recent article by *Bloomberg* reported that China Renaissance investor, Richard Liu, sacrificed a seven-figure salary to focus on bitcoin and cryptocurrency, especially initial coin offerings."

I listened intently as they spoke. I still felt like a pawn. Our business was fueling their business interest. I wanted to know how I could make this new venture our business, without Don Carlos or the Chinese.

"Did Don Carlos shoot up my house?"

There were about ten suited businessmen in the meeting, including Trae and me. They did not look like the Chinese Triad you read about or watched on TV. They all looked like white-collar businessmen—legitimate businessmen.

"We have been using this cryptocracy form of banking for years. This is a system that can't be traced. Just recently the Chinese government has begun talks of licensing it, but I can assure you gentlemen, if we iron out the details, we can beat them to the punch. No one owns bitcoin yet. That's why we're sitting in this room, today, gentlemen."

Fuck me! *The Don wants to own bitcoin?* Me and Trae exchanged eye contact at that statement. However, the Don didn't need us for this. I needed to brace myself for what was coming next. This trip wasn't all about bitcoin. Was Don was fucking us over. But why? And for what?

Chapter Twenty-Four

RICK

"How's the baby this morning?" I asked Nina, kissing her on her neck. She was sitting in a rocking chair breastfeeding my son, who looked nice and greedy, sucking away. That little boy was smacking and holding on to her breast with one hand, while he constantly kicked his feet. Must be good.

"Very hungry," Nina said, filled with content.

We had made up since Rick Jr. had gotten through his medical crisis. He was in the hospital for almost two weeks. Plus, she was glad that Kyra had gone back to New York; she seemed perfectly happy—for now.

She had no idea that I would be going back to New York to be with Kyra when she delivered Destiny. There had been a long stretch of peace, so I decided not to break the news to her until just before it was time to leave.

Nina smiled. "Our son is fine. Why can't we stay like this always?" She was referring to how peaceful things had been around our house.

"Yeah, you like what I put on you last night, huh?"

Nina blushed. "That, too. I just want us to be like we are now. Always. Our baby is healthy; we are good financially. All the kids are happy. Promise we will stay this way."

I didn't say anything. I couldn't promise that. My thoughts went to the text I'd received from Kay. He wanted me to pull out the information I had kept for them. That same piece of information that made Mr. Li back off. With Kay and Trae both in China, Kay's house getting shot up and all the women in hiding, it sounded like we were in a little over our heads.

ANGEL

"Angel, it's raining too hard," Aunt Marva said, wringing her hands. "I can't drive in the rain." She began praying out loud. "Lord, help us to get this baby to a hospital safely. Amen."

"Aunt Marva, I can drive. Her pains are coming too close together. I don't think I can make it to Mount Sinai. We have to find somewhere closer."

"Stop talking like I am invisible," Tasha said, puffing and holding the bottom of her stomach. "I hear—heh, heh, heh, heh, heh, heh. Oh God! That was a hard one!" She damn near screamed. She was sitting on the sofa with her bag packed.

"Dang, Tasha, you'll upset the kids. Haven't you done this shit before?"

"Angel, now is not the time! This shit hurts like it's my first."

I burst out laughing and that broke up some of the tension. Tasha laughed, too. It made me realize in about seven months I'd be in the same position. "Okay, okay. I know the severity of the pain. Just breathe through the pain like they teach in the childbirth classes."

"What the hell do you think I'm doing?" Tasha said, trying to breathe, moaning and yelling all at once.

"I'll look out for the kids," Marva said, looking helpless. "I'm not riding with y'all."

Kyra was hesitant as well. "You'll be all right, Tasha. I'm praying for you. I'll help watch the boys, but I suggest y'all leave now. The ambulance obviously can't get here."

Leave it to Tasha, the drama queen, to go into labor during one of the worst rainstorms on Sag Harbor. This tropical storm must be the stepchild of Hurricane Irma.

I googled, *nearest hospital to Sag Harbor*, and Hampton Bays Hospital appeared to be the closest. Since I was the designated driver, I had to keep my cool, tropical storm and all. I kept thinking of Kay. He always remained calm or better yet large and in charge.

Unfortunately, sheets of rain were pummeling the street when we opened the door and came outside. The winds were so high, I had to struggle to close the door behind us. I tried to hold the umbrella over Tasha, and it blew away and we both were getting wet. The sound of high winds whistled through the trees, which leaned to the side.

One of the goons was waiting outside the door. He made him the scariest looking one in the group, with the jagged knife scar across his face we called him Scarface behind his back.

"Where are you going? You're not supposed to leave the house," Scarface barked in his strong Mexican accent.

"She's in labor. We called an ambulance almost a half hour ago. We can't wait any longer. I'm taking her in my car."

"What hospital? How far from here?" Scarface asked.

"She was supposed to go to Mount Sinai Hospital, but we can't make it in this rain, and her contractions are coming really close together. We're going to the hospital nearby. It's about a half hour."

"Okay; but let me drive you."

Tasha moaned and groaned, and I had to keep my focus and keep her focused. "Hold on, Tasha. We're going to get there safely."

"Get me to the hospital in one piece, Angel."

"Bitch, I got you. Ain't nothing changed. We've had each other's backs since day one."

TASHA

I had been in labor before, but this one was by far the worst. I was fearful of Scarface driving like a bat out of hell through the pouring rain, but I was in so much pain, I couldn't even worry about a car accident. I just wanted to get this baby out of me, and I prayed it didn't happen in the car. "Here comes another one!"

Angel rushed inside the emergency room to get help, while Scarface sat and waited by the car door with me. For the first time, I wasn't afraid of him.

Once the orderly wheeled me up to the maternity ward, the nurse examined me, then called the doctor. She asked Angel to leave the room, but she didn't. The doctor came in, threw on some white rubber gloves, and did a vaginal exam. It felt like he stuck his arm up into my tonsils.

"Is the baby okay?" I asked through a veil of red pain.

The doctor had stopped examining me and put a monitor on my stomach. He finally replied, "Your baby is fine, but it's lying transverse, instead of head down or even hips down for a breech birth. We can't turn the baby, so we're going to have to perform a C-section."

"A C-section?" *Oh, no!* Nothing was going as planned. I wanted Trae to be here when I delivered, but that wasn't happening. I had planned on doing natural childbirth like I did with the boys. That wasn't happening. Now a C-section? Could my luck get any worse? There was nothing I could do but go for the ride and pray that my baby girl and I would be fine. For the first time, I understood what Aunt Marva said about a woman being close to death whenever she had a baby.

"Can my sister come in and be here with me since my husband is not here?"

"Only a husband or partner can come in when there is a C-section."

Angel pulled the doctor and nurse to the side, whispered something, and the next thing I knew, she was covering herself with a white gown and mask. She squeezed my hand. "I got you, girl."

The last thing I remember was a mask going over my nose and mouth.

***

Waking up woozy, I heard my baby's first cry. It was loud and feisty, as if my baby was mad. "It's a girl," the doctor said. "Time of birth: 4:04 p.m."

"She's beautiful!" Angel said, tears streaming down her face as she aimed her camera.

I couldn't see my new daughter because of all the sheets covering my body. The doctor was stitching me up. "I can't see her," I complained in a panic as I remembered that dream!

"Wait a minute, Mom," the nurse said. "We've got to clean her up and weigh her. She's a big one."

Finally, the nurse wiped the blood and mucous off her and brought my baby to me.

"She weighs eight pounds. Twenty-one inches in length."

My baby was wrapped in a white receiving blanket. I released a sigh of relief. My heart melted. My daughter looked more like Trae than our sons. She had his eyes, his mouth, and even his ears. She had my complexion and a head full of hair.

"She looks like Trae chewed her up and spit her out," I whispered. In that dream, I had given birth to a son who looked like Kyron. I thought of the second therapy session I had listened to just before I went into labor. The one where Kyron said he'd came inside of me and had hoped I'd gotten pregnant by him again. I breathed another sigh of relief. The DNA test had been correct. Trae was the father.

"What are you going to name her? Princess?" Angel asked. "Her daddy is going to be crazy in love with her."

"Taylour. Taylour Macklin."

Chapter Twenty-Five

ANGEL

I had never witnessed a live birth before, other than the home video Kaylin shot when I birthed Jahara. I never liked to look at it that much, so this was like the first. Just seeing my little niece draw her first breath, and to hear her first cry, I was awestruck. But I had to admit, it was nasty! The cut, and then all six hands digging around in her stomach. *Yuck!*

"I love you, girl," Tasha said drowsily. "I'm sorry I cussed you out."

"No you're not! But you did good. You know you my sister." We hugged, holding onto each other longer than usual.

I felt like I was on a different level after watching Tasha give birth. It was a spiritual awakening. What I saw was scary, but beautiful. I knew Tasha was glad that it was over. She had been on bed rest the past couple of weeks, dealing with Trae coming home and having to leave again, and not to mention those fucking tapes. There was only so much a sister could take.

"Get some rest, Tasha." She nodded and immediately dozed off.

I checked on the baby in the nursery, then headed to the elevator. I decided to go out to get a bite to eat. I was surprised to find Scarface still waiting in the waiting room.

"Is Mrs. Macklin okay?"

"Yes, she had a healthy baby girl. They have three boys, so we are all excited."

"Good, Good." Then he did the sign of the cross. These cartel men could kill you in the morning and go to mass in the afternoon. That was just tradition with them. Still, I thought it showed the human side of him; he stayed for Tasha's delivery and appeared to be genuinely concerned.

"Well, I'm going to stay here with Tasha. You can go back to the house."

"No. I can't leave either of you alone. I'll have to get the other men to take turns, so we can be on rotation until you leave the hospital."

"Okay, give me your cell phone number, and I'll call you, so I can be in your phone. I may be here until she's ready to be released."

He nodded.

CHARLI LI

"You're not doing what I asked you." I had called my private investigator, Calvin Braggs. "Will I have to get someone else?"

"What do you mean? You have your updated ID and your passport."

"Where is Tasha Macklin? You were supposed to keep a trail on her."

"I don't know. I'm here in New York, and the trail has gone cold."

"I thought you knew how to hack hospital records. Has she had the baby yet?"

"She hasn't delivered at Mount Sinai. That's where she was supposed to deliver."

"Has she been to see her ob-gyn, Dr. Brown?"

"No, not since last month. She could've changed doctors."

"Have you seen her near her apartment?"

"No."

"What about at Mr. Santos' house?"

"His house is boarded up."

"Why is it boarded up?"

"I'm checking now."

"You're definitely not on your job. I thought you were a hacker and could get into records, cell phones, and bank accounts. I'll give you one week. And if you don't have any up to the second reports I'm terminating my contract." I slammed down the phone. I had already contacted a bomb expert to bomb Tasha's car, but I had to make sure she was in it alone.... once we found her! I also wanted the dogs to mutilate her. And I wanted to take the baby through the system and get her arrested. Whichever tragedy came first, that would be her fate; but now, she had practically disappeared. I wanted to take her out or get her locked up, and I didn't care how it happened. I wanted her. She needed to suffer for the rest of her life or die.

I went on social media and did some trolling. I tried Facebook, Instagram, and Twitter, but I couldn't find Tasha. I couldn't even find her friend, Angel, or the other ones.

What was I going to do next? My patience was running thin.

RICK

"Kyra, just one more push and the baby will be here," I said, acting as her coach and the proud father-to-be. I took a white washcloth and wiped the sweat off her forehead.

"I'm tired," Kyra cried. Between cussing me out, and screaming and hollering, it had been eight hours since the doctor induced her labor.

"I can see her head! Just one more push–"

"One more? You said that two hours ago." Kyra blurted out.

"One more push, and I promise she'll be out," Doctor Glenn said.

"Rick." She looked at me with pleading eyes.

"C'mon, baby. You've got this."

Kyra took a deep breath, grunted, and bore down with all her might. I was helping her push with her shoulders. Finally! Her head, shoulders, then the rest of her body slithered out. I was searching for her toes and fingers.

"She's here, baby," I said, kissing her. I whispered into her ear. "You've made me a very happy man. I love you Kyra, and I want the world for you."

Kyra started crying. "She's beautiful. I love you, too." I looked down at my newborn daughter, who was wailing at this new cold world she was thrust into. She looked like Rick Jr. more than she looked like me.

"Welcome to the world, Destiny Kyra," I said, looking into her big brown eyes, which were already open.

Let me call Nina and tell her the news.

ANGEL

"Seth, how was the tour?" I was trying to talk over the static. I knew this type of phone didn't have the best connection, but I couldn't stay off it. I had never been this paranoid in my life. To keep from being traced, I'd had Scarface buy me five throw-away cell phones.

"Mrs. Santos, I've never seen anything like it!" Seth said jovially. "I know you checked us out on TMZ and all the sites for the music. All the buzz is about Game Over Records. We killed it!"

"Great." I was faking my smile so hard my cheeks were burning. Although he couldn't see me through the phone, I was hoping he could feel the grin. I tried to sound enthusiastic. It hurt me to hear this, although I knew it was good for business. Begrudgingly, I must admit, Seth is a keeper. I kind of hoped he would have failed, which is insane because that would have hurt the business. I resented the fact that I was no longer in control. And then he had the nerve to say, "We killed it." Ooohhhkay. *He's stealing my job and now he's stealing our slang.*

I had to catch myself. Everything was getting on my last nerve. I was getting cabin fever, and I wanted to know what the real world—my world—was up to in my absence. I hadn't heard from Kaylin, and Tasha had not heard from Trae. They said two weeks, and we were at twelve days. What was going on with our men? I tried not to worry, but I wasn't having much success. They had been to Mexico and other countries in the name of business. They had money in the Cayman Islands. They both traveled to China before, so they weren't new to this. So why were my nerves a horrid mess?

I thought about what was really irritating me. Babies, babies, babies. So many babies. Huggies, cute little dresses, bassinets, waking up to crying every night. Thank God, not a lot of baby bottles since both moms were breastfeeding. We had a damn day care going. I had one, Tasha had four, Kyra's two and Jaz with Kaeerah. Too many kids and five women stuck in one house. I was going stir crazy. Jaz and I had started homeschooling all the children to take up part of the day, get some order and burn some energy. When we were youngsters, we used to talk about us getting a place together, raising babies and having husbands who were best buds, but who would have thought it would have been under these circumstances?

In the meantime, Kyra was all booed up with Rick, who acted as if he was going to move into our already crowded situation. Tasha was so wrapped up with baby Taylour; she was in her own world. These girl babies are so sweet, but I wanted a boy. I wanted a baby Kaylin this time around. Rambunctious. A spiders-and-worms-scrunched-in-his-hand little boy. I had been a stepmom to Kaylin's firstborn son, Malik, but I wanted to give my man a son. I was looking forward to the day when Kaylin would hold his son by me.

To pass time, I did what everybody else does, troll the internet and play games. I often checked on the police sites since our house was shot up. I was curious to see if the police had found anything, but the police didn't give a damn about our problems or our house. And I wasn't expecting them to find anything. Then suddenly something caught my attention.

Amber Alert: Mother, Tasha Macklin, has kidnapped her baby girl from the hospital against medical advice. She is being sought by authorities for questioning.

"Get the fuck outta here!" *What the fuck?* This had to be a joke. I was there when she was released. There was no hold on her or the baby.

I rushed into Tasha's bedroom, where the twins and Caliph were playing quietly on their tablets, and she was just putting the baby down for a nap.

"Tasha, send the boys over to my room, so they can play with Jahara."

Tasha had a knowing look on her face, one that said she had been expecting something bad to happen. "Hey guys, go over to your Aunt Angel's room and play so Mommy and Auntie Angel can talk."

As soon as they left, Tasha grabbed me by the arm. "What is it? It's our men, isn't it? I've had this funny feeling in my gut. Do I need to sit down?" Her face was filled with anguish.

"No, I haven't heard from them. Have you?"

"No." She shook her head.

"I hate to be the bearer of unwelcomed news, but I want you to look at something." I showed her the tablet, and for a second, her face went almost white.

Finally, she spoke up. "I've had this recurring dream—that someone is trying to take my baby from me. Ain't nobody taking my baby from me."

"Who could it be?"

"It's that psycho bitch, Mari. What the fuck is wrong with these chicks today? She's called Trae and me trying to stir up shit. Besides, she's got connections with the courts through law enforcement and obviously that fuckin' therapist."

"How about if I call the hospital or the authorities and get this straightened out?"

"No, never! I remember how me and my siblings were taken from our parents. I am not allowing anybody to take my child or children for that matter. Don't you call anybody! Somebody is up to something."

"But your situation is different. You're not on drugs or an abusive parent. Let me make a few calls, Tasha."

"No, Angel! Trust me, it doesn't matter. Once a black baby gets into the foster care system, it is hard to get them back. They take our babies for no reason."

I couldn't say anything. I thought about the mass incarceration of Blacks, and the high number of children in the foster care system. We looked each other in the eyes and were speechless. "So, what will you do?"

"I'm getting the hell out of here."

"And going where?"

"I don't know. Anywhere I can hide out by myself with the baby until Trae gets back. I will need to leave the boys with you. Is that all right?"

"Hide? By yourself? What in the hell? Tasha, you're talking crazy now!"

WAHIDA CLARK

Chapter Twenty-Six

CHARLI LI

"What do you have for me, Calvin?" I asked my private eye, handing him an envelope with cash. He was sitting across from my desk in my new office. Alexa McMillan, who ran my front office looked at him suspiciously. Being in downtown Manhattan, my establishment looked and felt like a Fortune 500 company.

"We still in business?" he questioned, lifting an eyebrow.

"Depends. Did you find anything regarding her financial activity? Did you check her bank accounts, credit cards, any type of online accounts?"

"Nothing. But Tasha Macklin's baby's birth was registered, and she was born at Hampton Bays Hospital, not Mount Sinai."

"Was there a home address?"

"Yes. The address of the apartment, but no one's there. I haven't been able to pin down a current location yet, but we are on the lookout for her and the baby now."

"Great. You find her, you'll find Mr. Macklin. And see if you can get the cameras at the hospital to see when she delivered and who was with her when she came in."

"Got that. I'm on it."

"How come no word on Mr. Macklin?"

"Your instructions were to find Mrs. Macklin."

"Find out where he is within the next 48 hours and that will be an extra $10,000."

Mr. Macklin, the love of my life was here in the city. I could feel him. I was getting closer.

MARI

I was just about to give up until I got the text highlighting the Amber Alert. My girl Dr. Gillis was a bad bitch! She knew I took Kyron's murder hard, so she was willing to do anything for me. And now, with her help, I had a baby to look forward to. I dialed her number.

"Hey, lady!" I forced myself to sound cheery.

"Hey, diva. How have you been?"

"Oh, fine, now that I got that text. I have to give it to you. It's brilliant how you were able to get that Amber Alert issued."

"Gurllll, it wasn't a simple task. But now, if she takes the baby to the doctor for shots, there will be an alert and the baby will be detained. The alert is like identity theft, but it's better. It's character assassination."

"You are one bad bitch." I stroked her ego.

"I told you I got you."

"Where did she deliver the baby?"

"Hampton Bays."

"Hampton Bays?" *What the hell are they doing up in the Hamptons? I need to find Trae so I can begin my negotiations of getting the baby from Tasha, legally. I know she delivered Kyron's baby. That's what all this hush-hush and hiding out is all about.*

"Renee, we've got to do dinner. My treat. I owe you big time for this."

"Yes, you do. How about the tapes? Were they any help at all?"

"Yes, more than you will ever know." *Maybe Trae's disappearance means he has left Tasha's ass*, I thought. "So, let me make sure I understand. Explain how the authorities will find the missing baby when there is an Amber Alert."

"Well, the mother might take the baby to the doctor if it's sick, or if she has to get the immunizations. Other than that, you'll have to wait it out."

"Where would the birth be registered if it was in New York?"

"At the State Department of Health."

JAZ

"Hey Big Daddy, we miss you. I miss you. Kaeerah misses you."

"I miss y'all more. I'll be there."

"When, Faheem?

"Let me handle my business, baby."

I knew my man and something wasn't right. Why hadn't he been by yet? What the hell was he out there doing? What business was he referring to? "Bae, what are you doing out there? You want to fill me in? Faheem, we didn't relocate up here for you to get dirty."

"We'll talk when I see you."

"What!" I didn't like the sound of that. Faheem had fought hard to free himself from the game. Now my gut instincts were telling me that he was up to no good. "Look at how we're living? We're in hiding. Talk to me now, Faheem. Not later when you see me."

"Jaz. Chill. Let me tighten up a few things, and I'll be there. What have you been up to? What's Kaeerah been up to?"

"Don't try to change the subject, Faheem. Me and Angel have been taking turns homeschooling your daughter and the other kids. Now, when are you coming to see us?"

"Don't worry. I'll be by to see you soon."

"Don't worry? How can I not worry when we are in hiding? I need this to be over, Faheem."

"Over?" Faheem scoffed. "Is it ever?"

"Damn, baby. It's like that?"

"Jaz, I'll be there soon."

He still didn't answer my question. As soon as I hung up, I went online and put in an order for a half-dozen guns. I could do that because I already had my license.

KYRA

I had never been this happy! Our baby girl was in the bassinette by our bed sleeping, and Rick was sleeping next to me. This had been the happiest two weeks of my life. My man being there when I delivered our daughter meant the world to me, and it strengthened our bond. Now that I was older, I saw and felt things I didn't feel when I had Aisha.

We couldn't have sex for six weeks, but I was already horny. I began to rub and kiss him all over his body.

His eyes flew open. He yawned. "Kyra, what's up?" Rick asked, looking down at his growing erection and smiling. "We've got to wait four more weeks, right?"

I wound up giving him a hand job. I would've given him a blow job, but I just didn't like the idea of knowing he was with Nina.

"Why can't it always be like this between us?" I muttered.

Rick said, "How about just living in the moment? Enjoying the now."

"How about you make a choice now."

"I'm in love and have babies with two different women. I love them both. I can't choose now or ever, and I won't."

SEVEN

I was so glad that Kevin had gone to Miami to some music conference that Diddy was hosting.

After I bathed and put Carlito to bed early, I took a bubble bath and slipped into a black, fitted Emanuel Ungaro dress. I had seen Taraji P. Henson rocking it in the *Marie Claire* magazine. I wore open-toed, trimmed-in-rhinestone Saint Laurent stilettos by Anthony Vaccarello. I was smelling good with a squirt of Bond Central Park perfume. I pulled out matching diamond earrings and a Chanel necklace which draped softly between my décolletage.

I picked up my cell to call Faheem, and he answered on the second ring. "Hello," I said.

"Who is this?"

"Seven."

"Siete." The Spanish rolled smoothly off his tongue. "What's up?" He had my heart racing at Siete.

Damn, ever since the shower I couldn't believe how bad I was yearning for him, Trae, Kaylin and I was even looking at Kevin in a whole new light. My hormones had been raging. Kevin was personal, but Faheem was all business.

"I'd like to talk to you."

"I have a minute. Talk."

"It's a business proposition. I need to see you in person."

"Where's Kev?"

"Gone for the weekend. This will be between you and me."

I asked Faheem to meet me at my house in the next hour and a half. Two of my spots were robbed and workers were killed. I needed muscle, and I needed to consult with someone familiar with the game and who wanted what I wanted. To take over. I saw it in his eyes. He was just like me. He had an unquenchable thirst to rule the streets. And from what I learned, he was all about his business. Unlike Kevin, who knew that our business was at risk, yet he was off to some music conference somewhere and still talking about taking it slow.

As soon as he walked in, my heart leapfrogged between my legs. My panties were soaking wet. I saw the look in his eyes when he saw how well I was dressed. I flung my long, curly hair to the side. I had him and that was exactly what I wanted.

"Calm down," I told my kitty kat under my breath. This here was all man standing in my house. I took a deep breath and began to talk business.

FAHEEM

When I got the call from Seven, I was somewhat expecting it. I had been popping up at her trap spots, so I knew it was a matter of time before she'd want to ask questions. I had to admit, she was tempting. Young. Exotic. Lineage Street Royalty. I was intrigued, and I was ready to play. But the business was to gain her trust and then pull the plug on her. I hadn't figured out how I was going to handle Kev.

Although Seven was dressed to kill, and looking like she wanted to fuck, she went straight into business mode.

"Why are you checking on my spots?"

I smiled. "I'm not checking on your spots per se. I'm just checking out the competition."

"I'm delighted to hear you say that; it brings me to the business at hand. Instead of us competing with one another, why can't we help each other eat?"

"I'm listening."

"And again, I'm delighted that you are. Let's move over here." She motioned to the round table where she had a laptop open. "Here is my proposal."

I took my seat.

"Now what you see, I'm sure you are familiar with, is a map of the city. Red is my territory, blue is . . ."

Seven proceeded to lay out her plan for a city takeover. This chick had a shrewd mind, which included getting rid of Kevin. That was some grimy ass shit on her part, but it was to be expected. Without a doubt, she was the daughter of a mob boss.

Chapter Twenty-Seven

RICK

Rick, Congratulations! I know your daughter has been born, but when are you going to get back and see about your son? Your bloodline who will carry your name. Nina's text was nice-nasty, but I had a more important text to respond to. Kay had texted me from China: *Time to release that formula.*

Shit! Now? That was my response. *What the hell is going on?* This was way too soon. We were supposed to sit on this for at least another year or two. And it was our last option. Our ace in the hole and we were giving it up already? This was the formula for a new drug more addictive than crack cocaine, heroin, and meth.

I knew this meant Trae and Kay were in more than a little trouble. It meant life or death.

"Baby, why are you packing?" Kyra asked, drowsily. She had woken up before I could finish. Destiny was in her arms and the baby was nuzzling, nursing a little, then dozing back off.

I was glad I was there with Kyra when our daughter was born, and I felt like we had a new bond. I hoped by me being here, Kyra could finally see how I could divide my time between both households. But since receiving the text from Kay, playing house was over. It was time to focus and get back to the business of the streets.

"I've got something to handle."

"You're lying. You're just trying to get back to Nina."

"If I was going to see Nina, I would tell you. I ain't hiding shit."

"Whatever, Rick."

"Then pack your shit and roll with me."

"I ain't going nowhere. You know I can't."

"Then trust me and wait until I get back."

ANGEL

"I've made some calls to some of my lawyer friends who work with Children Services Court," I said, going into Tasha's room. Tasha was hastily packing a suitcase, including baby clothes and pampers. "There is a child endangerment referral out on you through Child Protective Services. They say your baby was born with substantial amounts of valium in her system."

Tasha went off. "You know damn well that's not true. I didn't drink. I didn't even take an aspirin while I was pregnant. You were there when she was born. You saw how alert she was at birth. Somebody is setting me up, and when I am sure who it is, I'ma tax that ho's ass!"

"I believe you. Who do you think would do something like this?"

"I told you! That bitch Mari. I know it's her." Tasha pulled herself together. "She's all up on Facebook, acting like she's a widow now, and like she's getting ready to adopt a baby. Who does that?" Tasha paused and pondered her situation. "If Trae was here, I could turn myself in, and he could keep the baby while I cleared my name. But he's not here, so I have to do me. I need a gun and about ten-grand."

"A gun? Girl, what you need is to call your husband before you do anything."

TASHA

What a difference twenty-four hours can make. I had to think fast. How could I get around the guards, who kept us under watch around the clock, as well as cautious ass Angel?

I mumbled a prayer asking for protection and guidance. As soon as I opened my eyes from the prayer, I knew what I had to do. I had to take a chance. I called Scarface and explained that the baby and I were in danger. I told him about the Timeshare we had in the Poconos and in the Catskill Mountains. He agreed to help me get out in the middle of the night and take me and the baby to safety.

"Will we be safe there?" I asked.

"You should be safe. Do you have a gun? Do you have a car?"

"No. Can you get me one? I also need about four-grand. I already have six. We can drive two cars and leave me with one."

"Done. I'll come and move you tonight. But I will have to get authorization to check on you every couple of days."

"Thanks! I really appreciate your help."

I just realized that my fate lied in the hands of a cartel member. I wasn't afraid of Scarface, and he sensed it. *But my boys! Would they be okay with me gone?*

***

That night at 2:00 a.m., I was packed and anxiously waiting for Scarface. Worry began to gnaw at me again. What if I couldn't get a signal on my burner phones to contact Angel? What if I couldn't get online out in the mountains? What if I couldn't get out to get food? What if? What if? What if? I hadn't heard from Trae yet. What was so hard about him calling from China? People did that shit all day long. *Something ain't right.*

Where was my King? I had to make my move. I grabbed my things and Taylour and we headed downstairs.

* * *

Scarface knocked on the door softly. It was a little after 2:30 a.m. I tiptoed to the front door, holding Taylour, wrapped in a big goose blanket.

"Are we ready to go?" I whispered. "Here's all of my things." I pointed to the bags against the wall.

Scarface surprised me and stepped inside the door. He handed me a phone. "Someone wants to talk to you."

"What?" I was perplexed. He pushed the phone into my face.

"Tasha, bae."

Shit. I couldn't believe the voice I was hearing. It was my King! I had never felt more love for my man. This baby made me love him even more, if that was possible. But that still didn't stop me from giving Scarface the screw face and the finger. He knew all along he wasn't taking me to no damn mountains.

"Trae, baby, is that you? Daddy, your baby girl is here. Why haven't you called me?" My mind and my tongue were racing a mile a minute, forgetting that I was getting ready to go into hiding, once again.

"Yo, slow down, Tasha. I only have a few minutes. Why the fuck are you trying to leave the safe house? What's going on with you? I need for you to stay where you are. I'm coming home."

I told him everything I knew about the Amber Alert fiasco. I told him I was scared to death and didn't feel safe.

"Tasha, trust me. There is no safer place than where you are."

"Is your business finished? Don't come back until it is. Don't give them an excuse to have you go back over there and leave us again."

"No, the business is not complete. It won't be complete if I gotta stop what I'm doing to come back home and make sure you stay where you are. I don't know what is going on with my wife. But I can't guarantee you and the baby's safety if you leave that house. Seriously, you're in a safe house, Tasha. I can't focus on this business way over here across the fucking continent and you on the other side somewhere calling yourself hiding with four kids by yourself."

"I was only taking the baby, Trae. Someone is trying to take our baby. It's all over the police websites and the Internet. I believe Mari is behind this Amber Alert. This bitch got me spooked. You think I'm supposed to just sit here and wait for children's services and the police to come take my baby?"

"Don't worry about that shit. I'll take care of it. Just stay there with Don Carlos's men. They will take care of you. Listen to me, Tasha. Don't go and do something crazy. Do not leave that house! Stay your ass right there. Do we have an understanding?"

With Trae finally calling me, my spirit was feeling more at ease. I missed this. I missed him.

"Tasha!"

"Okay, baby, damn. I am not going anywhere. But can you call me more often? Is that asking too much?"

"I'll make the arrangements. Just stay put, Tasha. Now tell me about our daughter."

"She's beautiful. She looks just like you had her and not me. She looks more like you than the boys. We got us a baby girl!" I picked up that Trae was relieved, not only to know I'd given birth to the baby, but most of all, that it was definitely his child.

"I'm sorry I wasn't there to see my little princess when she was born."

"That's all right. Angel stayed with me. I had a C-section, and I never want to have another one. Taylour —that's her name— her middle name, I'll let you pick that, she gave me a time, but she was worth every minute of it. She weighed eight pounds— even though she came a few weeks early. Can you believe it? Did you watch the delivery? Please tell me you got it."

"Watch? I think I could deliver the next one, I watched it so many times."

TRAE

What the fuck was Tasha talking about? An Amber Alert? Mari trying to take the baby?

Where was she getting this shit from? Was my wife losing her mind? Is this the result of this trip? I needed to have Kay get Angel on the phone so I could find out what was really going on. But for now, I was glad that the Don's men had enough sense to get on the phone and call me.

When we first arrived in Beijing, everything seemed to be copacetic. We were being shown around to all the new construction sites symbolizing the growth of Beijing. We were staying in a five-star hotel with red and gold walls and beautiful, antique, jade vases and hand carved furniture. We had an escort, Mr. Wong, and a bodyguard, Mr. Chin, who were driving us around in Bentley taxicabs. Talk about luxury on steroids.

At the business meetings the first week, the executives representing Bitcoin Project said they were pleased to do business with Don Carlos. This was business that didn't involve banks, and it was the new money system. Then they walked Kaylin and me through the process of setting up our own accounts. Kay even got some networking in by negotiating bringing his artists from Game Over Records to tour Beijing and Shanghai, since the youth loved Hip-Hop over here.

They gave us a brief history lesson on how the Chinese viewed America. America used to be strong, but now they owed China a shitload of money. But they still liked doing business with Americans; one of their top consumers.

We had one more day in China before we would fly back to the States. I was just about to breathe easy. I needed to get back to my wife and my family, especially my princess.

But then about eight men in uniforms showed up at our hotel rooms around 10pm. I assumed they were the Chinese police.

"You! Mr. Macklin and Mr. Santos, come with us. You are wanted for questioning."

They spoke perfect English.

KAYLIN

We finally learned that even though Mr. Li had told Trae that no harm would come to him and his family, he still sent someone to take Trae out right there behind the wall. He was not a man of his word. And I had a problem with that. This was now personal for me.

I thought about the final confrontation Mr. Li and I had when I pulled out my trump card. Because of that little piece of information, he couldn't have me if he wanted to.

Mr. Li jumped out his chair. "You want to go to war with me? You are nothing! You think you can come into my house, shut down my operation, and get away with it? You fuckin' porch monkey! Are you ready to go to war with me?" The veins were popping around his neck, and he was damn near foaming at the mouth, looking at me through glossy eyes.

"Do we have a deal?" I asked him again.

Finally, he said, "I have some stipulations of my own. You have forty-eight hours to leave the state. I don't want you back here, and if I hear anything about you in my backyard, the deal is off. Whatever business we had is done and forgotten. Mr. Santos and Mr. Macklin, you no longer exist."

"I have no problem with that."

After twenty-four hours, I realized we were being detained. I hadn't kept my word because I had to go back and forth to California to get Trae out of jail and to get Tasha and the kids to New York. Obviously, Mr. Li didn't keep his word that he would leave our families and us alone. The Don had been right. There had been a price on our heads. But now it looked as if Don Carlos had handed us to Mr. Li on a silver platter. I hated it when Red was right.

"It's not funny, Kaylin. I'm not feeling this trip." She told me. "And you are not listening to me. I'm scared."

"Red, come on, yo. Scared of what? I'm going to be good. I will be back with you before you know it."

"Baby I went online and looked up Beijing and my heart dropped. China is the so-called People's Republic, but it is a Communist country. Our Black men don't have rights here in the states. With all the wholesale killing of Black men, and the police always getting away with it; what chance do you have in China if something goes wrong?

Chapter Twenty-Eight

SEVEN

I kept thinking back to that night when Faheem came by the house. I went over every word he said in our conversation. I remembered every detail. What really endeared me to him was while I was on the phone negotiating and Carlito woke up and started crying. I was headed to get my baby, when Faheem halted me by holding up his hand.

Surprisingly, Faheem went in the bedroom and scooped Carlito up, brought him back into the living room and soothed him, walking him back and forth while I talked business. My baby fell back to sleep quickly. He took Carlito back into his bedroom, and then returned to the living room. That meant everything to me and I could see where Kevin got it from. This man was not only the leader of his crew, he was a husband and a father. His wife sure was one lucky chick. *I wonder if he creeps around on her?* If not, I would damn sure persuade him to.

I ended my call. "We are in!" I raised my hand and gave Faheem a high-five. One of those types of high-fives you give when your point guard scored that dunk. "They are calling us back with the meeting place and time. Damn, I'ma boss! If I had you on my team a few years ago, I'd probably be retired by now."

Faheem gave that smile. "I see a lot of me in you, Seven. We never retire. We may take a breather, but retire? Never. What's your story? Why are you doing this? You have a son. A legit business. Are you sure you are ready to take this risk?"

"Not you too, Faheem! I have my reasons. But for now, let's revel in the moment. I'm giving you the keys to the city, Faheem, my city."

"We don't have the keys yet. Let's not get ahead of ourselves."

"Okay. Okay. I hear you. Anyways, I wanted to say that you're pretty good with children."

"I love kids," Faheem said simply.

I had heard good things about him from Kevin, who practically worshipped him. Faheem had left the game to raise his only daughter. He'd recently lost his only son, so I'm sure Carlito made him think of his deceased child. Hell, he could help raise Carlito if he wanted to.

After Faheem left, I spent the night masturbating while fantasizing about us getting together. I loved his swag, and I imagined him taking control of me when we made love. However, he didn't seem moved at all by my perfume, my sexy dress, or my flirting. I couldn't get a read on him.

JAZ

I was so horny; I couldn't keep still. I needed my man. A sex toy would not suffice. I called Faheem and it went straight to his voicemail. Where the hell was he?

I felt sorry for Angel and Tasha, who didn't have their man at home. Kyra had Rick until recently, when he had to leave— probably for his other baby mama. But Faheem was right there in the next city, and I hadn't seen him in eleven days, but who's counting? I was going crazy!

He called, but he hadn't come by the house. I sent him a text:

I need to see you ASAP. Don't call because I won't answer. I need to see you.

Two nights later, I was getting madder and madder. The kids were down for the night and I had just indulged myself with a bubble bath and I deep conditioned my hair. The house was quiet since it was almost one in the morning. I was lying across the pull-out sofa channel surfing. My phone beeped with a text.

I'm at the front door.

Yes! My threat worked. I jumped out of bed, fixed my hair, applied some lip gloss, sprayed the first perfume I saw and grabbed my robe. Quietly and quickly, I made my way to the front door and snatched it open.

"Baby!" I shrieked. "I miss—"

He covered my mouth with his mouth. "Shh," he said. "You have a houseful of people and I can't stay."

That made each touch even more tantalizing. We shared one of the sweetest kisses we'd had in a long time.

"You smell good enough to eat. Your skin, it's so soft and smooth." Faheem started circling my nipple with his index finger. "I miss you."

"Not more than I miss you."

"You think so?"

"I know so."

He slid his finger between my thighs. "Why are you so wet? You better had been fantasizing about me."

"Don't flatter yourself, babe."

He pinched my butt cheek.

"Faheem."

"I said you better not have been fantasizing about no other nigga."

"Who else . . ." I moaned as he played with my clit. "I'ma be thinking about."

"You tell me."

"Faheem. Baby." I was holding on to him for dear life. Enjoying the finger fuck that made me want to throw every one of my sex toys away. Before I knew it, I was squirting all over his hand.

"Damn, baby. You do miss me. Check out how fast you came."

"You thought I was playing?" I moaned. I slid my hand down to his dick. He was good and hard. "What's good, big daddy?" He nestled his face into my neck, and I unzipped his jeans and worked my magic. This time it was my turn to let my fingers do the fucking.

"Do you love me?" I squeezed the base and played with the head.

"You know I do."

"Then love should bring your ass home more often." I turned his hard dick loose.

"Oh, so you done got yours, now you want to break bad?" He picked me up, and I wrapped my legs around his waist while reaching over to lock the door.

It was funny, because we were trying to make the least amount of noise possible, while bumping into furniture. He carried me toward the kitchen. "Where you sleeping at?"

"The pull-out sofa. It's my turn. When we let Aisha and Kaeerah have it, they play all night, running back and forth to the kitchen, so we had to put them upstairs where we can watch them."

My husband laid me back onto the kitchen table. I was propped up on my elbows, legs in the air. You talkin' 'bout gettin' ready to get it in. I had goose bumps.

FAHEEM

Jaz ain't know who she was fuckin' with. Shit, I missed fuckin' my wife. She wasn't the only person missing somebody. I was getting ready to give her that you-just-getting-back-from-the-streets fuck, on top of that you-glad-to-be-home-and-miss-and-appreciate-your-family fuck. That's what mode I was in.

"Oh, so it's like this?" Jaz said as I lay her back onto the table. "We gonna break the table." She giggled.

"Shut up and put them legs up on my shoulders." I shoved down my jeans and boxers at the same time. I pushed up inside her wet and waiting pussy. Nothing beats a man knowing he got some pussy at home waiting for him.

"Babeee," Jaz cooed as she welcomed the dick inside.

"What's up?" I kept my voice low and steady, gaze fixated on my movements as Jaz's breathing was getting louder and the pussy was feeling hotter and wetter. It was feeling good. No...more like heavenly.

"You. Are. What's-up, bae." She was trembling first and now coming a second time. The table was even shaking. I kept my hardness up in her as she got her nut off.

"FAAHEEEEM! Oh, god. Oh, god," she kept repeating. Finally she fell back limp, creaming all over my dick. I began stroking her as deep as I could.

"Faheem." Her voice was shaky as she tried to put her legs down.

"Nah, I don't think so. Put them legs back up there. You miss me, remember? Why couldn't I come home, remember? You needed a good fuck, remember?" I had locked her ass in place and was going deep, right when I couldn't remember where I was at, I began to skeet. And skeet. And skeet some more.

Dayum.

I lived for moments like this. I looked down at Jaz and the way she was breathing. I knew she was about to come again. I was done. Depleted. My dick was soft. Jaz raised up, wrapped her arms around my neck and I lifted her up in the air and gave her a kiss. I told her, "You pregnant for real this time."

"I love you and we miss you."

"Then go wake my daughter up. I want to see her before I go." I eased Jaz onto the floor.

"Go? Faheem, you just got here. What do you mean go? Go where, Faheem?"

I leaned in and took another long and passionate kiss. My baby really did miss me, and she was worried. She had reason to be worried because my mission in the streets had my undivided attention.

Chapter Twenty-Nine

JAZ

" "Jaz, go get my baby."

"Faheem, no. You're not going anywhere. Can't you at least spend the day with us?" I felt as if I was hyperventilating. I was losing him. His focus was in the streets. It was obvious what he had been doing for the last ten or eleven days: Reacquainting himself with the game.

The old Faheem had resurfaced, and there wasn't shit I could do about it. I was a day late and a dollar short.

"Jaz. Go get Kaeerah."

I felt sick to my stomach. Faheem left me Dr. Jekyll and came back as Mr. Hyde.

"Can I have a little more time with you first? Before you say bye to your daughter and leave us?"

"When I come back next time, I should have us a new place."

"Faheem, why didn't we discuss this first?"

"Jaz, it isn't up for discussion. Go get my daughter, and while I'm talking to her fix me something to eat, right quick, please."

I got through the next couple of hours in a daze. I felt as if I was about to fall out. He took Kaeerah upstairs and they said their goodbyes. He came back downstairs and into the kitchen where I was starting the dishwasher. He eased up behind me, wrapped his arms around my waist, and kissed me on the cheek.

"You're taking really good care of our daughter. She's very happy. Thank you. I'm going to get up outta here. I love the both of you."

With that, he was gone.

FAHEEM

I really needed that time with my family. Here it was forty-eight hours later and that visit and sexing was fresh on my mind when Jaz called me.

"Faheem." Jaz was crying. "I'm headed to the hospital. I've been bleeding clots and cramping to the point that I'm doubling over."

"What? Where are you now?"

"Angel is texting you the address. She's taking me to the hospital."

I was in Jersey City when I got the call. I called Angel, but she didn't answer. Finally, the text came through. I made a wild U-turn and high tailed it to the hospital.

* * *

"Jaz, what's the matter? What is the doctor saying?" I asked before I even got into her room good.

"Hey, Faheem." Angel gave me a hug and then left the room.

"I don't know what happened," Jaz sputtered, helplessly. "I had a reaction to the pills."

"Pills? What pills?"

"The birth control pills."

When Jaz said birth control pills, I felt as if I had been kicked in the balls. I don't think she meant to say it. I think it slipped out because she panicked. I had been thinking we both were on the same page, and these last four months or so, I'd been trying to get her pregnant. I thought we both wanted to be pregnant.

Jaz started crying. "I'm sorry, baby, but I felt the time wasn't right."

"Jaz, what the fuck are you saying?"

It turned out that Jaz had been about five weeks pregnant. A reaction to some birth control pills brought on the hemorrhaging which led to a miscarriage. The doctor gave her a D&C and said she would be discharged in the morning. I was livid, but this was not the best time to express my anger.

Jaz was sedated, so it would have been useless for me to tell her how I really felt. I needed her to be 100% attentive when I spoke my mind. So, I got comfortable and decided I would wait this out. I sat in the chair for the next three hours as Jaz slept peacefully. I got to thinking about how instant and unexpected your life can do a total 180. Just ninety days ago I was a stay at home soccer dad living in a Georgia suburb. Now, because of my love for the streets, I signed a deal with the devil. I couldn't even blame it on Kay and Trae needing my help. I could have turned it down. But I didn't, and I felt no regrets. It wasn't like I was doing it for the money. But that helped of course. I was really married to the rush of the streets. And the risk. I knew the risk. I was throwing the dice, betting on my life, my freedom, and more importantly, I was gambling with the lives of my wife and daughter.

"Why are you frowning? What were you just thinking about?"

I looked up at Jaz, who was trying to sit up in bed. "How are you feeling?" I asked. She looked weary, even though she fell asleep almost four hours ago.

"I'm okay, I guess. I'm groggy and my heart is heavy. Why were you frowning?"

"Why, Jaz? And without discussing this with me."

"Faheem, I thought I was doing what was best for us."

"Without us discussing it? Then what if I said, what I'm doing is what's best for us as well?"

"That's not fair, Faheem. These are two totally different situations."

"The fuck they are. Why would you choose this time to get on the pill?"

Before we could get into it any deeper, we were interrupted. "I'm nurse Eva Choi. What's your last name?" she asked Jaz as she confirmed it against her wristband and chart.

I got up to take a walk before I said or did something I would regret. I was already into enough shit.

All night I remained at the hospital, but I didn't go back to her room. The next morning, Jaz was blowing up my phone. She was discharged and I was right there in the hospital but didn't let her know it. I followed them home. And when the gates closed, I kept on going, heading back to Jersey.

MARI

After I took Dr. Gillis to lunch on Sag Harbor we went to the Hampton Bays Hospital. I talked her into using her authority to see what she could find out about Tasha Macklin since there was an active Amber Alert.

"Are you sure you're okay with doing this?" I asked, looking Dr. Gillis in the eyes.

She nodded adamantly. "Yes, I can do this."

With that, she took her badge and ID, then went to talk to whoever it was that she needed to talk to.

About a half hour later, she called. "I couldn't find anything," she said, "I'm headed your way."

I didn't tell her, but through serendipity, I'd hit the jackpot. No, it couldn't be, but it was. At first, I almost couldn't believe my eyes. Yes, I recognized Faheem in the parking lot as I was waiting in the doorway of the lobby. I knew I would run into them somewhere, somehow. I didn't care how long it would take I wondered what they were doing down in this area. The first thing that came to mind was vacationing. A long one. Then I saw Angel heading my way, pushing an empty wheelchair. I stepped aside and hid from view. Dr. Gillis startled me as she came up behind me.

"Sorry I couldn't come through for you."

"Thank you so much for even trying. That says a lot about you." I flagged my hand in dismissal. I knew what I had to do next. I needed to see what the gang was up to. After all, if they were vacationing, it wouldn't be a problem for me to stop by and say hello.

"Thanks for breakfast," Dr. Gillis said, trying to keep up with my brisk pace.

"The next one is on you. But girl, there has been a change in plans. I'm going to take a taxi."

"A taxi? Do you know how much that is going to cost to get you home?"

I laughed. "I think I spotted an old friend, girl. I'll call you."

"Oh, I see. Where is he?"

"No. You are not going to embarrass me. Don't wait up," I teased her. Faheem was pulling off.

"Yeah, right. I know who your heart belongs to. Just be sure to call me when you get in so that I know you are safe."

"I will." I jumped in a cab and ordered the driver to stay at a distance but to follow Faheem's car. I didn't see what Angel was driving. There was a black suburban on Faheem's tail. That was odd. I followed them as far as I could, until I saw them go onto the bridge to Sag Harbor. Much easier for them to be located. Wherever Angel was, I had a feeling Tasha was nearby.

CHARLI LI

"Are you sure?" I repeated myself as I looked down at the report, blinking my eyes in disbelief.

"Yes," Calvin Braggs said. "Mr. Trae Macklin and his business partner, Kaylin Santos, are in Beijing. They are being detained at one of the Black camps."

"What did they do? Why are they in Beijing?" I was appalled. What had Trae gotten himself into? Black camps or black jails were known for torture. I wasn't going to stand by and allow Mr. Macklin to be subjected to that. If any torturing was to be done, I would be the administrator.

"Are you ready for this?"

"Calvin, tell me everything. Don't ask me questions."

"It looks like there are allegations that they were enemies of the state. They both have work visas. Your father found out they were there; he already had contracts out on their families but cancelled them once he learned of them being in Beijing. I don't have to tell you how far your father's reach is. Your father is headed over there as we speak."

My heart clutched. I was speechless. This time, my father had gone too damn far.

"What do you want me to do about Tasha Macklin? I know where she delivered her baby, so she's probably in Sag Harbor."

"Put that on hold. I've got more pressing matters to tend to." I passed him an envelope.

I went online and put in a plane reservation to Beijing. I also put in some calls to the Chinese Embassy and people I knew in high places. I just hoped it wasn't too late. I had to save Trae Macklin.

JAZ

Look in the dictionary under fuck-up, and I can promise you that my picture is right there. Leave it to me to fuck up a perfectly good situation. Me and my stupid ass started taking these pills not knowing that I was already pregnant. In rejecting the pills, my body also rejected the fetus. This miscarriage had me feeling at my all-time lowest. I really needed my soulmate to be with me, to comfort me. I called Faheem all day the next day, but it kept going to voicemail. Each time he didn't answer felt like the wedge of a knife slicing through our marriage and my heart.

The look on Faheem's face was burned in my memory when I told him that I was on the pill. I might as well have said I had cheated on him. Forget about when I was cooking meth and selling it, and he had to get me out of that. This was the ultimate betrayal in his eyes. I knew how bad he wanted another son since Lil' Faheem's death. I admit . . . I was the selfish one.

All day I kept crying. I couldn't stop. I sent Kaeerah to play with Aisha and Jahara, since they basically were their own sitters. Angel and Kyra agreed to keep her while I stayed holed up in my bedroom.

Suddenly my door opened, and Tasha came in. "Jaz, how are you holding up? Angel told me what happened," she said in a soothing tone.

"I'm not holding up, Tasha."

"I wouldn't suggest holding in your emotions. Talk about and share your feelings, or else you are going to wither away." She began rubbing my back. "You know I can relate. I remember when I had my miscarriage before the twins and before Taylour."

This chick. I couldn't help but smile. I looked at Tasha with surprise. "Are you saying that you were upset about the miscarriage when you were most likely pregnant by Kyron? You have lost it." I couldn't believe my ears.

"Yes, I know. I did lose it. I mourned that baby, too."

I sniffled. Tasha handed me a Kleenex. We sat there, both wrapped around our own thoughts, or should I say mistakes.

"I really, really fucked up this time, Tasha. I mean, think about it. Think about the circumstances. He wants another son so bad right now. He feels that it will make him whole again. And I get pregnant and lose the baby because of some birth control that I was taking that he didn't even know about. I fucked up big time. Ain't no coming back from this shit. I don't see it."

"Don't say that. You know Trae and I have been to hell and back. Marriages must be able to take knocks. It makes the both of you and the love and respect for each other stronger. And it builds character. Trae swears we are unbreakable, and I believe him."

"That's good for you. But Faheem is acting like I murdered his seed in cold blood with an AK. He's acting like I got rid of the baby in my stomach on purpose. Tasha, I didn't even know I was pregnant."

"Don't worry. He'll be back. You know how Faheem is. He blows up, but then he calms down. And before you know it, you'll get pregnant again."

"I wish. I'd give anything right now to even believe a smidgen of what you just said."

"He'll be all right." Tasha reached down and hugged me. "Well, heaven just got another angel."

"Tasha, heaven is right here on earth, not in the sky after you die. Faheem ain't tryna hear that shit. You know who I'm married to. His son is gone."

"Jaz, trust me. You will get pregnant again. I promise you. This is why Taylour is so special to me. She came out of the worse time of our marriage. Trae was in jail, the whole Kyron mess, and yet this beautiful baby girl was born."

Tasha didn't make me feel any better. She didn't know Faheem like I did.

SEVEN/FAHEEM

I had carved out a square of the city that contained the prime dope district. The Kings had a section. Bo had one, me and Kev, and the last one was ran by a little bit of everybody; whoever had the balls and the muscle. But I wanted all four. What I proposed to Faheem was that he take two and I take two. Allow The Kings to have any place outside of what was now called District Seven.

All Faheem and his team had to do was move in and execute.

We had the best product and the best price. I figured fair exchange wasn't robbery. It wasn't a total hostile takeover. However everyone did hear the same announcement, "This is the Seventh District and all business comes through District Seven. Everything will be fair, and we will make sure that we all eat. Spread the word and be glad that we didn't kill you! Now, together let's get this money!"

Three nights earlier, my first big shipment was robbed. And it was a huge lost for us.

It had started pouring down raining, and I didn't want to go back home to an empty house. I looked over at Faheem. "That was a big L, Faheem."

"Don't sweat it. You win some, you lose some. It happens to every muthafucka at one time or another. It's the only way to learn how to make sure it doesn't happen again. Don't be so hard on yourself, me or the team. At least we didn't lose any bodies. But we still gotta find out who took our shit. That's when shit is going to get ugly. But until then, I got this. You stressing over it ain't going to change shit."

"I'm trying not to stress, Faheem. But that's easier said than done. Where are you headed to? You want to come up for a drink? I damn sure feel like I need a stiff one."

"A drink? What you got to smoke up there? I ain't got nothing on me."

I parked the ride and we headed upstairs. Since I kissed him, he had been staying away. I liked that I had made him uncomfortable. We came inside, shut the door and went our separate ways.

This was it. I was going for it. He was finally ready to get this lovin'. Faheem was about to be the third man I'd slept with.

The nanny and Carlito were sleeping peacefully. I hurried to shower and put on a negligee and a silk robe. I freshened up with some more Coach perfume. Ready.

"Seven!" I heard him call my name, sounding impatient. Hold your horses, big daddy. I got even more excited.

"I'm coming now." With each step I took, my heart was beating so loud I could hear it through my chest.

Faheem was standing at the front door, the smell of weed filled up my nostrils. "I gotta run."

He looked me up and down before I could ask him why: and just like I thought he would, he took control of me. Faheem started kissing me with one of the most passionate kisses I'd ever had. His lips felt like pillows. We were so close to each other I could feel his joint through my robe. He was definitely hung. We kept kissing until I felt myself climaxing. *What the hell?*

"Fafa..heeem….in!" I cried out his name.

Faheem let me go, kissed me on my forehead, and left. I stood there in a daze. I'd never had an orgasm from a man kissing me. That was a first. My legs felt weak, so I stumbled over to the sofa. I fell into a deep sleep. When I woke up hours later, my body still had that feeling of bliss. I wondered if Faheem and I could take it any further.

WAHIDA CLARK

Chapter Thirty

BO

"Y'all know this is my favorite Chinese joint! As much as I come in here, y'all can't even give me a plastic cup for free? No extra duck sauce?" I joked with the owner, I called Mr. Chow. I don't even think that's his name, but he had been answering to it since I had been coming to the little hole in the wall restaurant in downtown Trenton.

I grabbed my food and the two containers of iced tea. As soon as I stepped out of the door, I heard, "Yo, take a ride with me, dawg."

I looked up, and by the colors the two niggas were wearing, they were Kings. My man's tone was firm but friendly. I could tell this was strictly business.

"Man, I ain't got no time for young boys. A nigga tryna get back to the crib and eat." I tried to walk off, mad at myself for getting caught slippin'. I had bags in both hands. I couldn't get to my gun, and it was broad daylight.

The main King got in my face. "Make time, Duke." He flashed his burner to let me know he wasn't playing.

I looked at the gun and laughed. "Nigga, do what you gonna do."

"C'mon, Bo, don't make this hard. If we wanted to kill you, you know you'd be dead already."

I knew he wasn't lying. These young boys had Trenton fucked up. These niggas were pulling mass killings in broad daylight and having shoot-outs in public places like this was the Wild West. They didn't give a fuck!

A blood-red Charger pulled up in front of us. The vibe I was getting wasn't hostile. After what we just pulled off, I was expecting some clap back, but not like this. This was formal and obviously thought out. So now I was curious.

"Get in."

"Only if I get to keep my gun."

"Only if you don't think about using it."

"Only if you don't give me a reason," I shot back.

The main King chuckled, and they pushed me in the car. That had to be the friendliest kidnapping in history.

* * *

We had pulled up to somebody's crib in Lawrenceville, past the mall and shopping centers. We were in the theatre room, and it damn sure didn't feel like a kidnapping. We were blowing massive amounts of the finest exotic you could smoke and playing tunk for five dollars a game. I was over $250.

B-Murda, the top King, finally got Faheem on the phone.

"Yo, Fah. We got your man Bo," B-Murda told him. He then hit the speaker button.

"What? You got my man, Bo? What the fuck does that mean?"

"Faheem, these youngins kidnapped me. They want to talk to you." I was choking on the exotic.

Faheem must've thought I was playing because he hung up the phone. B-Murda called him back.

"Yo, who the fuck is this? How the fuck you get my number?" Faheem sounded agitated.

"Be easy, fam. It's not that serious, yet. But you can make it so. I just want to talk to you. Bo is just insurance that shit don't get ugly, feel me? We need to come to a mutual agreement."

"Who is this? And no, muthafucka, I don't feel you. But I'm about to see you fo' sho! Where you at?"

"Meet me at Cadwalader Park at three o'clock and remember, yo, check that famous anger of yours," B-Murda said.

FAHEEM

Damn. I got shot. And now they got Bo? How that nigga get caught slippin' like that? The Kings were the only ones willing to clap back. But shit, it could have been much worse. So far my mission for phase 1 had been a success.

Three o'clock. I looked at my watch. It was 1:05. I called Snell and told him to round up a team and where and what time to meet.

At 2:30, I arrived at the park and drove around. Ten minutes later, Snell and three shooters arrived. I looked in the backseat and they had more than enough fire power. I didn't have much longer to wait. A blood-red Charger whizzed by us, did a U-turn and came back. I recognized B-Murda and Reese as they got out and approached me. Bad ass youngins. Thinking they grown now.

B-Murda looked around at all the ice grills and the glittering chrome of locked and loaded pistols and chuckled. "I see ain't much changed with you, Faheem. Still ready for war when words are enough," B-Murda remarked and we dapped up. "When did you decide to come back? And why with such the hostility and urgency? I guess this was a side of you I never got a chance to witness."

"Where's Bo?"

"Fam is good, believe me. This ain't no kidnapping. More of a social ploy. I knew if I didn't resort to drastic measures, I wouldn't get your attention," B-Murda explained.

I stepped up close to him. "So what kind of game you playin'?"

"No games, yo. This is business, and I'm hopin' we can come to an understanding . . . for both of our sakes. I already know how you get down, Faheem, and I know how you used to have shit on lock. Niggas been buzzin' ever since you came back, so I already knew you had plans. But after your team ran up in my territory, I was able to peep what those plans are. You still got it. But it's enough for all of us. So, regardless of District Seven, just so you know, shit done changed a lot around here." B-Murda tried to be firm without being disrespectful.

"Yeah, what's changed?"

"The Eastside is King City now and I run it," B-Murda replied, in the tone of a man sure of his power so he didn't need to flaunt it.

"And you can still run it. It's just that I control all of the product."

B-Murda's eyes turned cold. "Apparently, I know who you are, but you don't know about me. I got soldiers in these streets like roaches with the heart of suicide bombers, except they don't die; they ride for the cause. Shit is real, so a war ain't to either of our benefit."

"No need for war. Like I said, all product coming into the city needs to have my stamp on it, and if you want to trap out of District Seven, it's your decision."

I couldn't help but to respect how the young boy was bringing it. I could tell he had a good head on his shoulders. "Do you like quality?"

"Yeah but—"

"Is the price right?"

"Yeah."

"Look, I don't mind you eating, but for now we have to eat at the same table."

"If I say no?" he asked.

"Then I hope you can survive a drought. It'll be a fuckin' desert for you. 'Cause nothing moves through this city except through me."

TRAE

Customs had detained us for almost twenty-two hours before they put us in a van and drove for hours to what was known as the Black Jail. Was I nervous? Hell fuckin' yeah. First off, I didn't know what the fuck was going on; and second, from what I understood, when a nigga was detained over here, there was no trial, no hearing, nothing. Now, that's the shit right there that had me nervous as hell.

I had no control over anything.

We arrived and were taken inside. They took Kay to the right and me to the left. He and I had been caught up in some tight situations and managed to wiggle our way out of most of them. But from the look and feel of things, this Black jail shit was obviously on a whole 'nother level.

How the fuck did we manage to get detained in China? Ironically, over here it's called the Black Jail. In the US, Blacks are thrown in jail.

* * *

Obviously, the good cop, bad cop routine was universal. Regardless of how bleak our situation looked, I never had to worry about Kay, and he didn't have to worry about me. We never outed each other. We were brothas to the muthafuckin' end. Wasn't no snitchin' shit in our blood. The good cop wanted to know why I came to China. The bad cop wanted me to tell him who I was here to see and why.

Thankfully, I had nothing to hide. I didn't have any narcotics in my possession. Hell, I hadn't toked on a blunt during our entire trip. Muthafuckas took my phone. I should be calling Benny, my lawyer, right now. "Can I call my lawyer?"

"The request has already been submitted. I'll let you know when you can have a call. In the meantime, would you like a cup of green tea?" the good official said. He was medium height and had blond hair. Odd for a Chinese man.

"No." I shook my head. I didn't know what they might put in a nigga's drink. I would dry fast if I had to. Fuck that!

"We understand you were detained in the US not too long ago," the bad official interjected. He was tall for an Asian, and he wore his hair cropped close. His head was a perfect round shape.

"Yes, but I was released on a technicality."

The official became quiet as he looked through the black folder embossed with Chinese letters and a big red seal on it.

Then he came at me using a little more force. "Our intel says that you murdered a man while you were detained. How were those charges dropped? How does that process work there in America?"

Then it hit me. Mr. Li. He's behind us being here. I paused. *Stay calm.* Never let muthafuckas see you sweat. "I'm sure your same intel revealed that it was self-defense. Another inmate came at me because he was ordered to kill me. It was a planned assassination while I was in custody."

"You must be a very dangerous man," he said, before picking up the black folder and greeting two new officers. They moved over to the desk in the corner where they spoke rapidly in Chinese.

What the fuck are these muthafuckas sayin'? I knew I had to get the fuck up outta here ASAP!

KAYLIN

I knew my wife was trippin'. It was like Trae and I had disappeared off the grid. Red told me not to come. She actually predicted that something like this was going to happen. Women are intuitive like that. We don't want to listen because we are 'the man of the house' and we have to do what we feel is best. But, once again, my wife was right and here I was caught up in some shit.

With all the recent terrorist attacks around the globe, I knew customs and everybody else had to crack down, but because we came here as businessmen, under the invitation of the business holdings of Don Carlos's IEE Enterprises, we had no problems when we came through customs. We were met by escorts arranged by Don Carlos and certified by the Chinese government.

But now these officials were treating us as criminals. They had taken our suitcases, our wallets, our laptops, our cell phones, cash and credit cards. They went through our belongings as if we had terrorized the White House. They were going through our shit with a thoroughness that only the Feds could appreciate, and we had nothing, not even a matchbook that belonged to China. I was glad our shit was squeaky clean, per se. They separated us, and I was put in a tiny waiting room that only had a long desk and three chairs. I was on one side, and two other guys were seated in front of me on the other. The medium-height official was holding a black folder with a big red seal. I had no idea what was getting ready to happen. So naturally, I was in defense mode.

"What are you doing in the country?"

"I came to do business on behalf of IEE. You have all of the verification before you."

"You have a work visa to be in the country, but it has expired."

"I'm the owner of Game Over Records. And yes, I have a work visa, but it hasn't expired."

Don Carlos made sure we had all of the documentation we needed. If the shit was expired, either their team wasn't thorough, or he was planning on us getting detained and hauled off by customs. Either way, somebody better have some good answers.

"Is that why I'm here because of an issue with a work visa? We need to halt this conversation until I get my attorney on the phone. Can I use the phone now?"

"How did you get the money to start a record label in the US? You do that rap music?"

I needed to talk to my lawyer, and these muthafuckas was stalling, purposely.

"I received an inheritance from my grandfather, which is how I started my business. And yes, I promote and sell hip-hop. We were here last year. We are planning a stop here in Beijing on our next tour."

Trae nor I would mention a word about the new bitcoin and cryptocurrency market. The new money and dope game. The Chinese government was now trying to license—meaning control—it all. Officially, we were here about entertainment and setting up a tour in China for our Game Over artists.

"You've been identified in your country by the FBI as a BIE."

"What is that?"

"Want to be terrorists. You know like Black Lives Matter. Maybe you are friends with them."

"I'm far from a terrorist. They are not terrorists."

"Black Identity Extremist," he stated.

"Black Identity Extremist? I don't follow you. If I know my black identity, I'm an extremist? Anyone seeking justice for the injustices done to the black man and woman is a Black Identity Extremist. What kind of shit is that?"

"Mr. Santos, our intel says that you are a threat and an enemy of the state."

"I'm a law-abiding American citizen. I'm a businessman. I came here to do business in and with China."

Suddenly it hit me. Mr. Li. China is his territory. But how did he know we were here?

TRAE

They escorted me into an administrative office. They still hadn't given us a phone call. When we stepped into the room, two members of Don Carlos's bitcoin team were suited up with briefcases and led me into a room. I was glad to see familiar faces, but I was pissed off at the same time.

"What the fuck is going on? Where is my partner, Kaylin?"

"He's next door. He's fine."

"We are here to see you. Don Carlos sends his assurance that everything will be fine, and he apologizes for the inconvenience. But you are a key component to this operation and will be released shortly."

"Operation? What operation? Why the fuck are we being detained? I need to call my lawyer."

"Mr. Macklin, Don Carlos simply asks that you remain patient and trust the process. Unfortunately, you are the bait. You are the top name on Mr. Li's agenda."

"What fuckin' process are you talking about? How long do y'all plan on keeping me here? I was supposed to be back in the States by now." I was seeing red. This muthafucka went on to explain why we were being detained in a place where they could kill us and there would be no repercussions. We wouldn't even be missed. What he told me sank my heart to my feet. I couldn't believe it. To make a long story short, I was being used as bait to lure Charles Li in.

And according to them, he was on his way to China, but he had a couple of stops. Once he arrived and they had him, I was free to go. All I had to do was arrange the meeting. I couldn't share any of this knowledge with Kay until after it was all said and done.

"How am I supposed to set up a meeting?"

"Use his attorney or his daughter, Charli Li. She's already inquiring of your whereabouts and taking steps to facilitate your release. It's exactly what we wanted to happen."

I was livid. What was being done to me and asked of me was bananas. Use his daughter Charli Li? Shit, I was trying to fix my marriage and they wanted me to jeopardize it for the same bitch I fucked it up wit' before. At this point I was more scared of Tasha than I was of the Black Jail. The second Tasha get wind that she was involved, my ass was toast.

Chapter Thirty-One

ANGEL

Time flies! A couple more years, and we would be knocking on thirty. Dirty thirty is what they call it. The four of us had been friends since the eighth grade, and our dream was to live in a brownstone together like the cast of *Living Single*. But that wasn't how we'd been thrust together.

I'd been cramped up in this small ass house, with all of these post-partum, mood swinging chicks, busy ass kids and newborns crying . . . long enough. I needed a change of scenery. And the tension was building. Teeth smacking, mumbling, doors slamming, things were coming to a head. Them niggas better hurry up and make something happen before we were up in here fighting. If it weren't for homeschooling, Jaz and I wouldn't be vibing at all.

I was going crazy being stuck in this house. Actually, everyone was going crazy. It was just like Kaylin and Trae to have us caught up in some shit. Now here we were, stuck together like some damn cockroaches.

We need some fun up in here. I was thinking that after we got the kids and babies to bed, it would be on! It was going to be a party! Yeah! That was what these hos needed . . . some weed. It's settled. Pajama Jammie Jam it is. That would lighten up everyone's mood, and if it doesn't then I'ma start smackin' these hos back into reality.

"Hey, guys!" I said at dinner. "I think we need to have a girl's night. We are long overdue." I gave them my puppy dog face.

"Where the hell are we going to go with all of these kids?" Kyra asked.

"I'm talking about us. Here. Put the kids to bed and we break out the wine glasses, the weed, you know, like old times. A Pajama Jammie Jam!"

Tasha was the first to pipe in. "Yeah booooyeeeee!" She said in her Flava Flav voice. "Now that sounds like fun. My man ain't here to take me out. And since he's not, he better come with a real nice bank roll for putting me through this shit." She looked off, probably thinking the same thing I was, like all the shit we'd been through with these niggas. Murders, kidnappings, jail, robberies. Our relationships and our marriages had been crazy!

But that was what we signed up for when we got with them. Loving them came with all the crazy and stressful bullshit. And as crazy as it sounds, I still wasn't walking away.

Kyra, who was looking depressed, worrying about her Rick situation, suddenly perked up, snapping her fingers, and seat dancing. "Hell yeah, let's do it!"

Jaz had the worst attitude of us all and had been upset since Faheem wasn't fucking her or with her because of her birth control shenanigans. She too perked right up at the mention of my Pajama Jammie Jam. "Oh, as long as we have some decent food, I'm down."

What does Jaz think decent food is with her vegan ass? "I don't want no tofu!" I told her.

"Girl, I make a mean hummus!"

"I don't think so. We need some chicken wings and margaritas and some weed. Where we going to get some from?" Kyra interjected.

"We can watch a movie."

"And we got to binge on *The Comedy Get Down*." Tasha was pumped up. She rubbed her stomach, which was still sore from the C-section as she lay on the sofa bed.

"Okay, we can play charades," Kyra suggested, or should I say she always suggested charades. "Or we can keep it hood. Get that spades game going, dawg! Sheeit, you talking about doing it how we used to." She stood up to high-five her cheating partner, Tasha.

"All right, all right; it's on. I'ma make sure we get turnt up." I was excited. "And don't worry about the weed. I got that covered."

Seeing my girls happy made me happy. Shit, we had all been through hell and back and once again we were going through some shit, so it was only right that I turned their frowns into smiles.

TASHA

I still had plenty of baby weight to lose. I honestly thought I would've snapped back by now. Especially since I was breastfeeding and my little fat momma was six weeks old. She was already giving me attitude. My boobs looked and felt like half gallon jugs. All I can say is ugh. Don't get me wrong. I was enjoying the bonding and naturalness of nursing, but damn! I was living in Trae's big pajama shirts. But for tonight, I did my hair and even slapped on a bit of makeup, which was not my thing. I hadn't put on any real clothes since the baby shower. I didn't even know what size I wore.

We lucked up and got the kids tucked away a little after nine. Which felt like a complete relief more than any other night we put them to bed. I guess because we were actually doing something together for fun. We all reported to the living room in our jammies with our comforters and pillows. It looked like a real sleepover, just how we used to do it. It brought back great memories and I could honestly say it felt damn good to be with my girls despite our current circumstances.

Kyra connected her Bluetooth to Shaheem's Beats Pill speaker for me. I was streaming from Tidal, my main man Cool DJ Red Alert and it was on! Everyone hit the floor.

 My C-section had me a little nervous to get down like that, so I volunteered to be the DJ and kept all of my favorite music in rotation. Yes, I am a selfish DJ. I was playing what I wanted to hear. I had to laugh at my girls busting their dance moves. It made me realize we were getting older, but we were still young at heart. Fuck that shit! Angel was talking about dirty thirty. Thirty ain't old, and we ain't even there yet! Shit, thirty is the new twenty! Period!

I put on Cardi B's Bodak Yellow and all the hood rat came out of each one of us. Tongues hanging out, asses shaking and hips gyrating while screaming, "Money moves!" on cue. You couldn't tell my girls shit! We were bad as hell and we could still get down! I enjoyed hearing them laugh. It made me feel free. It made me feel like everything was okay and that I had not a worry nor a care in the world. I knew they felt the same way. We needed this party.

Jaz must have thought that we were really in prison, serving us jail house caramel popcorn balls and her homemade pizza. That girl was trippin'. After we danced until we could dance no more, we binged on *The Comedy Get Down*, which had my side hurting as well as my scar from the c-section we laughed so hard. I don't know which mood killer suggested we watch, *Best Man Holiday* but that shit was a total dud.

When ol' girl from *The Players Club*, the wife (Monica Calhoun) who was dying, started singing "Silent Night," I was no more good. I cried from deep in my gut. I was sobbing so hard it made each of us realize how important our camaraderie was and we started hugging each other. That shit was like a domino effect, everybody was tearing up. I never wanted it to take such a heartbreaking situation to happen for us to value our friendship or marriages.

I wish my husband was here with me.

"Why are we crying?" Jaz asked through tears. "One minute we laughin' all loud and now we are all crying." And we all burst into laughter and couldn't stop.

Kyra started crying. "I miss Rick. I do love him. But why? What am I going to do? How can I love him when he's putting me in such a fucked-up situation?"

"At least none of your marriages are on the brinks like mine. I fucked up!" Jaz started crying. By the time Aunt Marva joined the party, all four of us were boo-hooing.

"Ain't this about some shit." She announced standing in the middle of the floor looking at us as if we were crazy.

"God woke me up and led me to tell y'all this. He has the strangest ways of getting our attention. Everything happens for a reason, season, or a lifetime. I'm leaving in the next day or so. Y'all don't need me. Y'all have each other, and I think that's more important for right now. And y'all still have a few more lessons to learn from all of this, but you'll be fine. Lean on each other for strength. That's what family does."

It was just like Aunt Marva to kick some old woman wisdom to us. It was much needed, and I now found the positive in us being cooped up in this house all together.

"Come here." She motioned for all of us to get up. "Let's get a group hug. And let's take a selfie." We all burst out laughing.

"What do you know about a selfie?" Jaz asked.

"Don't worry about what I know about them."

We took the selfie, and then Marva began praying, "Heavenly Father, keep their husbands safe so they can return to their families and continue to build even stronger families and grow the love between them, Amen."

"Amen," I said silently. I didn't mind praying, but when an older person prayed it struck something in me and made me feel safe, like I could make anything happen.

Chapter Thirty-Two

RICK

W hen I was in the Witness Protection Program, I learned about the shadow government, the Dark Net and the Dark Web. The Dark Web or Dark Net is a subset of the Deep Web, where there are sites that sell drugs, hacking software, counterfeit money, knock-off prescription pills and a lot of other shit you couldn't even imagine. The shadow government are the rulers behind the scenes; it's not the elected officials, like we tend to think. And I now moved in the shadows with the shadow government.

I moved out of the Witness Protection Program on my own. I was not in the type of program where you take the stand for snitch-related shit. Fuck no! My program was the government's Deep Undercover Intelligence (DUI). So, for the most part, I didn't have to worry too much about someone coming for me. It was like I never existed. And I walked away with three new identities and all of the paperwork that went with them. However, I did need to be careful. I wasn't stupid. I tried my damnedest to stay under the radar. I made sure I didn't get so much as a jaywalking ticket. But this shit with Kay and Trae and a formula that seems to be more harm than good, and now Kendrick was blowing up my phone asking me about it. I was two seconds shy of blocking this nigga's number. That's how much he had been calling. I don't know he got my number. The nigga aint even know me like that.

In the meantime, I was awaiting further instructions from Kay or Trae. I was in the dark as to what their next move or mine was. But one thing was for sure, if I didn't hear from them in forty-eight hours, I would have to get in contact with the Chinese Embassy.

My phone rang. I was hoping it was them niggas calling me from China. But it was my baby instead.

"Hey, Rick, it's me. Aisha."

"I know your voice. How's my big girl doing?"

"Good. My mom said I had to ask you, when I asked her if I could come out to Las Vegas. That's where you are, right?"

She giggled.

"What, come again, road dawg." She knew that's what I called her every time we would go somewhere.

"I said I want our next trip to be Las Vegas."

"I got you. But why Las Vegas?" She giggled some more. "I'll tell you when I see you. It's a surprise, okay?"

"What?"

"Riiiii-ck! Wait till you come back. When are you coming back?"

"In a few. Put your mother on the phone."

"Rick? Hey, bae." It was Kyra. "When you coming home? Both of your ladies here miss you."

I loved hearing Kyra's voice. I loved everything about her. Especially when she said she missed me. But if she missed me so much and she loved me so much, then what was the problem? Why weren't we together?

KYRA

Marvin. Tyler. Rick. Yup! I only had sex with three men in my life. Marvin and Tyler were my high school sweethearts. Eventually, Marvin and I got married. Marvin went to prison, and I thought I had moved on with my life; that was until he came home, and his first stop was to find me. We eventually moved to LA with Trae and Tasha; all of us wanted a fresh start. But Marvin started back using drugs.

Long story short, that's how I wound up shot in the head. I was out chasing behind my husband when he was on a drug run one night. The nigga was so fuckin' high, he left me for dead. Yes, dead. The next thing I knew, I was waking up out of a coma, and I had amnesia. I found out my identity by a former UCLA classmate who recognized me. But it was Rick who saved my life.

* *

I was dreaming that I was riding in a car. However, when I opened my eyes, I was. How did I get here? The last thing I remembered was looking for Tasha Macklin, and then standing on the porch in front of Rick. I had recognized him. Tears were streaming down his cheeks, and then everything went black . . .

That was crazy. Yes, Rick happened to show up at Tasha's at the same time I did. How spooky is that? After I blacked out, he took me to the hospital, then got me back to Tasha and Aisha. He had saved me once again. Everyone thought I was dead. I can only imagine what that must have been like.

Rick left us early last week. And I missed him. I felt better now that I'd talked to him. He said he was out working. At first, I didn't believe him. But something was up with Trae and Kaylin, and he was being very tight lipped. These men are so damn secretive. If we didn't know what the hell was going on, how could we help if help was needed?

For some reason, I picked up the phone and dialed a number I had known for a long time but didn't feel the need to use it because I was like fuck that bitch.

"Hello?" Nina said.

"Hello," I said. "This is Kyra."

There was silence.

This shit was more awkward than ever.

"How's Little Rick?" I had to break the silence since I called her. I could feel Nina's defense slowly coming down.

"He's doing better. He's gaining weight." Then she paused. "How's Destiny?"

I lightened up, too. "She's growing, literally bursting out of her newborn clothes."

Nina started laughing. "She sounds fat like her brother. Rick told me you are breastfeeding?"

"Yes. And he told me you were breastfeeding little man."

"I am."

Before I knew it, we were talking about sore nipples, breastfeeding, and how good breast milk was for our babies. A mother's weakness was her babies, and it wasn't strange to see how us talking about our babies brought us together for a moment. The energy was positive, and the conversation was filled with some laughter, but I couldn't just allow that lump in my throat to stay there. I had to say something. Something I had been dreading.

"Nina, I love Rick and I know you love Rick, too," I blurted.

There was silence once again.

"I do. I do love him," she finally said.

"This I know, but from the looks of it, he loves us both and there's not a damn thing neither one of us can do to change that."

As bad as I hated admitting that, I knew it was the truth. Rick was in love with two women, and I couldn't blame him. I had to keep reminding myself of that. He was in love with me before I fell off the face of the earth, and he never stopped loving me, even when he started loving another woman. Was I pissed? Hell yeah! But could I blame him? Unfortunately not.

"So, what are you saying?" Nina asked.

"I'm saying why keep this back and forth going? Rick loves me and he loves you. He's never going to stop fuckin' me and he's not going to stop fuckin' you. He's never going to leave either one of us alone so why keep going at each other's throats when Rick clearly doesn't give a fuck about our bickering. He's still going to do him, regardless of how we feel about it."

I had said a fuckin' mouthful and I couldn't believe how I was coming, but a bitch was tired. Tired of all the drama. Tired of all the negativity. As you get older, all that extra shit is for the birds. All I wanted to do was continue to grow and glow and be happy.

"I feel everything you're saying, but this hurts, Kyra. This really hurts," she said.

"I know. How do you think I feel? We're in love with a man that's in love with two women. We both want him to ourselves and that's just something we can't have, but instead of looking at the negatives, let's look at the positives. Rick is a damn good man, and a damn good father. Instead of fighting each other, let's come together, stick together and raise our kids to the best of our ability. Hell, if anything we're winning," I told her with confidence in my voice.

"How so?"

I could tell that I was going to have to school Nina on a thing or two, and I had no problem in doing so because I wanted to be stress and drama free from this point on.

"Look at it this way, not only is Rick a good man and great father, but you just got yourself a new best friend. I know it gets lonely not having anyone around but the kids. And on top of that, Rick has no problem with taking care of us. How are we not winning? I mean, if we're not beefing, we could be enjoying each other's time, shopping, going out for drinks and god knows what else. Shit, we can even leave the kids with his black ass."

Nina chuckled at that last remark but then surprised me with what she said next. "I can't tell you how long I've been trying to find a way to have this conversation with you. I looked at you as my enemy, but in reality, you're just a woman like me who's feelings were wrapped up in such a crazy situation."

She was spot on with her response because both our feelings were wrapped up in Rick's good dick having ass.

"So, are you down for starting over? Putting all the bullshit to the side and moving forward? Rick isn't going anywhere. He's not about to leave neither one of us alone."

Now the ball was in her court. I knew that I was done fighting. I gave Nina a few minutes to get her thoughts together because I knew this entire conversation had her at a halt, but it needed to be done and not on Rick's time.

"I'ma give it a shot," Nina finally said.

Chapter Thirty-Three

JAZ

I texted Faheem. Again, for the fiftieth time.

We need to talk. Please come see me.

It had been weeks since my miscarriage, so I wasn't thinking about sex. I just needed to know what was going on in Faheem's head. I wanted him to hold me. I needed to know just how bad I fucked up, so I could at least have a beginning point on how to fix it. As of now, I had nothing.

I knew he was back out there grinding in the streets. He knew just as well as I did, the risk that goes with that. I didn't know what had my spirits down the most, him in the streets, or me having the miscarriage because of taking some deadly birth control pills behind his back. The two sins were neck and neck. Both resulting in possible death. Our child was a testament to that.

My phone vibrated. It was Faheem.

"Hey," I said, fighting not to choke up.

"Jaz? What's up? Y'all okay?" Faheem sounded gruff, as if I had just woke him up. My heart sank to my stomach. *Where is he sleeping?*

"I'm still spotting."

"When do you get checked out again?"

"Thursday."

"Good."

"Kaeerah has been asking about you. Come see us. Plus, we need to talk."

"Tell her daddy loves her, and I'll be there in a couple of days." With that, Faheem hung up.

Was our marriage over or what? It definitely felt over.

CHARLI LI

I had already spoken to my contact at the Chinese Embassy to verify that Trae was being held at the Black Camp. I was not leaving him in there to rot. I just couldn't do it. I was too in love with Trae. I'm talking deeply in love with Trae. He was my man. Or at least he would be once I got finished with my plan. I immediately began to pack. My first stop would be the Chinese Embassy. I had to beat my father over there. Thank God, Beijing was his last stop.

TASHA

I knocked on Angel's bedroom door. We had five spacious bedrooms. One for me, Angel, Jaz, Kyra, the boys, and the girls. Using a sofa bed, we had turned the dining room into sleeping quarters. It was like one big sleepover all the time. We were enjoying ourselves under the circumstances. Aunt Marva had just moved out. She said it was too much activity here for her. But if we needed her, all we had to do was call and she'd be back. With Angel being pregnant and Kyra and me just having our baby girls, the kids would be all around the same age, growing up together.

"Have you heard anything?" I asked Angel. The men where initially supposed to be gone for two weeks, but I told Trae not to come home until everything was resolved. And clearly, he had taken that to heart. At this point, we hadn't spoken to them in over a month.

"Tasha, please. I know you are on pins and needles just as much as I am. If I heard something I would have rushed and told you."

"Girl, I know it. It doesn't hurt to wish. This shit is beginning to feel like déjà vu."

Jaz suddenly entered, carrying a large cardboard box. There was an air of the old Jaz about her, not the vulnerable, broken down, man-done-left-me recent Jaz.

"Hey, let's have a meeting in the living room," she said. "Call Kyra in, too. We all need to talk," Jaz added.

Kyra came out of her room, and we all went downstairs. We all gathered around Jaz, who had taken charge for the time being. She seemed to be getting back to her old self since the miscarriage.

"Look, I don't know about y'all, but I feel like we are sitting ducks just being here." Jaz got straight to the point. "I don't know what the fuck is going on. But I do know that Faheem is getting us a place, but if he doesn't come through soon, we need to map out a plan to get our own place and get the fuck outta here. And from what I'm piecing together, your husbands may be detained over in China for all we know."

"Don't say that, Jaz," Kyra said. "You don't know for sure."

"The hell I don't. I was able to pull a little bit of info from Faheem. There are only eight men surrounding this house, and I don't trust them. There are four women and eight children, two of them babies in here."

"What are you talking about, Jaz?" I asked.

"Being ready that's all. We can't trust those muthafuckas. We are going to have to be proactive up in this joint." With that, Jaz went over to the corner and pulled out the cardboard box and opened it. Inside were four guns.

"Look, I've been going to the gun range since I got back. We had enemies we made in Atlanta, so I wanted to be prepared. I can't take y'all out to the gun range, but I can simulate how you shoot and teach you. Hell, we can watch a YouTube video if we need to. All I'm saying is, it's better to be safe than sorry."

"Jaz, I hope we won't need to use any firepower, but I'm in," I said.

"Okay, ladies, we gon' have to get suited and booted up in this piece. There's a burner for each of you. Today is lesson number one. How to *properly* hold your weapon."

This bitch was bored to death and her mind was now playing tricks on her. She was going stir crazy.

Chapter Thirty-Four

CHARLI LI

As soon as I arrived, I saw one of my old business partners, Han Shou. Over the years, we'd done a lot of business in Africa with technology.

"Hello, Han," I said in Cantonese, which was what I used to speak with him, although they mainly spoke Mandarin in Beijing.

Han did a double take. He didn't recognize me. I could see the look of confusion in his eyes.

"Han," I teased, "Don't tell me you could forget this face?" I puckered up my lips and batted my eyelashes. "It's me! 2009 we hosted the Shanghai Technology Conference? Attorney Charli Li, of Li, come on! Li and Ross," I said, lifting my eyebrows. "Remember when we did business in Nigeria? I may have changed a little, but my voice is still the same."

"Oh, Ms. Li. Charli Li. I . . . I. You look—look great!" He was stammering, obviously embarrassed that he didn't know who I was. "I thought that you and your father wouldn't arrive for a few days?" He humbly bowed and I bowed back.

As I happened to look in my pocket mirror to tighten up my lipstick, I saw three Chinese men walking backward so they could look at my behind. The way men had been looking at me in the States and since I landed in Beijing let me know all that work was worth it. Han was more confirmation. He was all smiles and still drooling.

"Yes. I've arrived early on a client's behalf. Do you know the new consulate?"

"Yes, of course. His office is to your left. The one with the big double doors. Here's his information." He handed me a gold embossed business card for the consulate and a white and tan card for himself.

"Thank you, Han. It was good seeing you."

"How long will—"

I turned around, not giving him a chance to finish his sentence.

The consulate sent me to the equivalent of the Police Liaison section in Washington DC. After that, they sent me to this place and that place. I swear I will give my all to begin the fight of my life.

MARI

I just found what I believed was the house here on Sag Harbor. Several times I drove by hoping to find any traces of the kids, Kay, Angel, Tasha or Trae. I finally parked almost a block away and hid my car under a large oak tree. I used my binoculars, and I still didn't see any kids. Just men patrolling the house. This had to be it! I noticed a small shack in the rear, where the men were going in and out. *What the hell is happening? Whose house is this?*

I concluded that this may be a little out of my league. It looked too risky for me to try to go in there by myself, or even with Children's Services. I turned my car back around and made my way out of the neighborhood. I needed a plan B.

FAHEEM

Before Rick arrived, I felt sick inside. This was a nightmare. I would've never knowingly put my wife and family in harm's way. No amount of cash or thrill to get back in the game would compensate for the safety of my family.

As I sped on the turnpike, I struggled to keep my eyes on the road and keep an eye out for the police at the same time. Rick kept reminding me to slow it down.

Frightening thoughts were racing through my head. I love Jaz, my queen. I didn't know what I would do if anything happened to her or our baby. Hell, all of them up there were family, and Trae and Kaylin put their trust in me to keep them safe.

As for Seven. It's just strange. This chick showed up and all this shit started happening. The enemy sending a woman to infiltrate and then take you down was the oldest trick in the book.

I explained to Rick that I had already spoken to Don Carlos, and he assured me that updated information on Trae and Kay was forthcoming. I called Scarface and told him I was on my way. He said everything would be fine, and Don Carlos didn't want to alarm the ladies, so he said to leave them be. Bullshit. If they thought they were going to hold my family hostage, they had another thing coming. Once Rick said he got the text about releasing the formula, I knew things were not good. We had our families in the belly of the beast.

Oh, Allah, please keep my wife and daughter and the rest of my family safe.

Chapter Thirty-Five

TRAE

Beijing, China

"Condition the mind. Condition the mind. Condition the mind," I chanted in the darkness. Each day that went by, I was feeling stronger and stronger. I liked the peace and clarity that fasting brought me. While locked up in Cali, Faheem sent me this book called *How to Eat to Live* by the God, Elijah Muhammad. The book was on point. Because of it, I would experiment with fasting at least once a month. I felt good. It gave me what I can only describe as a natural high. I believe it's because you can think clearer. The only catch is, you have to keep the peace, or you will no longer feel good. And right now, a nigga ain't feeling good.

I was sick of these muthafuckas. They kept questioning me. I had gone through weeks and weeks of this bullshit. They would get us up in the middle of the night to ask us questions. It was as if they were intrigued to have some niggas up in their prison. Don Carlos's lawyer assured me that they were simply going through the motions and for me to be patient.

"What's this about the nightclub you owned in Los Angeles?" They kept asking that one over and over. As if they wanted to open up a fuckin' nightclub.

"What about it?"

"I understand you were raided for drugs being dealt out of there."

"That was cleared up and the club was reopened just before I was falsely accused and incarcerated."

"Do you still own the club?"

"No, I sold it."

"How could you do that when you were locked up?"

"My attorney handled the details. When are you going to let me use the phone and call my lawyer?"

"We are still waiting to hear from the head office. Take him back!" Two officials rushed in and spoke some words in Chinese. Then I was rushed back to my cell.

KAYLIN

I dreamed I was at home with Angel, and she had given birth to the new baby. A baby boy! I had known all along Angel wanted a son, and I wanted her to have one just as much. I love my firstborn, Malik. Nothing would be better than having a son with my soulmate, my queen, Angel. With Malik, I couldn't wait until my baby boy was born, but with his mom and her bullshit, I couldn't have the relationship I wanted with him. But now it looked as if I was about to get full custody. I was smiling when I felt someone roughly shaking me. I woke up, looked around, and saw I was not at home.

"Get up! Time to get up, Mr. Santos!" one of the three officials barked. Hell, there were always three of them. It felt like the middle of the night with the dark mud walls and ceilings. I had no clue what time or what day it was.

"I'm awake. Where is my lawyer? I need a phone call."

"We want to know if you're an enemy of the state?" he inquired causally, as if asking if I would care for a smoke.

"I'm not an enemy. Y'all know I worked for Mr. Charles Li, who you know very well, prior to this trip, and he gave us clearance to come here anytime. And this time we are here on IEE business holdings. You know that as well."

"That proves nothing! Right now, all we have is your word!" he yelled. His voice bouncing off the wall.

"Can I call my lawyer now?" I stood up. The other two officers stepped in front of the first officer. "I need to call my lawyer. And I need to talk to my partner." I didn't know how we were getting out of this shit. And I wanted to know if they allowed him to make a phone call. "I need to speak to someone at the American Embassy."

They turned and walked out.

"I need to make a phone call!" I yelled out.

CHARLI LI

The meeting with the assistant to the consulate, for a small fee, gave me the information that I was looking for. I was furious, as I dialed my father's number. He was behind this debacle that had me clean across the country and sucking another man's dick.

Once again, I was shown the depths of my father's hatred and vitriol when he wanted revenge. My father had ordered men killed before by the most brutal means. But the hatred he had for Mr. Macklin—whom he blamed for the pit bulls attack was just too much. It equaled the hatred I had for Tasha. I couldn't wait to make her suffer by my own hands. I had every intention of making sure she had the same nightmares I had about dogs ripping my face off. My father went a step further and figured it would be easier to just kill everyone with the last name Macklin.

The people my father hired to kill Trae told my father that he and his friend left the country and were headed to China. The next thing you know, my father was on his way there. That's why I had to move fast. There were only two Black men attending the secret bitcoin meeting. Nothing too much happens in Beijing without me being able to find out. And from what I gathered, they were there promoting Mr. Santos's record label, Game Over Records.

"Enemy of the State." With his influence and connections, my father was able to get this word to the Republic of China government that Trae and his accomplice were just that. That's why they were detained. He wanted them held in custody until he got there. But he forgot that I was his daughter, and this was still my playground. So, I was able to move a little bit faster than he. I felt like the Chinese Olivia Pope.

* * *

"Ms. Li. We have drafted the documents needed to accompany you to the detention camp to get the two Americans suspects released."

"Suspects of what? They haven't been charged with anything."

"Ms. Li." Han attempted to calm me down. "I have what you need." Han held up two folders, waved them in front of my face, and he led me outside.

I let out a sigh of relief. It was one of the moments I had been waiting for since I arrived in Beijing. I had found an ally in Han. All it took was some head and my hand to get him to give me what I wanted. Han put me inside the Chinese Embassy in front of the appropriate official who helped me get what I came over here for. My father would be arriving tomorrow evening. If he hadn't made two stops, he would have beaten me here. I had to get them released before he arrived. Anyhow, with my business completed, all I needed was to see my man. Trae hearts danced in my eyes. I couldn't wait for my escort to arrive for Han and me to be driven to the godforsaken Black jail.

* * *

"Whatever you say, do not call me by my name," I'd told Han beforehand. "As a matter of fact, I'm Ana Ming."

When Trae and Kaylin walked out, they were unshaven and gaunt looking. I'd never seen Mr. Macklin that thin, but they didn't look broken. They held their heads high as they walked out the Black jail. While we were waiting for their release, their belongings had been loaded up into the back of the van.

"Get in the backseat," Han ordered.

"Who are you? Where are you taking us?" Trae asked suspiciously.

"To the US Embassy. You want to return back to your country, don't you?"

"Of course, I do. It's just that no one told us anything."

"Well, get in before they change their minds."

Trae and Mr. Santos climbed in the back. And they looked relieved. I sat in the front seat with Han. I was holding my breath.

KAYLIN

I was glad to be out of there and glad to see our shit in the back. I needed my watch. It was daylight and I felt confused. I definitely wasn't relaxing until my feet hit US soil. "Who sent y'all to come get us?" I asked the man because the chick wasn't saying a word. She wouldn't even look at us.

"Everything will be explained to you when you get to the Embassy. I'm just the driver."

"Pull over. I need to take a piss," Trae demanded.

The driver looked over at the chick in the front. She nodded and then put a call in to whoever was following us. The driver pulled over on the narrow roadway and let us out. Trae jumped out and I was right behind him. Immediately all doors from the two cars behind us flew open as several uniformed officers jumped out and stood within a short distance.

We walked over a few feet and gave each other dap. We hadn't seen each other in over a month.

"You all right?" Trae asked me.

"Why are you so fuckin' calm? Do you realize what just happened to us, and there's still a chance we may not get out of this muthafucka? What the fuck is going on, nigga. If you know something you need to spill it."

"I'm getting ready to tell you now."

"Don't tell me shit but who are those people and where are they taking us? To another jail?

"That's Charli, yo."

"Who the fuck is Charli?"

"Charli Li. But listen, they are waving us back to the van. I can't tell you everything now, but Don Carlos wants me to get her to set up a meeting with her father. I have to use her. We set it up, he gets there, and we out. That's all I can tell you right now. Trust me. When we get to the Embassy, we are supposed to receive further instructions."

"How do you know this?"

"Don Carlos sent some attorneys to see me. I'll tell you more. Just follow my lead. Trust me."

Trae turned around and took a piss. The officers were staring us down and one headed our way. Trae zipped up, and we got back into the van.

JAZ

We pulled up in front of my new house around one in the morning. For now, I would be residing in Morrisville, PA. I saw what this was. Nice and convenient. Faheem's old stomping grounds were right across the bridge in Trenton. This was one of the old dope boy moves. Move out of the city and into the burbs.

Niggas had been doing that for years. Faheem was getting dirty, and I needed to figure out how to stop him before it was too late.

I couldn't wait to get in and get settled. Mainly because on the way back, Faheem and I engaged in very little conversation, and I had lots of questions.

"Faheem, do you have to run the streets tonight?"

"Run the streets? Who the fuck do you think I am? Ain't nobody runnin' the streets."

"Well, whatever the fuck you are leaving the house to do. It ain't to pray or go to the grocery store. What else you doing at one o'clock in the morning? And don't speak to me like that! Your family has been locked away for damn near two months, not seeing or hearing from you." I was so furious that my voice quivered.

"If you want to spend time with me, then say that. Don't accuse me of running the streets. I'm not running the streets."

"Don't flatter yourself. And if that lie makes you feel good, I'm for it. Remember, what you do in the dark will come to light, Faheem. You got a house in Morrisville, and you been in the streets for the last two months. You running the streets. I can only call it like I see it."

"I don't got to report to you or no fucking body else. And yeah, shit do come to light. You a prime example of that, Jaz. Like I said, I don't have time for this bullshit right now. I'll be back when I'm back. Y'all staying here, and you should be good. Rick heard from Kay a few hours ago."

I gasped. "They're on their way back?"

"Not sure. They're fine and said they will be in touch. They aren't here yet, so don't tell Angel and Tasha. I don't want to get their hopes up. Me and you will talk when I get back. Other than accusing me of running the streets, how are you? You aiight?"

"I'm glad to get some good news. But other than that, no. Me and you need to talk. We both made major decisions without consulting with the other."

"At least I didn't lie."

"Right. You just didn't say anything. That's a lie."

"You ain't gettin' off that easy, Jaz. You fucked up! Big time."

"You back in the streets. That's fuckin' up big time! Unless you can convince me that your why is bigger than your family, I'm leaving you."

"Whatever. Don't wait up for me."

"Faheem! Don't make me do this."

And he left. This muthafucka left!

Chapter Thirty-Six

TRAE

On the flight to Shanghai, we sat three rows behind Charli. She never acknowledged us. Instead she was acting as if she was on some diplomatic shit. Every time she got up, she had two guards on her heels.

Kay nudged me, "Yo, that white chick. You saying that's Charli? The Chinese bitch?"

"Later," I mumbled. The less Kay knew, the better his role was played. And more importantly, we were the only niggas on the plane. I trusted no one, so I didn't speak; and Kay, being the thorough nigga he was, peeped it and so far was following my lead, other than being shocked at how Charli looked.

We finally landed in Shanghai. We were almost free; my instructions stated that we were not to leave until I arranged a meeting with Charli Li. We were ordered to remain seated until all the other passengers deplaned. Charli came back to where we were seated unescorted.

"Hello, Mr. Macklin."

"I need to meet with your father immediately. I'm not leaving the country until I do."

"Can I at least get a thank you?"

Before I knew it, I was up with my hands around her throat, trying to squeeze every ounce of breath from this bitch's lungs.

"Nigga, chill out!" Kay was in my ear. "Let her go! You just said you needed to see her father. I want to go home to see my daughter. And I know you do too. We are almost there. Don't let your temper fuck that up, nigga. Let her go."

I did, and she fell back onto one of the seats, frantically gasping for air. I honestly was trying to kill her. A stupid play on my part.

"Set the meeting up, Charli." I glanced at her. She started smiling and slowly stood up.

"Is that what Don Carlos ordered? I must admit, you are a very, very, valuable pawn right now. I hope you are prepared for the international stage. You need me more than ever."

Four officers entered the plane and made their way to us. She was handed a folder as they held a conversation in their language. I stood there confused. What the fuck did she mean, is that what Don Carlos ordered? A pawn?"

"Yo, Trae. Let's get on the next flight and get to where muthafuckas speak English. Talk to me, nigga! How can we get outta here sooner than later? And that's Charli? How the fuck did she turn white?"

"I don't know. Maybe it's make-up. I need you to follow my lead, nigga."

"Gentlemen, follow us," one of the officials interrupted us.

We were led out of the airport to a private hanger, where we boarded a van with tinted windows. No one said a word as we drove for exactly three hours and twenty minutes. We pulled up to an office building and the driver and his partner got out, leaving me and Kay alone.

"Yo—"

I cut Kay off. "Charli was right. I am a pawn. Now, I'm the bait. I was supposed to get over here, turn Charli, and then get her to set up the meeting with Charles Li!"

"Now they want us to set up a meeting with the muthafucka who has a marker on our heads?" Spittle formed in the corners of Kaylin's mouth; he was that angry.

"We got played my nigga."

"You mean to tell me that bitch is the only thing standing between me getting home to my family? And you just fucking choked her." He was now choking me. And I was fighting for air. I finally managed to get him off of me.

"Yo, what the fuck!"

"Nigga, I swear, you better get the fuck out of this van and fix this shit. I'll be damned if I'ma let your temper get me killed. Nah, nigga. I ain't going out like that. Take that fuckin' temper, and that big ass ego of yours and do what you gotta do. You my brother and it's nothing I wouldn't do for you. You better fix this shit and fix it fast."

* * *

Kay was right. I almost fucked up, but I knew I didn't. I could tell by the way she looked at me that I could still work my plan. One of the officers came back to get us. He had his gun aimed at us as he snatched the van door open.

"Get out! Turn around. Place both hands on the van and spread your legs." He patted Kaylin down first. "Don't move!" He kicked my leg, motioning for me to spread my legs wider.

As he used one hand to pat me down, he mumbled, "She is talking about calling the meeting off. If she does, Don Carlos said you are a dead man. Fix it. All he needs you to do is get him to come to the meeting, then you go home to your family." He grabbed me roughly and yelled, "Move! Go inside now."

KAYLIN

I ain't never seen no shit like this before. Niggas wouldn't believe in a thousand years, that we went through this. This was a dangerous game and we were playing with the big dawgs. If we got out of this, our resume was going to be lit. Don Carlos had a man on the inside. That made me feel a little better. Having all my eggs in one basket—Trae— that shit was bleak as fuck! I swear, I'ma kill him myself if he fucks this up.

When we entered the building, we all took the stairs to the second floor. We were led to a huge office set up like a suite in a 5-star hotel.

"How long will we be here?" I asked one of the men.

He shrugged. "Give me your cell phone."

"It's not charged. I can't use it." He snatched it from me and checked it. He gave it back.

"You. Come with me," he said to Trae. They left out. Leaving me alone. I went to open the door, but it was locked. "Fuck this shit!"

TRAE

Kaylin was pissed off. I'm glad they did separate us. But even gladder that Don Carlos had a man on the inside. I was taken across the hall from Kay and I wasn't surprised that Charli was sitting in there waiting on me.

"Have a seat, Mr. Macklin. We need to talk." The goon stood by the door as Charli remained seated at the small coffee table.

"I'm not doing anything until I take a shower. And Charli, give us our shit."

"We need to talk now, Mr. Macklin."

"Get our shit, Charli. If you need to talk now, you are going to have to talk to me in the bathroom."

Her goon came toward me. She raised her hand and spoke something in her language. He bowed and left as I made my way to the bathroom and closed the door. I looked around at the marble fixtures. Fuck the shower! I turned the water on in the Jacuzzi. I needed to scrub off that prison, the plane ride and I needed to shit, shave and think.

As I lay back enjoying the water massage, I knew there was no getting around it. For me to get her to do what I wanted her to do, I had to make a sacrifice.

CHARLI LI

He picked the wrong time to show his arrogance. Me granting him his wishes made me look weak in front of my men whom I told to leave the room while I dealt with the situation. Mr. Macklin's life was at stake, yet he's more concerned about a clean set of clothes. Obviously, he was confident that I had his back. I had news for him. Before I made another move, I took out my cell phone and turned on the camera and placed it where I knew Trae wouldn't be able to see it.

I tapped on the bathroom door and stepped inside, purposely leaving it cracked so that my cell phone could catch whatever I needed it to. He was in the Jacuzzi. "Are you almost done? We're waiting on you?"

"I like the new look."

His words caught me by surprise.

"Turn around." He was gazing at my ass, at least what he could see.

"What about my face?"

"Turn around. I mean, that's what you got it for, right? For muthafuckas to look at it."

"We are waiting on you."

He stood up, body dripping wet. His dick hanging. My pussy wouldn't stop throbbing. I wanted his dick. I needed it. I needed him. But now was not the time.

"Turn around." He stepped out the Jacuzzi, and I don't know what came over me, but I did turn around, but it was to leave out. He placed his hand over mine as I was turning the doorknob.

"You had some serious work done on your ass. Why? It was fine the way it was. At least I thought so."

"Mr. Macklin, we have business to discuss." I went to slide out of the cracked door.

My hands were moist from the nervousness that came over me. I fought so hard to get him back and now that I was in his presence, I didn't know how to handle it.

He shut the door, but I opened it back as I remained facing it. The door play was the least of his worries now that his hands caressed my ass. I closed my eyes. My throat was dry. I was frozen in place. I had dreamed and fantasized about him doing exactly what he was doing this very minute. In my fantasy, we were in our home together and in love. But we were in Shanghai playing a dangerous game.

"It feels so real." He was palming all over it. "These fake asses usually are hard?"

"It is real." My voice trembled.

His hands glided up to my breasts.

"These were fine too. Why, Charli?"

Oh, my heavens. His fingers were roaming all over my breasts. He was now pressed up against my ass and he had an erection. And for once I was at a loss for words. The only sounds that escaped my lips were moans.

"I'm trying to stop, but you feel too damn good." He flipped up my bra and turned me around, palming my left breast roughly as he bent over and began to suck on my nipple.

"What . . . not now. No. I mean . . . Oh yessss, Trae." I shivered. The flimsy lace of my panties was no obstacle as he used his fingers to rip them off and slid three inside my wetness and began to vigorously finger fuck me. I thought I had died and gone to heaven.

TRAE

"Trae Macklin, you have me so wet." Charli was trembling as she cocked her legs wider. I was fingering the shit out of her pussy, trying to make her come so I wouldn't have to fuck her. I could hear Tasha screaming in my head, "Did you fuck her? Did you fuck her?"

"Fuck me, Mr. Macklin. Fuck me now. I swear to you, I will give you whatever you ask of me," she whispered. Her goons were right outside. "I promise you. You have my loyalty. Fuck me now."

Damn.

I turned her around and picked her up, laid her on the cold bathroom floor. I entered her in one powerful thrust. She let out a squeal.

"Give me all of my dick. I need this so bad," she urged, wrapping her legs around my waist. "Give me all of my dick."

I untangled her legs and placed them over my shoulders and got in the push up position. I continued pounding the pussy, making sure she got every inch. "Oh, shit!" I gritted.

"I love you so much. I swear I do." We both came at the same time as we heard pounding on the bedroom door.

What the fuck did I just do? I saved me and my family. That's what. But at what cost? Hurting Tasha, again? It was just business though, that was all. Just business. That was what I had to keep in my mind to make sure this shit didn't eat at me. Either way, I would make sure she never found out about this shit.

KAYLIN

Trae obviously handled his business with Charli because I was basking in the red-carpet treatment. I was in the Jacuzzi. I had a lobster meal and two ladies came in and offered me a fuck. I respectfully declined and instead I opted for a massage and a manicure and a pedicure. I was so damn proud of myself.

They had just dropped off some bubbly and strawberries as Trae, Charli and I sat around the conference table.

"Why can't we use the phone?" I asked Charli.

"We can't afford to compromise the mission, Mr. Santos. The meeting has been arranged, and in forty-eight hours my father will be here."

"We have to wait forty-eight hours to let our families know that we are fine? They haven't heard from us, Charli. C'mon now. And we have to stay locked in this suite?"

"No more than forty-eight hours, Mr. Santos. I'm sure you can bear to be locked into this suite. This meeting cannot be compromised. Whatever you need, just let me know."

"I need to take my ass home. Yo, excuse us. Let me have a word with Trae."

Charli stood up. "A few more hours, gentlemen."

This was my first chance to talk to Trae since I choked him up in the van. As soon as she left out, I moved to where he was seated at the end of the table.

"How are we going to get the fuck out of here?" I whispered.

"They aren't telling me shit other than be ready to leave at a moment's notice," he whispered back. "So, stay ready."

"I'm ready. But what are you supposed to say to Li? What is this meeting about? Why is it so important?"

"I was told I would be given instructions. Until then, wait it out."

"This don't sound right. It doesn't feel right. It makes no sense to me."

"Me neither. But ain't shit we can do but wait it out."

"Have that bitch get us a burner. Just in case."

"I tried. It ain't happening."

"Shit! The dick obviously wasn't that good."

"Fuck you man!"

CHARLI LI

I failed myself. This was supposed to be all business. And I damn near compromised the mission. I was worried, but then again, I wasn't. I set out to do a mission of my own and that one would soon be fulfilled once I clicked *send*.

My father finally arrived at the designated location in Shanghai. He looked well. But his demeanor was smug. We were seated at the dining table in relative silence. From time to time, he would glance at me out of the corner of his eye. I couldn't take it anymore.

"Why the silent treatment, Father?" I asked out of exasperation.

"I have to travel all the way to Shanghai to have dinner with my daughter, who doesn't even live in Shanghai."

"Father, you know where to find me. And let's be frank with one another, as soon as you learned that the only man I've ever loved was over here, you began to plot and scheme."

He placed his fork down and shook his head. "I can't believe I'm hearing this. I don't understand you."

"What's to understand, Father? That you drove the only man I love away?"

He chuckled. "Don't be ridiculous. Love? A common low life for my only daughter? And what would you have me do, Charli?

Ignore the damage that he has done to this family? To you?" He motioned at my face. "You are requesting a lot from me, as you continue to disgrace yourself and the organization that I built. And over a married black man mind you. I shouldn't have come."

"I will deal with this my way, Father. What I need from you is a free hand in doing so," I demanded.

"What are you proposing, Charli? And this better be good. I've traveled very far."

"You were coming anyway. But you know me; I will do whatever it takes," I shot back. He held my gaze to gauge how serious I was and to see if I was going to back down. But I wasn't. Mr. Macklin was way too valuable to me and the team I'd assembled.

"I won't allow you to kill him, Father. Do you want me to hate you for the rest of my life? If not, don't touch him."

"Is he really worth all of that—I think not. Therefore, there is no need for me to meet with him. I am going on with my agenda."

CHARLES LI

I tossed my dinner napkin across the plate, signaling to my spoiled daughter that this meeting was over. I was totally disappointed that she was trying to stop me from crushing these two little cockroaches. And realizing that I had to crush her next. Her loyalty to me had been compromised. I left her at the dinner table looking angry. I made my way to the restroom down the hall. As I unbuckled my belt and unzipped my slacks, I felt a breeze. I turned around, and I felt a sharp pain across my throat.

KAYLIN

Charles Li? Damn. What a way to go out. And he walked right into the trap? The boss got his throat slashed while his dick was hanging out of his pants. In a matter of seconds, Charles Li was gasping for air and choking on his own blood. The assassin holding the knife, placed the bloody blade to his lips, confirming or signaling that this was a silent assassination carried out Carlos Cartel style. Another man motioned for me and Trae to follow him. We were whisked down the stairs and into a car.

Our business in Shanghai was done.

FAHEEM

Reunited. I peered through the binoculars as the helicopter smoothly touched down on the helipad of Don Carlos's mansion on the outskirts of New Orleans. His mansion was housed on what looked like an old plantation. The porch wrapped almost around the entire house, or shall I say the veranda. The Louisiana heat was as thick as gumbo as it swirled around Kay and Trae from the force of the helicopter's blades. Their shirts and pants being beaten by the breeze. But it was cool and crisp inside, the way I liked it. As soon as they hopped onto the golf cart, I headed downstairs for the celebration. I made my way down to the large study with cathedral ceilings and Mammoth Mahogany bookcases against each wall. Everyone was already there except the three of us. I was called in to have my first meet and greet with the Don. He figured this would be the best time. I got the impression that he wanted me to learn a few things and be there for moral support with Kay and Trae.

There were eight Carlos Cartel members in the study. I made nine. Don Carlos, ten. He was seated in a big, cocaine white, leather chair. When Trae and Kay stepped through the wide double doors, he stood up and started clapping and the rest of the room stood and joined in.

I could see that both my mans had lost a little weight. Those Chinese muthafuckas obviously weren't feeding them.

As I took a seat in the back of the room, I watched as Enrique, Don Carlos's nephew, kissed Trae's left hand first and then Kaylin's. All them muthafuckas went down the line.

Once words were exchanged and done, it was revealed that Don Carlos used Trae as bait to get to Charles Li. And once I learned that Charles Li was gone, I understood the importance of the festivities. Now that Charles Li was out of the way, Don Carlos was the man. Both, Trae and Kaylin were pissed at how it all went down, but what could they do? What could they say? They were safe, they were home, and their families were safe. And they had a shitload of money and credibility. They sacrificed their lives for the Mexican Cartel. Don Carlos reminded them that he told them up front that sacrifices would have to be made. If Don Carlos was as genuine as I took him to be, then their sacrifices would never be forgotten.

Trae and Kay were now made men.

Chapter Thirty-Seven

RICK

When I pulled into the Philly airport, Trae and Kay where already waiting. I couldn't front and act like I wasn't happy to see the crew. I jumped out the Suburban. "Y'all early. Let me find out niggas are anxious to get home."

"Nigga, I already see that you got jokes. Your ass is late!" Kaylin teased.

"Awww, man." I gave them hugs. "It's good to see y'all niggas."

"It's good to be seen," Trae said. "You have no idea."

Their eyes said it all. They were both relieved and happy to be home. I couldn't wait to get the 411. They had enough drama for a television series.

"Damn!" Kaylin said. "I hate I put my family through this. Y'all don't know how thankful I am to have niggas like y'all on my team. The shit we just went through was unreal."

He was right. The shit we were all into could cost us all our lives. It was one thing for us to get into some shit, but to have our women and kids in the mix with us was a hard fuckin' pill to swallow. But if I had to, I'd leave Kyra and Nina with them anytime.

TRAE

I was so happy to be back. I knew Tasha was probably sick of Sag Harbor, but I wanted to stay. I didn't want to go back to the apartment. Rick rang the doorbell for us, and we stood to the side. It was almost 10:30 in the morning.

"Okay, okay, here I come." I heard Jaz fussing. We heard the locks turn, and Jaz opened it up. She looked shocked, confused and happy all in one.

"Oh my God! I'm so glad to see y'all! Trae. Kaylin." She grabbed us both at the same time, forcing us into a group hug.

I put my fingers to my lips. We both wanted to surprise Tasha and Angel. Our ladies had been through enough and hopefully this was the end to all the madness.

I went to the room that Faheem pointed out was Tasha's.

Jaz knocked on her door.

"Come in," Tasha said, sounding sleepy.

Jaz cracked the door. "I've got a surprise for you." She stood to the side and let me step in.

Tasha was lying in the bed, breastfeeding my baby. She'd never looked more beautiful. *Damn.*

Her hair was pulled up in her typical ponytail, knotted on top of her head. Her skin was glowing. She was a little more plump and I loved every bit of it. My wife was stunning. She was wearing a muumuu but had the top unbuttoned and had this fat little hand grasping her breast. I'd never noticed how beautiful the sight of a mother feeding her baby was. But after this experience in China, everything was amazing to me.

"I'll let you guys be alone." Jaz smiled, then eased back out the room.

"Trae! Baby!" Tears of joy fell down Tasha's cheeks. She squealed as she pulled her big breast out of my baby's mouth, causing white milk to squirt all over. My daughter started crying and kicking her legs since we were interrupting her meal.

"Taylour Macklin, I want you to stop fussing, baby. It's time to meet your father." She stood up with my baby and handed her to me, and I gazed down in sheer love. Damn, a nigga was in awe. It was like I was looking at myself. Taylour was the female version of me. She was gorgeous! She had a headful of curly hair. My eyes. My nose, and my ears. Immediately, my fears of her being Kyron's baby were a distant memory. Taylour had dimples and her chubby legs were like little, fat, turkey drumsticks. Taylour, my precious daughter, looked up at me, stopped crying, and started smiling.

She knew her daddy already!

"Aw, look at daddy's princess," I cooed, rocking her back and forth. She immediately fell asleep. Now I could see why they said men loved their daughters so. This girl had already grabbed my heart out my chest and wrapped it around her finger.

Tasha and I kissed for the first time in months. The entire time, we were holding our baby in our arms. It was comical to have Tasha feeling me out, making sure I had all of my body parts. As if I was a soldier just back from Iraq or some shit like that.

"I'm good, babe."

"You're so skinny. Are you sure?" Tears rolled down her cheeks.

"I'm fine. Just glad to be back home where I'm supposed to be. With you and my kids."

Those words rolled off my tongue so naturally. It felt good to be home.

KAYLIN

My plan was to serve my wife her favorite breakfast in bed. She loved my homemade waffles, topped with fresh strawberries, bananas, and caramel drizzle. I was fucking with the electric stove, cooking me some turkey bacon and eggs. While I was messing with the waffle iron, the turkey bacon started smoking and the fire detector went off. Angel came rushing down the stairs, yelling, "Aisha and Kaeerah! I told y'all not to cook anything! Why must you insist on being hard-headed?"

"Why the fuck don't y'all have a gas stove?" I was fanning the smoke, hoping the smoke detector would quit that shrill refusing-to-stop noise.

Angel stood frozen in place, speechless, holding her chest. I'll never forget the look on her face when she realized that it was me who was trying not to burn the house down. I had to open the window to air out some of the smoke and to get rid of that loud irritating noise.

"My baby's home!" she finally spoke and kept saying it over and over. "My baby's home!"

"I was trying to serve you breakfast in bed." I was mad because I was burning shit up.

It was clear she didn't give a fuck about eating. Her only concern was me, her man. She rushed and jumped into my arms and I didn't deny her embrace as we held onto each other for what felt like an eternity.

* * *

All eight of us were seated around the dinner table. The kids were seated at the smaller table next to us. Jaz and Kyra had cooked a big pot of gumbo with lobster, crab, chicken and sausage. That's what our lives had become. One big pot of gumbo. Our friendship and our love had been tried and tested but we had survived through it. These last couple months had tightened us all up.

Most of all, it felt so good for all of us to be together. Faheem, Rick, Trae, me and our wives and kids. Kyra even seemed at peace with Rick. How long that would last remained to be seen, but he was really into Kyra, and I saw the love. His new baby stayed on his lap, and Kyra's eyes were filled with bliss.

We, the men, still needed to have a sit down and figure out what the next move would be. Up for discussion was our new bitcoin business and getting new houses for our families; but for right now, it was just time to enjoy everyone being around each other. We hadn't had this much fun since Tasha and Kyra's baby shower. This was how life was supposed to be.

Angel and Tasha never stopped grinning the whole time we ate. Their eyes just glistened every time they looked at us take a bite of food. They watched us closely; they were so happy to see us eating.

"Eat up. There is plenty," Tasha kept saying while fixing Trae another bowl of gumbo. "Plus, I want to get y'all nice and full so that we all can talk. Y'all owe us an update. We need to know what our next move is, while we are all here. Things need to be ironed out. These kids need to be in school. I got things I want to do like live in my own house. You feel me, Trae?"

"Can we enjoy our meal just like you suggested? And can I have a few more moments to enjoy my wife, please?" Trae was fixed on Tasha.

"Of course, you can," Jaz said.

"Thank you, sister."

"But!" Jaz waved her hand in the air before continuing. "Tasha is right. We need to have this conversation sooner than later."

Angel had tears in her eyes as she fixed me a second bowl with an oversized slice of cornbread on the side. "Yo, Red. You trying to kill me?"

The women had really tightened up their shit. Even the children got along well. I had anticipated hearing horror stories of the whole house bickering and fighting. But my hunch was all wrong. They obviously all got along well, considering the circumstances.

*****

Jahara, my little princess had been all over me right up until bedtime. Something was bothering me, though.

"What's the matter, Kaylin?" Angel asked. She always knew when something was on my mind.

I heaved a sigh. "How are you really holding up? How's J holding up?"

"Jahara is the best of both of us. She's good. We both are good for now. You are home, and for the moment, I feel safe. I wouldn't trade nothing for you and our life. I don't have any regrets."

"That's why I married you."

"Playa, please. You told me no at first." Angel sat up in the bed.

"Red, quit lying on me. Why do you keep saying that? I didn't tell you no."

"Kaylin, stop it. We will continue this conversation another time. Tell me how much you missed me." She slid down next to me with the slinkiness of a lioness. She rested her chin on my chest and was gazing in my eyes.

"No. I want to talk about me telling you no."

"Kaylin, stop playing. Tell me how much you missed me."

"How about I show you?" I had to take this time to enjoy my wife. My pregnant wife. Her breasts were pleasingly plump. Like cool, slippery water balloons between my fingers. Her nipples were hard. Then we heard a knock at the door.

"Dad. Dad."

"Shhhh—" Red placed her hand over my mouth. "Play sleep," she whispered in my ear. "This is my time."

I moved her hand away. "What's up, J?"

"I can't sleep."

"Come on in, baby."

"She ain't no baby! She's a cock blocker."

"Go unlock the door and let my daughter in."

Red jumped up and hit me twice with the pillow before unlocking the door and letting our daughter in.

TRAE

While at the dining table, we did manage to bring the ladies up to speed with almost everything. There was no way I was about to tell my wife or any of the ladies I had to fuck Charli in order for us to get home.

We told them the Cartels were beefing and wanted us to pick a side, Kendrick was sweating us to release the Fentanyl formula, which was the new drug that was fifty times stronger than heroin, and about Charli Li pulling strings to get us out of China. We didn't say she was there. They had to admit that it was a bit much but since they wanted to know what was going on, we gave it to them. We told them we are now made men. There was no turning back. We were living foul, and they were a part of it.

Kareem, Shaheem, and Caliph wrestled with me until bedtime. When I wasn't holding my baby girl, the boys were all over me. I hadn't had a chance to really be with my big baby— my wife. After she nursed the baby, she lay her in the bassinette; she dozed right off.

Tasha grabbed both of my hands and looked me directly in my eyes. "Trae, I was thinking that I'd never see you again. But I kept praying, trying to stay positive. And you're here. You know my head is spinning, and I want to talk. You threw me for a loop when you said that bitch Charli came to the rescue. What happened? What did she say to you? Did you fuck her?"

I shook my head. I didn't want to talk about it. I wouldn't talk about it. "Baby, we'll talk about the business tomorrow. I'm home. I just want to be with you."

"That bitch, Trae—"

I placed my lips to her ear. "I'ma have to handle her. She's not going to leave us alone, Tasha. I just have to map it out."

Even though Charli came to my rescue, she still had a motive and I knew she wasn't going to leave me alone.

She and Mari were both on some other shit and I was tired of my family being fucked with.

Tasha simply looked me in my eyes. "Handle her at what cost? Our luck is bound to run out one of these days, and my biggest fear is that moment that I'm told that you are not coming back home to us."

I took Tasha in my arms and kissed her. "That's why we have to enjoy each other to the fullest, while we can. Fuck her. Fuck doing business, fuck everything for the next seventy-two hours. I'm home, baby. And I want to enjoy you. Can we just fuck? I think I'll be straight after that and should be able to think a little clearer."

She giggled. "Seventy-two?"

"Seventy-two."

"That's a lot of love making. But you do owe me."

"I want to thank you for my three sons." I kissed her. "Thank you for my beautiful daughter." I kissed her again. "Thank you for being my soulmate." I climbed between her legs and entered my wife for the first time in two months. She mumbled something about not getting pregnant. I don't know why she was telling me that because the pussy was feeling so tight, wet and hot, I had no control. I think I may have fucked her all of three minutes before my knees began to buckle.

"Trae," Tasha moaned. She could feel that I was about to come. She pushed me off her. I rolled onto my back and she climbed on top. I was through the minute she began rocking back and forth. She slid off my dick and sat on my face.

I licked and sucked her clit until she begged me to stop. Then I flipped her over and hit it doggy style. Watching that ass jiggle, watching me slide my dick in, out, and then disappear inside of her again, made me pop that question. "Whose pussy is this, Tasha?"

She yelled out my name and that's when I pulled out and shot my seeds all over her ass and back; something I realized I didn't do with Charli Li.

Fuck! I didn't pull out.

ANGEL

I don't know how I always got caught up in the bullshit. I got a text from Jaz telling me to meet her at a random address, and when I pulled up, it was a fuckin' psych ward. I sent her a text.

Where are you?

OMW outside. She replied.

What the fuck was she up to and why was she including me. As I climbed out of my car, I saw her exit the building and approach me.

"Here are a set of keys, Angel. Just in case. And as my attorney, you must keep this confidential."

"Keys to what, Jaz."

"My two-bedroom condo. Follow me," she said. My heels click-clacked against the pavement as I tried to keep up with her and understand what was happening. She grabbed up Kaeerah and they moved out of the house she shared with Faheem? And we were at a crazy house, and I needed to keep this confidential; why?

"You coulda brought me a drink, some green tea, a latte, or something. If you want me to listen to whatever you are about to lay on me."

FAHEEM

I received a text from Kay telling me to call my daughter. We spoke every day, so I couldn't help but wonder what was up.

"Dad, come home. I have to tell you something," Kaeerah whispered.

"Tell me what?" She had me whispering.

"Come see me in the new house. I gotta ask you something."

"Ask me what?"

"Mommy said I can go to the school around the corner. What are you going to say?"

"We gotta talk about that."

"That's why I said come over to me and mommy's new house."

"Y'all not at the other house anymore?"

"No, Dad. I will text you the address. I want you to tell her I don't want to go to the school around the corner. Okay, Dad?"

"Text me the address."

"I will. Don't tell Mommy we had this conversation. You are coming tonight, right?"

"Yeah, I'll be there."

"I'll wait up and let you in. Love you, Daddy."

"I love you, too."

I had to go see what was going on. Immediately, I got in my car to go see Angel and get the key; I didn't trust Kaeerah to stay up. I had to drive more than two hours to get to Angel's and one more to get to Jaz's new spot. I already felt like I had been up for the last two days.

It was just past midnight. This was my favorite time of night to drive around the city. When I jump on the Turnpike, my head begins to clear. An old practice that I used back in the day. I pulled in front of Jaz's new condo, parked and got out. There was a light on downstairs. I knocked. I knocked again and waited. I took the key out and used it. Jaz was at the door with a burner pointed.

"Yo, it's me!"

"Shit, Faheem!" She dropped the gun to her side and held her chest with the other. "You scared the hell out of me."

"That's why your ass should be where you are supposed to be."

I brushed past her to get in the house. "What are you doing here, Faheem? How in the hell did you get a key?"

I took off my jacket and placed it on the sofa.

"Give me my key, Faheem."

"I didn't come here to fight, Jaz." I grabbed her hand.

"Why did you come?"

"I came to fuck my wife." I pulled her to me.

"No, Faheem." She tried to snatch away from me.

"What do you mean no? Why are you talking crazy?"

"You know damn well why I'm talking crazy."

"I'm here. You got my attention." I lifted her up and headed for the kitchen.

"Put me down, Faheem."

"You're going to wake up my daughter."

"She's already awake."

"No, she isn't. She was supposed to let me in. She fell asleep on me. I sent her about four text messages, and all I got was crickets."

I sat Jaz down on top of the island in the kitchen. I was still pissed, but I couldn't stay mad at her for long. Yeah, I was fucked up over what she did, but I knew she was genuinely sorry, and all I could do now was try to get her pregnant again, regardless if she wanted to or not.

Chapter Thirty-Eight

FAHEEM

"This is what I came here for," I whispered in Jaz's ear as I leaned her back, so I could dig in the pussy a little deeper. I told her how hot and tight she felt. I told her how hard she made my dick, and she felt just the way I liked her to feel. I told her I loved her more than anything in this world. Her legs curled around my back as she was trying to take in all the dick she could and stimulate her clit at the same time.

"Faheem. This. Feels so good, baby." Jaz's moans were getting louder and louder. "Faheem. Right there, baby. Oh yes! Faheem. Right there. Keep it right there, baby. Faheem. Oh, shit, Faheem!"

She started coming.

JAZ

We made our way through the facility without speaking. I didn't know what to say; I didn't know how to explain it. I had to show her. We stopped in front of the door and looked through the glass window; her jaw dropped. I saw her eyebrows wrinkle in confusion and then her eyes stretched wide in amazement.

"Wha—what is Faheem...?" Angel's eyes were as big as saucers. She grabbed my wrist. "Why is Faheem...what?" She looked back through the window at Faheem who was pacing his bedroom floor having a deep conversation with himself.

"I admitted Faheem into this State Hospital." I said trying to remain stoic. "He um. Ever since Lil' Faheem. He just... He doesn't sleep and he wakes me up every night and he tells me these stories about Trae, Kaylin, and him, and how they are working *with* Don Carlos," I explained to her. I emphasize *with* because when I said *for*, Faheem made sure he corrected me.

She looked bewildered. We all knew Faheem had been out of the game and would never go back. He enjoyed his role as Mr. Mom.

"He talks about Seven—" I continued.

"From the baby shower?" she interjected.

"Yes and how she wants him. She invited him over, tried to seduce him. And Bo—"

"What happened with Bo?"

"Nothing, Angel, but he says he was kidnapped, and Faheem had to save him."

"Oh Jaz," she said and pulled me into a hug. I allowed a few tears to fall before I pulled back.

"I just wanted you to see...I didn't know how to tell you."

"I'm sorry, Jaz," she said, tears falling from her eyes. I smiled and wiped mine away.

"I need to get back in here," I told her. "You leave out the same way you came in."

"You want me to stay...I can stay," she offered, gripping my hand. The love and compassion she had for me was evident in her tone and eyes.

"No, it's fine. He can talk for a loooonng time," I said trying to make a joke of it. "He likes to tell me stories about how he fucked me on a kitchen table." I laughed. The truth was, we hadn't had sex since before my miscarriage.

"Okay." she said.

"Okay," I said and gently pulled my hand from hers. I took a deep breath and entered the room. Faheem rushed over to me.

"Jaz, where were you. I think I figured out who was following you."

"Nobody was following me, Faheem."

"Yes, they were, baby, remember?" he said. His deep gaze penetrated my soul.

*****

Now it was almost four in the morning, and we were sitting in the living room in the dark. I was curled up on my baby's lap as I listened to his tales. "So, what do you mean, you and the Don exchanged favors, Faheem?"

Faheem fumbled around with his phone, finally holding it in my face. It was a blank screen, but he said it was a wire transfer confirmation. His bank account was stacked, according to him. Really stacked.

"Okay, baby. What do you have going on that you are willing to risk everything for a few dollars? I know it's a lot, but make me a believer, Faheem. You are treading through very dangerous territory."

"What else is new, Jaz? This is what we do. Me and you. You don't remember Georgia? That shit ain't over, Jaz. I have to do the getting or get got. Bottom line. We can't ignore that. And getting rid of my enemies cost money. I either go at Steel and Oni's people, or wait for them to come at me. What do you want me to do? It's going down one way or the other. I need a big fuckin' war chest to make sure I win, Jaz. Working with Don Carlos allowed me to stack my war chest. I need you to understand that."

"But at what cost, Faheem? Did his daughter come with the job?"

"What are you talking about?"

"You know damn well what I'm talking about! Did you fuck her?"

"No."

He went on to tell me that Don Carlos told them what he wanted done with Seven. He wanted to bring her to her knees. Shut her down. And since she was already set up in Faheem's hood, they all agreed that he would be the perfect one for the job. That's why Don Carlos was so interested in Trae and Kaylin bringing their team to the table. Bottom line, Faheem felt that if he could make a shit load of cash and secure the territory for Don Carlos, he would be straight. Faheem admitted that he loved the rush of being back in the streets.

"What if she is the Feds, Faheem?"

"We would know it, Jaz. I didn't rely on Don Carlos. I had her checked out already. She's good."

"Now you really got me nervous."

"Don't be." He continued to ramble on.

Yes, all of Faheem's accounts in this story were a fantasy. Except for the fact that I did take birth control and I did have a miscarriage. Nothing else ever happened. It was a figment of my man's imagination. Faheem. My big strong King was broken. I was able to see firsthand how a mental disorder could take down the strongest of men and women. But I know Faheem; he will bounce back. And we will get through this. I don't know what or how it happened. One day my Faheem was gone, and this new Faheem emerged. When I saw him playing with who he said was Lil' Faheem, I knew I had to get help. My life hadn't been the same.

Fortunately, he was getting better and he got weekend passes. But when he came home all he did was tell me stories about how he is back in the streets, working with Don Carlos. But none of it is true.

TASHA

Angel, our attorney of record, went with Trae and me to the police department. We took the baby with us and met with a Jamaican social worker, Erica Monteith. She was there, representing the Department of Children Services. She undressed and examined Taylour in front of me as I looked on anxiously.

"Healthy, well-cared for baby," Ms. Monteith pronounced. "She is an appropriate size for her age. Breastfed? Nice." She wrote some notes, then studied my documentation.

Taylour kept looking at me, smiling her toothless baby grin and kicking her legs.

"This baby really knows her mother. Good bonding," the social worker commented.

I had the release papers from the hospital, showing there was no evidence of prenatal exposure to any type of illegal substance when Taylour was born. The Department of Children's Services dropped the allegations of child endangerment and the police department removed the Amber Alert restrictions. Praise God for that. I didn't know who pulled that shit in the first place, but I was willing to bet that it was that stinking ass Mari.

"So, Sergeant Toliver. I'm pronouncing that correctly, right?" Sergeant Toliver shook his head yes. "So, someone," Trae continued, "can put out a lie and an Amber Alert is issued at the drop of a hat? That's some bullshit!"

"Calm down, bae," I said, holding him by the arm. He was beginning to gain a little of his weight back and his arms had swollen up like they do when he's angry. I knew how dark Trae's temper could get, and he had recently been locked up twice, so

I damn sure didn't want him locked up a third time for getting it in with a police officer.

Trae still didn't calm down until Angel said, "I'll initiate an investigation." We were free to go, so we hurried to leave before Trae exploded.

* * *

The baby hadn't seen her pediatrician, Dr. Baker, yet. So, Trae rode with me to the doctor's office after we dropped Angel back off at the house. I had the clearance papers just in case the doctor had that same fake ass Amber Alert notice.

The doctor wanted to start Taylour's shots, but I declined. We still had time and we weren't stable yet. With me breastfeeding, her immune system was protected by my breast milk. The doctor confirmed that she would be fine for a couple of months. Trae's phone went off. He answered it while the doctor was still examining Taylour.

I heard him mumble, "Damn." Then he turned to me and said, "Tasha, this is something important. I'm going to have to handle this. I have to go but Bo is coming to pick you up."

"I know how to get to the house, bae."

"Tasha, we had this conversation already."

"Trae, we are almost done. Don't make me wait here for Bo. Drop me off or let me call Uber."

His face turned into a frown. "I gotta leave now. Wait here for Bo." He leaned in and kissed my lips. "Wait for Bo," he repeated and kissed me again.

He got up, went over to Dr. Baker, shook her hand, then said, "Thank you. Good-bye." And rushed out.

After the examination, I sat in the waiting room waiting on Bo. While I was sitting there, my stomach felt queasy and all knotted up, but I dismissed the funny feeling. Bo sent me a text. He was on his way and would be here in about twenty minutes. I sent him a text.

Don't get a ticket trying to get here. I'm good.

I figured now would be the time to use the restroom and change Taylour's pamper.

I made it to the restroom at the end of the hall. I used the bathroom with the baby in the stall with me. I washed my hands, then changed her pamper on the changing table. Someone walked in the bathroom, but I didn't bother to look up. As I was about to walk back out into the hallway, something hard was pressed into my back. My first thought was this can't be happening. I was imagining it. "Don't open your fucking mouth keep walking, or I'll shoot you." I immediately recognized the voice and understood why I had that queasy feeling in my gut.

It was Mari.

Trae was right. This bitch needed to die.

Chapter Thirty-Nine

MARI

I didn't give a fuck what that bitch Tasha or anybody said, that baby was Kyron's. Therefore, it was mine and I was going to do whatever I had to do in order to get what belonged to me. I was hiding behind a pair of big black shades and a floppy hat. That was the best I could do on such short notice. So far it worked. I spotted Tasha at the police department and had been following her ever since. I was there on a case of my own, so I was so surprised and then overjoyed when I saw Angel, Trae, and Tasha with the baby—Kyron's baby. My baby. Heaven was shining its light on me.

I saw them drop off Angel. Now I knew where she lived. If I had to, I would make her life a living hell as well. Angel was cool, but she was Tasha's friend, so her loyalty never lied with me. I made sure I stayed on Tasha's ass. I followed them to the pediatrician's office where I waited in the lobby. I saw Trae leave alone. He seemed as if he was in a hurry which was great for me. Tasha didn't have any back up. I knew that I finally got the break that I had been hoping for, and I thanked God for it. I already had a passport to get out of the country; we were going to visit a colleague of mine in London. I'd take my new daughter, and we would start life all over. This would make what I went through with Kyron worthwhile and complete.

I was so glad when Tasha finally came out to go to the bathroom, I didn't know what to do. I thought that I was going to pee on myself. I damn near beat her inside a stall. I used the bathroom and waited until I heard her get to the sink. Call me crazy, but a bitch had to do what a bitch had to do.

"Don't open your fucking mouth and keep walking, or I'll shoot you right here," I said in a low voice. "I'll grab the car seat. You grab the diaper bag. Do as I say. Head down the hall to the stairway."

"Mari, are you fuckin' stupid?" Tasha snapped. "What do you want? Give me my baby."

"Bitch, you better listen to me. Don't try me. Turn around and head down the hall. And you know damn well what I want."

"No, I don't."

"I'm holding what I want. Kyron's baby."

"What are you talking about? Bitch, you ain't stupid, but you damn sure crazy! Look at her. Trae spit her out."

TASHA

I still couldn't believe my ears. I didn't see Mari as the type of chick who would go to this extreme. I knew she was crazy. But now, I realized this bitch was bat shit nuts over Kyron's ass! She pushed me out of the bathroom as we walked slowly down the corridor. I was feeling petrified for my baby. I also felt empty carrying only her diaper bag and not her car seat. How could I get caught slipping like this? Most of all, how could Trae leave me and his baby?

"So, you were the one who put in the Amber Alert?" I asked, trying to stall for time. I had to get in the vicinity of other people, and I hoped these hallways had security cameras and that someone was sitting behind a desk watching everything. I wanted to kill this bitch right where she stood, but I had to think smart because she had my baby.

"No, I didn't, but I did see it. That was a sign; this baby belongs with me."

Yeah, she was a lunatic.

"Well, the alert has been dropped, because it was based on false allegations." I told her, hoping those words dug into her skin like a hot pitchfork.

"Shut up, before I shoot you."

"Shoot me? And then what? Before you make it out of here, people will be all over you." I was getting angrier by the second. If this bitch thought that she was going anywhere with my baby, she must have been smoking something. I was a geek about mine, and I would go to war over my kids.

I was grateful to see one of the office doors open and out came some people. Mari popped me on the back of the head so hard, my ears stopped up. I fell to my knees. Stunned. Groggy. All I could hear was a door slam. My baby. Oh my god, my baby.

"Miss? Are you okay? What happened?" I heard voices. But I was dizzy.

"No. Help! My baby. That woman kidnapped my . . . she stole my baby! She stole my baby!" I screamed. "Call the police! That bitch stole my baby!" I stood up and pushed the two people in front of me out of my way. "My baby! Help me! Help me please!" I screamed at anyone who would listen as I started running, trying to catch Mari.

MARI

Mission accomplished! I should have shot that homewrecker in the head instead of hitting her in it. However, she was right. A gunshot in a doctor's office? That noise would be so loud, I'd end up on the 6 o'clock news. And I'd come too far to do that.

So, instead I hit her, put the gun away, secured the car seat and diaper bag and left out. No one even saw me.

I made my way to my car, and everything was a mess. My keys were in my bag, on my shoulders. I had the diaper bag on the other shoulder and the baby in my other hand. I couldn't get to my keys. Hell, I wasn't used to having a baby around. I set the car seat on the hood of the car and took a second to peek at my little princess. Oh, my God! She's gorgeous! Her little beady eyes flew open from her nap, then they closed right back.

Just that quick, she had made my heart melt. Just so adorable. She was wearing a red fluffy dress, white tights, and little T-strap shoes. She had a red bow on the top of her hair, which was long for such a young baby. She looked just like . . .

"Shit!" I dropped the diaper bag to the ground and looked at my baby closely.

"Nooo!" I screamed. "Damn it!" She looked just like Trae. Tasha was right. Trae spit this baby out. "This can't be! This fuckin' can't be!"

"Hold it right there, ma'am. Drop the bag on your shoulders, raise your hands in the air. Step away from the vehicle. Now!"

The officer, or should I say officers had their guns pointed at me. I wasn't going out without a fight, no, fuck that! I had come too far to just let these bastards win! I may just go out guns blazing, and if I did, I would make sure their precious little baby got hit too. If I didn't have Kyron, then they wouldn't have their baby. If I was hurting forever, they were going to hurt forever.

SEVEN

My childhood wasn't normal; I had witnessed everything under the sun. Murders, kidnappings, drugs, money. The funny part was I was supposed to have been sheltered from those elements. My mother was very strict, and I attended private school. I was an only child so once my mother passed, I was left on my own.

I fell in love with math. I got excited every time I would help my uncle count his money. As we would count, he would drop little jewels on ruling the underworld. And each time he would pat my head and say, "Sina, one day you will have your own empire."

Chapter Forty

KEVIN

"**W**here the fuck is that bitch?" The dude with the yuk-mouth screamed in my face.

"I told you. I don't know!" My speech was slurred, and I could tell my jaw had been broken with that last blow. I could feel blood running down my face and onto my clothes.

With that, I was socked in the face again. I didn't know how many more blows I could take. Earlier that evening, I was at the car lot about to close up shop, when these three niggas held me up at gunpoint just as I was locking the door. Although they had on face masks and wore all black, I knew they were niggas by their voices.

I thought their motive was robbery, but they wanted Seven and wanted me to tell them where she was. Seven was hard-headed; I told her she had fucked up by coming out of the shadows. As long as she was underground, we didn't have any problems. We were all getting money. But no, she just had to be this big Queen Pin, and one of her rivals was already after her, going through me—her business partner. *I swear, if I get out of this, I'll kill her myself.*

I got caught slippin'. And the truth was, I didn't know where she was. I thought of Tasha's call from a month or so ago. What did I know about this girl?

"You know somethin', nigga. But if you'd rather die here today. So be it."

Once they were convinced that I wasn't going to say what they wanted to hear, they started on some ransom bullshit. They untied me and gave me back my cell phone.

"Call yo' bitch!"

I did, and it went straight to voicemail.

I was feeling weak, but I knew I was fucked if someone couldn't pay my ransom. I tried Seven's number again and got the same thing. I wanted her to answer because if she came here, they would kill her.

"Where the money? We know you got it." The one nigga with the thick football neck threatened me.

"Call Bo."

"I don't know his number. I didn't."

Dude came and slammed a gasoline can smack dab in front of me. "No. No. Wait!" I yelled. I was scared now. "Let me see my phone. His number is in my phone."

"I was gettin' ready to say. I know you worth something to somebody. To her, Bo. Call somebody if you want to get out of here alive. Tell them one mil', and they only have twenty-four hours."

I called Tasha and got the same thing. Voicemail. My hands were shaking. I could see blood on my hands smearing the phone as I dialed Trae's number. My heart was pounding.

Nigga, please answer the phone, I prayed.

"What's up?"

"It's not good, dawg." I knew my voice sounded slurred because of all the blood and pus in my mouth, but I knew Trae recognized me. "I can't reach Seven and these muthafuckas want one mil' in twenty-four hours. I—"

He hung up on me. I called him back. It went straight to voicemail.

The next thing I knew, one of the three men started pouring gasoline on me.

"No! Please!" I begged.

I thought about the warning Faheem had given me at the baby shower. *"Yeah, right. I know you think you got nine lives. But you done used up how many already?"* So, this was how it was going to end for me.

When dude with the football neck threw the match on me, the smell of my flesh burning, and the searing pain was overwhelming, and I was hollering so loud, I didn't know which was worse. The screams or the smell. I was being burned alive just like my sister Trina. I couldn't believe I was going out like this. I never saw this coming. After a while, the pain subsided, and then I started dreaming of the time I met Don Carlos.

I was feeling lucky, so I made my way down to Atlantic City. I even had on my lucky fedora. I ended up at the poker table and I had a really great night. It was so great that it allowed me entrance into one of the high roller suites. Once in there, I was doing what I do. I turned on my charm. The most beautiful chick I had ever seen came by and asked if I wanted a cigar. I wasn't a cigar smoker, so I was hesitant. The gentleman across the table said, "Here. Try one of mine." And from that moment on me and dude just hit it off. I smoked and talked shit until I could take no more.

I got my chips and dipped off. I was Gucci good walking away with 50 stacks. My sister taught me to always follow my gut. I got ghost but I remembered that I left Fedora on the rack in the suites. On my way back, it was like pushing 3:30 in the morning and I was overhearing a conversation as I was turning the corner. These dudes where speaking in a way that let me know whoever they were waiting on was in trouble. You had to have the key to get in, so whoever they were waiting on was good as long as he stayed inside. These muthafuckas were black Maryland cats. So I go in and there is only one person in the room. The cat who gave me the cigar. My dude. I didn't even have his name. I usually would have minded my business, but something told me to get involved.

"You came back for me?" He asked me, lighting up another Cuban.

"Nah, I left my jacket, but you got two out there waiting for you."

We made eye contact. He knew exactly what I was talking about. He said nothing. I grabbed a seat and watched him; he remained cool. He played a few more hands never missing a beat.

Finally when he was done with his hand, he gestured over to the pit boss who then collected the gentleman's chips. The gentleman nodded to me as if to say thank you and handed me a chip and they exited out the back somewhere. I didn't even know that was an exit.

That chip was my comp to a penthouse suite. The next morning someone was in the room and it wasn't no damn maid. It was the same man who gave me the chip, and now he was giving me a business card that said call me and a number. It said Carlos.

My friend. Who shared with me the Cuban cigars. Why would he burn me alive?

SEVEN

"Sina, lo sciento! Lo sciento!" The nanny kept saying. "Lo sciento! They took the baby! The baby!" She was crying and screaming out.

"Carmella, who took the baby? What are you talking about?" I was running around frantic for my keys while trying to understand what she was saying.

"Lo sciento! Lo sciento." She cried and hung up.

My heart was racing as I grabbed my keys and ran out of the office. Before I could close the door, I was greeted by two officers. "Sina Lolita King?" One of them asked me.

"Yes. I just received a call from the nanny saying my baby. They took my baby."

"Yes, we need you to come with us. There is a warrant for your arrest."

"A warrant? Where is my son?"

"We need you to come with us, ma'am. You can either go willingly or go in handcuffs? Which one will it be?"

"My son."

"Come with us and you can check on the status of your son."

I stood frozen in place. My son. The second officer opened the door of the SUV. I looked at both of them and got in. My mind was racing. Warrant for what? And what kind of SUV was this? I couldn't even see out of the windows. What precinct are they taking me to? Where are they taking me? These were not law officers. I was not being taken to a precinct.

The SUV pulled into a warehouse and both of the men got out and my door flew open.

"Is my son here?" That was my only concern.

"Follow me."

This was no precinct. There were no police cars or police personnel. There was nothing official about this building. I was led down a long, dimly like hallway with marbled glass floors. All I could hear were footsteps. But then I smelled something familiar. We turned the corner and the smell got louder. Freshly rolled Cubans.

THUGS: SEVEN

The doors opened and I couldn't believe my eyes. No fucking way. I got sick to my stomach. The cigar smoke was permeating the air and here was the two of them looking more alike than what I had imaged. Don Carlos and his grandson were laughing and playing. I wanted to yell out but I couldn't. This was that crucial moment where I had to remain calm and calculate my next move. That was what my father taught me.

My son was as happy as he could be. The toys and stuffed animals that Carlito was playing with held a Paw Patrol theme. My son was in love with Paw Patrol which meant my father had to be watching us closely. That caused me to lose my breath and that gasp for air caused them both to look up.

"Carlito! I told you Mommy was coming!"

"Mommy!" Carlito continued to play with the toys in each hand. He was having the time of his life not even bothering to come and give me a hug.

My father took a seat and motioned for me to sit down. I kept my eyes on my son. The silence was awkward, but I was not going to break it.

"You look so much like your mother."

"How dare you! You killed my mother. You left us for dead."

"Is that what you think? I didn't even know you existed until you were 13. I was looking for your mother, but she moved around a lot. As if she was intentionally trying to keep us apart."

"You are lying! My mother told me everything. She told me about how you seduced her. You knew that she was young, and you manipulated her. You made her feel that you were in love with her, but instead you were just using her. You always wanted power. She told me about you. She said you are power driven."

Don Carlos let out a chuckle. The type of chuckle that says, you dumb little chick. "Is that what she told you? Did she tell you about how we really met? At the club?"

"Club? What club?" In my mind, my mother grew up sheltered and boring.

"It doesn't matter. But listen, that's not why I was looking for you. You are blood. And family means more to me than anything. And what type of man would I be if my own family was in danger? Or wasn't protected?"

"What are you talking about?"

"Don't you get it? You really don't have a clue? I've been watching you since I've found you three years ago. You went cold on me for a while, so I had to put a marker on you. I never wanted them to kill you, just to find you."

This was fucking crazy.

"Do you remember how excited you were to get your first key? Come on, Sina. Every drug dealer gets over excited. You hit the jackpot! How do you think you got your connect from Columbia? I saw the small nickels and dimes you were moving. I am the one who put you on. You've been moving work for me."

"What are you talking about? Everything I got, *I got*. You never gave me shit!" I was so mad I was seeing red. How dare he say that my success was because of him.

"You are a baby in this game. More like a fetus, Sina."

He was pissing me off. "What do yo want from me? Why am I here?"

"I want to give you an opportunity. I see that you did well. The life you chose is not the life I would have chosen for you, but I did my best in making sure you were safe."

"Safe?"

"Yes, Sina. The Turnpike incident? And your Aunt Carmella loves the time she spends with the baby."

How could he have been playing me so close? That's fucking scary. I felt violated. Tears of rage burned my cheeks. "Why do you have me here? Do you want to kill me? What? What do you want?"

"I want you to stop. You deserve better. This is not a life for you. You are more than this. This life was my only choice. Why do you choose to run around like a common criminal? What happens if you go to prison? What about your son, Sina? I had to get it the hard way. I had no choice."

"What does that have to do with me? You gave me no choice. You left us for dead. And now you pop up to tell me to stop the one thing that I am good at. It's too late to step in and play daddy. I don't need you."

"You do need me. You just said the one thing you are good at; let me give you a promotion. I have operations way bigger than that elite business you call your self doing."

"Fuck you!"

"Watch your mouth!" He said that so loud that he startled both Carlito and me. I was a little shook and Carlito was quiet. You could hear a pin drop.

"Like I said. I have bigger operations that I need you to run. Legit operations. I have operations in Venezuela, Brazil; I have business in South America. I want us to be clean. I want us both to wash our hands. I want my grandson to grow up without this chaos. Attend prep school. Travel the world. You can have this, Sina. Don't you want this?"

I was at a loss for words. I refused to submit to my father. But yet, I wanted to. That scared me and it made me feel weak.

"The streets are not going to allow you to just walk in and take over. I won't allow it."

"My dear, Lolita. It is already done."

"What do you mean?"

"You no longer control any territory. I have already taken over. Go to your room, Sina. Game over. Seven is dead."

"That's what you think!" I needed my phone. I had to call Kevin.

I knew he would be there for me and help me out of this situation. After all, I felt in my heart that he wanted me just as badly as I wanted him. Soon, he was going to be mine, but first, he had to help me get rid of my father.

Chapter Forty-One

TASHA

What a day this was. I am so glad to have my baby back. I couldn't believe that my poor, harmless baby was caught in the crossfire of some bullshit Mari had going on. And Trae had just dropped two bombshells on me. First, he said my brother called saying that he was kidnapped and then he told me that he handled Charli. He finally deaded that bitch. Originally, I didn't want him to touch her because I feared the backlash. But fuck it, she would no longer be a threat to us and neither would Mari's crazy ass. The only thing was Don Carlos was already calling them to take the next flight out. I hoped this wasn't the backlash that I was anticipating.

KEVIN

The pain that shot through my body as I slid across the floor had me wishing I was dead. All I needed to do was get out of this house and get somebody to notice me. I didn't want to die. And it would be a miracle if I survived any longer. I kept saying silent prayers that I would make it. As long as I made it long enough to get my revenge on Seven a nigga didn't mind dying.

But that bitch was dead, the moment I got my hands on her. How could Don Carlos play me out like this?

KENDRICK

I was caught between a fuckin' rock and a hard place. Shit didn't go as planned with hitting up Kaylin's crib or that bitch ass secret spot, they thought a nigga wouldn't find out about. But thankfully, Mari got that muthafuckin' private investigator, so all I could do was wait for the fat white nigga to get at her with more information so that she could get at me.

"Yo, nigga you've been tweakin' for a while now. I told you when the time is right I'ma get at that nigga," B Murda said to me.

I wasn't trying to wait; I wanted them niggas dead and gone now! Kyron's death was eating at me and on top of that, Kaylin fucked me over with that formula, so now I had to make sure I made this shit up to B Murda and the rest of the niggas he rolled with.

"Plus, where the formula at? You got me looking all stupid and shit."

"You said Trae? Trae Macklin?" Ace asked.

I was surprised he was even talking to us. He felt fucked over once he realized this formula shit fell through and not in a good way.

"Yeah," I answered.

Ace nodded his head and rubbed his hands together. "He run with Kay and Faheem. This is good news."

This nigga had me confused a little. It wasn't a shock that he knew them, but how was this good news?

"What you talkin' about?" B Murda asked.

"I don't fuck wit' them niggas at all, and now they fucked over ya boy on some major work and bread? Nah, these niggas need to get touched. I had that lil nigga's son killed so it's only right for me to take the rest of the crew out."

It finally hit me. Faheem's son, Faheem Jr., was murdered by The Gresham Boys. *Damn!* This shit was about to get hectic and I wanted all parts. They took my cousin, Kyron, from me, and now I was about to take everything from them!

###

WAHIDA CLARK

NEW TITLES FROM WAHIDA CLARK PRESENTS

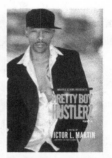

#READIT
WWW.WCLARKPUBLISHING.COM

HENRY D. MUHAMMAD(HAMILTON)
MS,LCADC,ICADC,CAMF

THE MAN

WITH THE
SOLUTION

**FROM
ADDICTION
AND MENTAL
ILLNESS TO
RECOVERY**

CPSIA information can be obtained
at www.ICGtesting.com
Printed in the USA
LVHW04202922112
704135LV00003B/301

9 781947 732445